Advance Praise for
MURDER BY MANICURE

Murder by Manicure

NANCY J. COHEN

KENSINGTON BOOKS
http://www.kensingtonbooks.com

KENSINGTON BOOKS are published by

Kensington Publishing Corp.
850 Third Avenue
New York, NY 10022

All Kensington titles, imprints and distributed lines are available at special quantity discounts for bulk purchases for sales promotion, premiums, fund-raising, educational or institutional use.

Special book excerpts or customized printings can also be created to fit specific needs. For details, write or phone the office of the Kensington Special Sales Manager: Kensington Publishing Corp., 850 Third Avenue, New York, NY 10022, Attn. Special Sales Department. Phone: 1-800-221-2647.

Kensington and the K logo Reg. U.S. Pat. & TM Off.

Library of Congress Card Catalogue Number: 2001090734
ISBN 1-57566-687-1

First Printing: December 2001
10 9 8 7 6 5 4 3 2 1

Printed in the United States of America

To Minnie and Harry

ACKNOWLEDGMENTS

Many thanks to my agent, Linda Hyatt, and to my editor, Karen Thomas, for making this book a reality.

Murder by Manicure

Chapter
One

"I can offer you a fantastic deal if you sign up for membership now," urged Gloria, an account executive at Perfect Fit Sports Club. Sitting behind a desk in her office, she gave her customer a patronizing smile.

"I'm just here to register for the three-month trial membership," Marla Shore explained. Crossing her legs, she surveyed the girl's svelte figure, coiffed hairdo, and flawless makeup. *You'd look better in a layered cut, pal,* she thought with the critical eye of an expert beautician.

"How can you turn this down? Don't you want to save money?" Gloria persisted. "Normally, our contract runs for three years with an initiation fee of two hundred and ninety-nine dollars. But if you join today, I'll give you a hundred-dollar discount off that price. It's a real bargain with the forty-dollar monthly fee."

Just what I want to do with my money—tie up another monthly payment for three years. Marla wondered how often Gloria worked out, or if she even bothered. Heaven forbid the girl should break a manicured fingernail on one of the exercise machines. Not that Marla was so familiar with the gleaming metal devices. Owner of Cut 'N Dye Salon, her main form of exercise was to take her poodle, Spooks, for his daily stroll. She felt as out of place in a fitness club as a white hair on a brunette.

"I'm just interested in the free trial," Marla replied. "Is there someone who will show me around so I can get started?"

Gloria pursed her lips. "As a member, you'd receive a tour by a personal trainer. Otherwise, you'll be on your own." She sniffed. "I might add that people who come in for the free trial period never sign up for membership."

Why is that? Because you're so rude? "I don't buy anything unless I try it out first," Marla snapped.

"If you pay the full initiation fee at the end of the month, you'll be sorry you didn't join today. I'll even throw in a coupon for a free massage if you sign up now."

"Don't you understand the word *no?*"

The girl's face closed like a clamshell. "People like you never come back after the free offer is over." Opening her desk, she pulled out a form and scribbled her signature. "Here's your trial membership card."

Grasping her bag, Marla muttered an expletive before stalking out. This place would never get her award for courtesy to customers.

She began her self-guided tour in the lobby, which held the front desk, a juice bar, and a comfortable lounge with leather armchairs. A glass partition walled off the wet section with its whirlpool and aquatics area. Offices and massage suites branched from the opposite side where a staircase led to an upper level.

Now you've gone and done it, she thought, glancing around in bewilderment. Coming here had been a gross mistake. She could feel it in her bones as surely as the January chill that penetrated through the green-tinted windows facing the parking lot. *Schmuck. You should never have let Tally talk you into this! It's your fault for gaining weight over the holidays.* Her best friend couldn't make it tonight, so Marla had decided to get oriented by herself. Then, when she met Tally here on Sunday, at least she'd know her way around already.

"Is it always so quiet on Friday evenings?" she asked the receptionist, a ponytailed brunette focused on a computer.

The girl glanced up, her jaw working a piece of gum. "Oh, no, honey. Everyone's at the competition over at Dayna's Gym. I guess you weren't interested in the prize, huh?"

"What's that?"

"A date with Mr. World Muscleman."

"You're right, I'm not interested. Where can I get changed? I came here directly from work but packed a bag earlier."

Pointing a finger, the girl said, "Walk through the wet area, and you'll come to the locker room." Her gaze surveyed Marla's denim jumper dress. "Are you new here, honey?"

"Yeah, how could you tell?"

A grin split the girl's face. "You have that lost look about you. Don't worry, you'll learn your way around. My name is Sharon if you need anything. By the way, I love your hair. Is that your natural color?"

Marla bristled. "Of course it is." Her brow furrowing, she patted her chestnut hair, curled inward at chin length. Even though her thirty-fifth birthday approached, she didn't look old enough to gray yet, did she? Maybe getting in shape wasn't such a bad idea. "I'm a hairstylist. Stop in at my salon sometime," she said, handing the girl a business card.

Glad she had worn rubber-soled shoes, Marla padded through the wet area, treading carefully along the slippery tiles. A whirlpool hissed and bubbled on her left, while on the right an aqua pool smelled strongly of chlorine. At the far end were doors to the sauna and steam rooms. *I don't need to go in there to feel the humidity*, she thought, perspiration rising on her upper lip. The place oozed dampness like a mangrove swamp.

In the rear, she pushed open the door to the women's lockers. Cool, citrus-scented air freshened the spacious area. Her quick glance noted polished wood benches, stacks of open cubicles, peach-and-turquoise floor tiles, and mirrored walls. Piped-in music played tunes from a popular radio station.

At least she was alone and could change in peace. But as she selected an empty cubbyhole for her street clothes, voices drifted her way.

"You're a murderer! I know what you've done!" a woman cried.

"I'm warning you, leave me alone or I'll file charges."

Marla's ears perked up. She recognized that smoky tone as belonging to Jolene Myers, one of her clients. Palm Haven was a small community, even though it counted as a western suburb of Fort Lauderdale, and she often ran into customers around town.

"I won't rest until you stop that torture," the unknown woman said. "Do you realize the pain and suffering you're causing?"

"Give me a break, Cookie. We're talking about laboratory animals here, for God's sake."

Marla rounded the bend and entered a tiled section with a row of sinks. Hair dryers and various toiletries sat on the counter. In front of a wall-sized mirror, the two combatants faced off. Jolene's eyes widened in recognition as she caught sight of the newcomer.

"Marla!" she rasped. "Will you tell this pest to get off my case? Our company goes out of its way to use the safest possible research techniques."

"Who are you?" the stranger demanded.

"Marla Shore. I'm Jolene's hairdresser."

"Oh yeah? Cookie Calcone here." Cookie, a diminutive woman, glared up at her. "Do you know what this twit calls harmless? Her scientists use the Draize Irritancy Test. They drip caustic substances into the eyes of rabbits to assess damaging effects. The test may last for days, while the animals are restrained to prevent them from rubbing away the chemical. Since their tear ducts work poorly, the stuff won't wash out. Blistering and ulceration of the cornea often occurs. Can you imagine the pain they suffer?"

"Well, yes," Marla began, but Jolene cut her off.

"Those tests are necessary. Better we should find out if a substance is toxic before it's applied to humans."

Cookie's green eyes blazed. "There are safer methods! What about the skin tests done on guinea pigs? Their torture lasts for weeks. Sometimes they kill themselves trying to escape. You can't tell me there aren't viable options." With a grunt, she tossed a short strand of strawberry blond hair off her face.

Jolene squared her shoulders. She wore a gray jersey top and matching shorts. With a towel wrapped around her neck, she looked as though she'd just come from a workout. "We've already begun using the Agarose Diffusion Method as an alternative to the Draize test, but sometimes animal trials are the only way to achieve reliable results. In that event, we anesthetize the lab animals when possible. We try to treat them humanely, but proving the safety of our products is paramount. Ultimately, we do what's best for the consumer."

Cookie snorted. "You just say that to justify the funding. Keep it up, and you'll be sorry."

Jolene's eyes glittered. "You're hot air without the wind, darling. You can't blow my house down."

"Oh no?" Cookie hunched forward, revealing the cleavage under her swimsuit. "I'll bet if your friends find out what you do, they'll shy away. You don't condone animal testing, do you, Marla?"

Fascinated by their conversation, Marla didn't expect to be drawn into it. "Uh, I suppose not. I haven't really given the issue much thought." Who did? In most cases, you bought products you liked without regard to their origins. She used items in her salon that produced the best results. It just so happened that many of them were botanicals. Would it make a difference to her if a particular brand employed animal testing in its laboratories? Probably not, if it made her clients happy.

"That's the problem," Cookie agreed, nodding vigorously. "Most people don't think about it. But if I tell them what your company is doing, Jolene, you can bet the media will be down your throat."

"Heck, I don't need this. I've had a bad day already. Dancercize class just wound me up tonight, and then I had a snack afterward—which didn't help. I'm going to relax in the whirlpool after my massage."

"Which massage therapist do you recommend?" Marla queried, rubbing the knots of tension stiffening her neck.

"Don't make an appointment with Slate Harper," Jolene advised.

"The guy asked me out and refuses to take no for an answer. He even showed up at my door one day. I've half a mind to complain about him to the manager."

"So why don't you?" Marla asked curiously.

Jolene glared at Cookie, who maintained a hostile stance, arms folded across her chest. "Because unlike this lady here, I don't like to make waves. I just avoid Slate, that's all."

Striding to a locker, Jolene grabbed a canvas bag sitting in an open cubicle. "You should take gelatin supplements, Marla. All that shampooing can weaken your keratin. I always take a dose before going into the whirlpool, and I had a manicure today, so it's doubly important." Scraping aside some yellow powder at her feet, she opened her sack and withdrew an unlabeled bottle.

"You know, we've gotten a new manicurist," Marla said, aware that Jolene hadn't liked their previous one. "Why don't you give her a try?"

"I'm happy with Denise at the New Wave. Hmm, that's odd, the cap is loose," Jolene murmured when the lid popped right off. At the sink, she downed two capsules with a palmful of water. "I've got to run. See you, Marla." Pointedly ignoring Cookie, she thrust her turquoise bag back into the cubbyhole and fled.

Left alone with Cookie, Marla felt acutely uncomfortable. The woman's gaze followed her around as though she were the quarry in a hunt. Changing quickly in a bathroom stall, she realized it would be necessary to bring a lock to secure her belongings in one of the lockers. For now, she'd take her stuff with her upstairs.

"What kind of products do you use in your salon?" Cookie demanded, trailing her to the staircase.

"We carry most of the popular brands. Now if you'll excuse me, I need to find a trainer."

Cookie's expression darkened. "Those animals will get their revenge, you know. Jolene's days are numbered. She just doesn't realize it yet." Leaving those ominous words hanging in the air, Cookie turned on her heel and headed for the pool.

Upstairs, Marla approached a reception area in the center of the workout floor. Behind the counter stood a tall young man with dark hair, slicked back from his forehead, and deep-set brown eyes. He grinned widely at Marla's appearance, undoubtedly glad to see another soul. No one else was visible in the aerobics studio, exercise stations, or free weight section.

"Guess you didn't want to see the competition over at Dayna's," he said in a pleasantly modulated voice. Wearing the club staff uniform, a green knit shirt and matching shorts, he displayed his musculature under a healthy glow of tanned skin.

"I'm Marla Shore, and this is all new to me. Are you one of the personal trainers?"

"No, they've left for the day. I'm Keith Hamilton, one of the fitness consultants here." He held out his hand for a brief, firm shake. "Is this your first session? I can help you, but I'll need to see your membership card."

Marla showed him her trial authorization. "I'd like an introduction to the equipment, if that's possible." Since he wasn't busy, maybe he'd be kind enough to accommodate her even though she wasn't a true member. Giving her most disarming smile, she tilted her head suggestively.

Apparently, he liked what he saw in her toffee eyes, because he took her arm and guided her to the cycle machines. "If you were a full member, you'd be entitled to a tour, body fat analysis, and free one-hour session with a trainer. But seeing as how you're on your own, I'll do what I can for you."

He winked, making Marla regret her flirtatious glance. She didn't need any amorous complications right now, not when Detective Lieutenant Dalton Vail was getting more possessive about their relationship. It didn't matter to him that commitment wasn't in her vocabulary at this point. She remembered the reason why every time Stan showed up to harangue her. After Dalton met her ex-spouse, he understood the basis for her fierce independence, but it didn't undermine his determination to pursue her. Unfortunately, every time their paths crossed, a murder was involved.

Focusing her attention, she concentrated on Keith's instructions as he introduced her to the StairMaster and Life Cycle machines, treadmill, and simulated rowing device.

"That looks like fun," Marla said, pointing to a Tectrix Virtual Reality bike. Like a computer monitor, a viewscreen mounted in front of the bike showed an animated scene of a road snaking up a hilltop.

"You can choose your own scenario. I like Tank, a military combat game. How fast you go depends on how fast you cycle, and you've got to steer around obstacles."

She raised her eyebrows. "I'll give this machine a try when I'm here Sunday with my friend. At least you have something to watch while you're pedaling." Reluctantly she admitted to herself that this might not be so bad after all.

"You're entitled to join any of the classes," he said, handing her an aerobics schedule. "Dancercize is popular with the ladies and not as strenuous as some of the other techniques. Now if you're interested, I can get you started with the body fat analysis."

"Sure, why not?" Marla knew she had nothing to worry about on that score. Tally was the one who always complained about her weight, even though the girl had a perfect figure to model the stylish clothes in her boutique, Dressed to Kill. Her friend's downfall was a craving for chocolate, whereas Marla's vice was caffeine. At least hers didn't add calories.

"This is the circumference method," Keith said, approaching her with a tape measure. "When you come back next time, ask Dave to do a bioelectrical impedance test. The fat machine, as we call it, is more accurate. Lift your chin."

Marla held still while he measured her neck. He stood awfully close, leaning inward until she could smell his lime aftershave. His face hovered a few inches away, his mouth teasingly within kissing distance. The hairs on her arms prickled. Did she just now realize they were alone together, and barely anyone else was in the building?

She held her breath until he finished, then squirmed when he wound the tape around her waist, tightening it at the back so his fingertips rested on her derriere.

"Shouldn't that be placed a bit higher?" she squeaked when he aimed for her hips. He'd twisted the tape around the biggest part of her butt. That wasn't her hip measurement, was it? And why was he pinching the tape so tight in front while staring down at her bared thighs?

"You're a thirty-four waist, thirty-seven hips, and thirteen neck," he stated, unabashedly ogling her.

Get real, pal! I'm not that big. You don't know what the hell you're doing. "So what's next?"

He put the tape away. "Take your shoes off and we'll get your height and weight on the scale."

Feeling oddly vulnerable in her tank top and shorts, she followed him to a corner and stepped onto the unit. His hand accidentally—or not—brushed her breast when he reached to move the lever.

"Watch it, pal. My boyfriend is a police officer," she muttered.

"Sorry." His grin displayed his lack of concern. "Five-feet, six inches, one hundred and twenty pounds."

"Wait a minute, my scale at home says I weigh one-eighteen."

"This one may be better balanced."

Marla put her sneakers back on while he did the calculations at his desk. He seemed to take an overly long time, confirming her opinion that this wasn't his customary job. Maybe he was faking it just for an excuse to put his hands on her.

"Your body fat percentage is thirty-one," he said, glancing at her. "The recommended percentage for a woman is twenty-two. What's your activity level at home?"

"I take my poodle for walks and work in a salon all day."

"Any regular form of exercise? Aerobic workouts?"

"That's been enough for me. I don't have time for anything else."

A frown creased his brow. "Would you say you walked your dog for thirty minutes, three times a week? I'll put you down for a moderate activity level then." At her nod, he did a further analysis. "Your lean body mass is eighty-three pounds, meaning you need to eat ten blocks a day."

"Huh?"

"One block contains ten grams of carbohydrate, seven-point-five grams of protein, and three-point-three-three grams of fat. It translates to about one hundred calories."

"So you're saying I need a diet with one thousand calories? I'll starve!" His numbers couldn't be accurate. She wasn't fat! Added to the insult, Sharon the receptionist's remark surfaced in her mind: *Is that your natural color?* Fighting an impulse to dash to a mirror and check for gray hairs, Marla managed a demure smile instead.

"I don't think you measured me correctly. I'll see what Dave says when he uses that machine you mentioned."

His eyes flickered momentarily with an emotion she couldn't identify. "Regardless of the recommended blocks for your diet, you need to be aware of proper eating habits, such as avoiding foods high in arachidonic acid. Giving guidance in this area is *my* sphere of expertise."

Rummaging in a drawer, he selected several papers, which he handed to her. "Make an appointment with me for next week, and we'll personally roam over the details of your diet plan."

His eyebrows rose suggestively, giving Marla the impression he wanted to roam over her person rather than discuss her health. Given Gloria's rude behavior earlier, she wondered if personnel problems were par for the course here.

"I'll be coming with my friend next week. Perhaps you can advise us both together." Compressing her lips, she scanned the pages detailing foods to avoid, which naturally included many of her favorite snacks, foods to include on her targeted diet plan, and sample recipes. She liked the one for spinach pie since it used ingredients that were easy to buy, unlike the energy bars that required fructose, nonfat dry milk, and soy protein powder, among other uncommon components. Maybe it was healthy for her body, but not for her purse. She wasn't about to stock items that weren't normally on her shelf.

Glancing at her watch, she cleared her throat. "I didn't realize it was so late. Guess I'll have to wait until Sunday to try this stuff," she said, gesturing at the exercise stations.

Keith turned on a smarmy smile. "Do you want to grab a bite to eat somewhere with me? We can begin discussing your diet plan tonight. I know a great natural food restaurant where we can get the best veggie platters."

"No, thanks. I think I'll pick up a Big Mac on the way home. With a large fries and a chocolate milkshake. Yum!"

Grinning at his horrified expression, she whirled around and headed for the stairs. She was halfway there when a blood-curdling scream from below halted her dead in her tracks.

Chapter Two

Marla raced down the stairs, nearly stumbling over her own feet in her haste to find the source of the terrifying screams. Arriving in the lobby, she noticed Sharon gesturing wildly from the pool deck. Careful not to slip on the wet tiles, she rushed inside the aquatics area. The receptionist's face resembled the color of an overdone bleach job.

Marla skidded on the damp floor. "What's wrong?"

Her teeth chattering, Sharon pointed at the whirlpool, which gurgled and frothed like a witch's cauldron.

As though in response, a flaccid hand bubbled to the surface and then sank.

"Someone's under there," Sharon wailed.

Not again. Marla's vision blurred as past events collided with the present in her stunned mind. *Get a grip. This isn't little Tammy. That tragedy happened fifteen years ago.*

She glanced up as Keith bounded into the room. "There's a body underwater. You've got to do something!" she told him.

Turning to the receptionist, he ordered, "Sharon, call nine one one."

Covering her mouth, Sharon fled from the aquatics section. A few minutes later, Marla heard an emergency announcement broadcast on the PA system: "Code Six in the wet area!"

Keith kicked off his shoes. "Whoever it is may be trapped by the drain. I'm going in." Charging down the steps into the seething water, he grimaced as the heat enveloped his legs. It wasn't that deep—four feet according to a marker—so the water only reached his ribs. Slogging through the swirling current, he stopped suddenly and reached down.

A few moments later, a woman's limp form rested by the side of the pool. Marla felt the blood drain from her face as she recognized Jolene Myers.

"She couldn't have been under long," Keith said, "or her skin would have sloughed off from the heat. She's not rigid yet. There's a chance." Dripping onto the deck as he knelt beside her still body, he began performing CPR.

"Can I help?" Marla asked, wringing her hands. Jolene couldn't be dead. She'd just talked to her in the locker room! Maybe she had slipped and bumped her head and could still be revived. If only her skin didn't have that bluish tint. It reminded Marla of the Barbicide liquid she used at the salon to disinfect her combs.

"Go find Slate. He's in the massage suite," Keith said, perspiring from exertion.

In the lobby, Marla confronted Sharon. "Keith needs assistance. Where's Slate? He must not have heard your bulletin."

Her chin quivering, Sharon opened her mouth to speak, but words failed her. She lifted a trembling finger and pointed to the right.

Reaching the massage area, Marla faced an empty check-in desk and two closed doors. Rapping loudly on the closest one, she fell back when it abruptly swung open. A tall young man wearing a staff shirt and shorts strolled out, his cool amber eyes assessing her. Marla got a quick glimpse beyond of a voluptuous blonde sitting on a treatment table adjusting her green knit top with the club logo. From the way it fit, she didn't appear to be wearing a bra. A pair of long legs showed below matching shorts.

"What can I do for you?" the man asked, plowing a hand through his short, disheveled brown hair.

"Are you Slate?" she asked.

"Yeah, what's up?"

"There's an emergency, and Keith needs your help by the pool. Didn't you hear the Code Six announcement?"

He glanced over his shoulder at the blonde. "Sorry, I was distracted. Amy, I gotta go." Without wasting another word, he darted off.

The girl slipped on a pair of tennis shoes and sauntered from the treatment room. Her overly made-up face expressed curiosity. "What's going on?"

"A woman had an accident in the whirlpool. She's unconscious, not breathing."

"Who?"

"Jolene Myers." If Jolene was a regular, the staff member might know her.

"Hah!" Amy chortled triumphantly.

Marla gave her a sharp glance. *Why are you so pleased, pal?* "I gather you know Jolene."

The girl gave a curt nod. "I manage the juice bar. She bought a shake and a sandwich earlier. Maybe she should have let the food digest." Her gaze cooled. "I'm Amy Gerard. And you are?"

"Marla Shore. A new member. Now if you don't mind, I'm going to see what's happening." Her ears picked up the wail of sirens outside, getting louder.

Beside the pool, Keith and Slate attempted to revive Jolene. They jumped aside when rescue personnel thundered through the front door and were directed by Sharon into the aquatics section. While the paramedics performed their patient assessment, a uniformed police officer approached Marla.

"Excuse me, miss," he said. "Can you tell me what happened here?"

Marla glanced uncertainly at the club attendants. "Sharon is the lady at the reception desk. I was upstairs when I heard her screaming. She found Jolene in the whirlpool. That's Jolene Myers." She pointed to her client. The officer scribbled in a notebook while she spoke.

"Do you work here?"

"No, I'm just a temporary member. *They* work here." She indicated Keith, Slate, and a couple other staffers who had joined them, including Gloria, whose supercilious expression had been replaced by one of mingled confusion and fear.

"Just a minute, please." The policeman strode away to confer with the paramedics, who had attached various devices to Jolene's prostrate form. Their faces were intent as they worked on her without apparent success. When they called for a stretcher, Marla's desire to flee struggled with her sense of morbid curiosity. Frozen limbs glued her to the spot until the rescue truck departed with Jolene aboard, and the officer returned to resume his questioning.

"Shouldn't you be talking to them?" she croaked, her voice hoarse. Now that the action was over, she felt an intense urge to sink down in a corner and cover her face with her hands. It might not blot out the images of Jolene's unconscious body from her mind, but she needed to crawl away to recover her composure. She'd started to shake—doubtless a delayed reaction. And the chicken wings she'd eaten on her way here were creating havoc with her stomach.

"Are you all right? You don't look so good," the officer said, his tone suddenly solicitous. "Say, haven't I seen you before?"

Marla gave him a closer examination. Her eyes widened when she recognized his ruddy face and kindly, pale-blue eyes. "Bless my bones, you're one of the guys who came to my house with Detective Vail after I had that break-in several months ago. I'm Marla Shore."

Light dawned in his expression. "Of course, you're the lieutenant's . . . friend. My name is Barkley."

"Well, listen, Barkley. Is it possible Jolene slipped and cracked her head on that ledge inside the whirlpool?"

"Medics said there were no signs of a head injury, ma'am. How well are you acquainted with the woman?"

"Jolene Myers is one of my customers at Cut 'N Dye Salon."

The stocky officer took notes while she spoke. "Does the lady have family nearby? Where does she work?"

"She's not married; her parents live up north; and she's a research supervisor at Stockhart Industries." A pause. "Jolene swallowed a couple of pills in the locker room, if that's relevant. She said they were gelatin capsules. She always took them before soaking in the whirlpool because she believed they'd strengthen her nails."

"Were you alone with her in the locker room?"

Marla hesitated. Should she mention the argument between Cookie and Jolene that had caused her client to become upset? Maybe not, at least for now. If Jolene had succumbed to an illness or accident, the discussion she'd overheard would be irrelevant.

"Another club member may have been there," she hedged, wondering where Cookie had gone. The woman was heading for the pool when Marla went upstairs. Had Cookie left the wet area by the time Jolene arrived?

"Jolene mentioned she'd been having a bad day," Marla continued. "After Dancercize class, she'd scheduled a massage and then planned to soak in the whirlpool."

"I see. If you'll pardon me, I've got to call my sergeant for instructions."

The officer turned and nearly collided with a tall, athletic man who'd just entered. The newcomer wore a charcoal suit, expertly tailored to fit his broad shoulders. A crimson-and-navy tie added a splash of color to his otherwise somber appearance.

"Lieutenant Vail, sir," Barkley muttered, giving a respectfully wide berth to his superior.

"Dalton!" Marla cried. "What are you doing here?" As a homicide investigator, Vail wouldn't be present unless foul play was suspected. "You weren't called in because—"

Detective Dalton Vail's steel gray eyes narrowed. "I was in the area and heard the dispatcher. I didn't expect to see *you*, however. Dare I ask why you're in the vicinity?"

She moistened her lips. "I, uh, joined the sports club. For a trial period. Today is my first day." Her glance strayed to his peppery hair, neatly parted on the side.

"No kidding." His mouth curled downward. "How amazing that someone just happened to end up unconscious."

Hey, pal, are you implying it's my fault? "Now wait a minute. Jolene's accident happened through no intent of mine. Just because Bertha Kravitz croaked in my salon and Ben Kline got his head bashed in after we met doesn't mean I'm a jinx."

"Maybe not, but a magnet for disaster is a possibility."

His eyes smoldered, and Marla recalled his earlier warnings for her to stay out of trouble. Warnings she hadn't heeded.

They stared at each other, his keen assessment making her knees weaken. His spice cologne and powerful presence made her heart race erratically. Damn, must she react like a hormone-driven adolescent? All right, so they hadn't seen each other for a few weeks. After Taste of the World at her cousin Cynthia's estate in December, they'd gone out together on New Year's Eve. Since then, busy schedules had claimed their spare time.

Someone cleared his throat beside them. "Excuse me, sir," Barkley cut in, "shall I take statements from witnesses?"

Vail dragged his gaze from hers. "Go ahead, I'll be with you in a minute," he replied, his deeply resonant tone sliding along Marla's nerves like warm brandy. Before he could continue his conversation with her, his cell phone rang.

"Lieutenant Vail," he answered. Listening, he nodded once, his face impassive. "I'm on it." He hung up, his demeanor grim. "That was our man at the hospital," the detective told her. "The lady didn't make it."

"Oh, no! Jolene is . . ." A lump rose in her throat. An optimistic part of her had expected Jolene to survive.

"I gather you knew the victim. I'll have to interview you, but I've got to give some orders first. Wait here." Pivoting, he strode away while punching numbers on his phone.

Marla stood by, wondering how she could help. There would be plenty of witnesses to question, judging by the uniformed staff clustered around. She didn't recognize everyone. Keith and Slate quietly chatted with the blonde, Amy, on the pool deck. In the lobby, Sharon sat at her post, her face a frozen mask of fear. Gloria leaned against the reception desk, watching the commotion. Her expression of cool disdain belied her earlier distress.

What about club members? Maybe someone had noticed Jolene entering the whirlpool.

No one paid Marla any attention when she headed for the women's locker room.

"Marla Shore! What's going on out there?" demanded a woman with intense moss green eyes, auburn hair, and a fiftyish face devoid of wrinkles.

Marla stopped short inside the entrance. "Eloise, I didn't know you were here." A successful mortgage broker, Eloise Zelman had become a regular at Marla's salon after Cynthia introduced them at Taste of the World.

"I was in the sauna." The older woman gestured to her salmon-colored shorts set. "I came in here to change and heard someone screaming. I was afraid to come out."

"Well, Jolene Myers dunked herself in the whirlpool and didn't surface. Keith pulled her out, but apparently too late. She drowned, or so I presume." Marla shook her head, unable to believe her own words. "Jolene is just too smart to let that happen. I've known her for several years." Realizing she was speaking in the present tense, Marla gulped.

"Jolene *drowned?*" Eloise's face paled.

"I should get her things and give them to Dalton," Marla murmured thoughtfully, eyeing a rack of plastic bags on a wall hook. Ignoring Eloise, who trailed after her, Marla obtained a paper towel from the bathroom. Careful not to touch the turquoise sack with her hands, she placed the deceased woman's belongings into the plastic bag, but not before peeking inside. Jolene's shorts outfit was on top. She must have changed into a swimsuit after her massage. A bottle of something called Bite No More was tilted on its side.

"How did it happen? Were you there?" Eloise queried, her pitch rising.

Flushing guiltily, Marla rested the plastic bag on the shiny tile floor. "I was upstairs getting a tour with Keith. Did you see anyone else when you came out of the sauna?"

Eloise fluttered a hand in the air. "I didn't notice anybody, but I'll ask Sam. He was in the steam room with Wallace Ritiker."

"Wally is here?" Marla knew the city councilman from her activities with the Child Drowning Prevention Coalition.

Eloise shifted uneasily. "Yeah, he and Sam wanted to talk about something. I wonder if they're still cooking or if they went to get dressed."

Where the hell had they been during the crisis? Marla refrained from asking. A woman screams, and everyone scatters. Nice group of people. She wouldn't want them around if she were in trouble.

"How many policemen are out there?" Eloise said, a worried frown creasing her forehead.

"The place is swarming with technicians." Or it would be soon, once Vail called in his team. Jolene's death may have been accidental, but she supposed the detective had to cover all the bases. *Time for me to skedaddle.*

Eloise put a hand on her arm. Her palm was moist and clammy. "Who was screaming before? Was it Jolene? Was she being attacked?" Her eyes widened with fright, or some other hidden terror that wasn't readily evident.

Marla shrugged her off. "No, Sharon shrieked when she found the body. The girl is upset. I'll go talk to her."

Eager to get away before Eloise hounded her with more questions, Marla scrambled to the exit. Outside, the force of police personnel had increased. Dalton Vail was at the hub, giving orders. Catching sight of Marla, he broke away and hurried to her side.

"Here's Jolene's bag," Marla said, handing it over.

"Oh, thanks." Vail passed it to a tech. "Look, I'd rather talk to you away from the crowd. How about if we meet later at Sterling Worth Café?"

"Don't you have to get home to Brianna?" His twelve-year-old daughter would be there alone. Marla knew that their housekeeper departed after preparing dinner for the pair.

Vail glanced at his watch. "Brianna is used to my irregular hours. I'll be here for a while yet, but I realize you have to get up early tomorrow for work. Is ten o'clock too late?"

"Not for you." She gave him a coy glance, pleased at the notion of having Vail's company to herself. Unfortunately, they always seemed to talk about suspects when they got together.

Crinkles appeared beside his eyes. "This is strictly a business date."

"Oh, sure." She raised an eyebrow in amusement, noting his darting glance at her figure. "We'll have our usual discussion about whodunit."

"There is no whodunit until the medical examiner issues his report. I need to gather information at this stage."

"Naturally," she agreed in a mild tone, although from the way he was looking at her, that wasn't all he wanted to cover. A vision of his tall, lean body entwined with hers flashed through her mind, sending a delicious shiver along her nerves. She hastily pushed the temptation aside. No time for that. This was business, remember?

She rushed home to shower and change into a black-and-jade silk dress before meeting him at the restaurant in Plantation.

Sterling Worth Café reminded her of a cozy Victorian parlor. They secured a table at an end row so no one could overhear their conversation. Settling into her seat, Marla drew a black shawl around her shoulders. It was cool outside, at least by her standards. Any time the temperature dropped below seventy, she froze. Too long living in the tropics.

A waitress came and took their order for dessert and coffee.

After they were left alone, Vail rolled his broad shoulders as though to relieve tension, then he pulled out a notebook and pen. "So tell me exactly who was present in the club tonight. Why were you there? I got the impression you don't have time for that sort of thing."

Marla stared pensively at her water glass. "Tally and I joined for the free trial membership. We need to lose weight and get in shape." Was she only five years away from the big Four-oh? At home, she'd examined her roots for gray hairs but had found none. Her weight scale hadn't been as accommodating. She'd gained two pounds since her last weigh-in. Maybe it was water, she thought hopefully, subconsciously sucking in her stomach.

"We ate too much at Taste of the World," she added wryly.

Vail grinned, transforming his craggy features from their normally impassive mask. "So did I. You and your cousin did a great job with Ocean Guard's fund-raiser."

"Did I tell you they offered me a position on the board?" Marla laughed. "As if I'd want to associate with that bunch of lunatics again. Cynthia can manage without me. Wait until I tell my cuz there's another suspicious death to investigate."

"I don't think she'll want to be involved this time."

"You're right." Their desserts arrived, and Marla swallowed her guilt over the calories. A few sweet mouthfuls of vanilla crème brûlée wiped away any remorse over the transgression.

"Gloria Muñoz was the first person I encountered at the club," she mentioned while Vail began scribbling. "She tried to sell me a full membership and became rude when I refused. Maybe Gloria works on commission, but her behavior was inexcusable. Sharon is the receptionist. She seems like a decent girl. Amy Gerard is the juice bar attendant. She didn't seem too upset by Jolene's accident."

"Go on."

A spoonful of creamy custard melted on her tongue. "Keith Hamilton is a fitness consultant. He tried to put the moves on me when he showed me the equipment. Oh, don't worry. I told him he'd better keep his hands off because my boyfriend is a police officer." She grinned at Vail's pleased expression.

"Slate is one of the massage therapists," she went on before he could comment. "Jolene warned me not to use him because he hit on her and wouldn't take no for an answer." Hesitating, she frowned. "Jolene had a massage before she went into the whirlpool, but I don't recall seeing another therapist in the massage suite. If Slate didn't take Jolene's appointment, who did?"

Vail's eyes narrowed. "I have a list of employees, so I can check it out. What about club members?"

"It was a quiet night because most people were at Dayna's Gym for some contest, or so Sharon told me. I met Jolene in the locker room, and she introduced me to Cookie Calcone. Cookie must have left after her swim, because I didn't see her later. Eloise and Sam Zelman were at the club."

Vail nodded. They'd met the Zelmans at Taste of the World. "Eloise said her husband was in the steam room with Wallace Ritiker," Marla went on. "She was in the women's lockers when she heard Sharon screaming."

Vail asked a few more questions before putting away his notebook. Then he attacked his dessert, a rich chocolate layer cake. He devoured it in a few bites before pushing his plate aside. Marla noted his unusual silence. His brows were drawn together, as though he were troubled.

Concerned, she reached out and touched his arm. "What's the matter? Do you know something about this case you're not sharing?"

Grimacing, he lifted his gaze. "No, it's not that. I'll have some late nights ahead, and that brings up a problem with Brianna. I don't want to burden you."

"Bless my bones, Dalton, how do you expect our relationship to progress if you don't confide in me? Of course I want to hear about your daughter."

He rested his large hand on top of hers. Its warmth seeped into her skin, conveying reassurance. "Brianna goes to dance class every Tuesday evening. Working late means I won't be able to drive her there. I suppose I could ask Carmen."

"Your housekeeper leaves around five, doesn't she?" A widower after his wife died of cancer over two years ago, Vail had hired part-time domestic help.

He nodded his head. "Yeah, after she fixes our dinner."

"What time is the class?"

"Eight o'clock."

Sitting back in her seat, Marla pursed her lips. Unfortunately or not, depending on how you looked at it, Vail didn't have a swarm of relatives in the area like she did.

Her next words tumbled from her mouth before she could retract them. "I'll take her," she offered, hoping she wasn't biting off more than she could chew.

Chapter
Three

"What's wrong, Marla?" asked Nicole, the dark-skinned stylist at the next station. "You're not your usual talkative self today. Did you stay out too late last night?"

Waiting for her next client, Marla scraped hair off a brush with deliberate strokes. "I met Dalton Vail for dessert. He needed information. Didn't you listen to the news? Jolene Myers was found dead at Perfect Fit Sports Club last night."

Nicole's jaw dropped. "She was your client, right? The attractive woman who worked at the chemical plant?"

"Tell me about it." Marla glanced furtively around the salon. Saturday mornings were always hopping, and today was no exception. Miloki and Giorgio were occupied with customers as were the stylists across the room. An assistant swept the floor while the new receptionist hugged the front desk. Clients strolled back and forth, sampling the bagels, sipping coffee, and greeting their friends.

Spotting her next client walking through the door, Marla leaned forward. "Jolene drowned in the whirlpool. The television report this morning said it was an accident, but Vail is waiting for the medical examiner's results. I was there."

"What do you mean?" Nicole asked.

"Just before she died, Jolene had an argument with a woman in the locker room. I overheard her plans to go for a massage before soaking in the Jacuzzi. Shortly thereafter, I saw her body." Squeezing her eyes shut, Marla blanked the painful images from her mind. "It reminded me of Tammy."

Nicole put down the water bottle she was using to spray-clean her counter. "Don't you go on about that again," her friend said, waggling a finger. "You've atoned for that tragedy a hundred times over."

Marla waved a hairbrush. "So how come bodies show up wherever I go? I've got more *tsuris* than those lab animals Cookie was talking about."

"Nonsense. Jolene's death had nothing to do with you, so don't complain you have too many troubles." Nicole's gaze widened. "Wait a minute. Whose name did you just mention?"

"Cookie Calcone. She was the one talking to Jolene in the locker room. Apparently, she's an animal rights activist because she was railing against lab research techniques used at Jolene's facility."

Nicole grimaced. "Anytime there's a cause worth defending, you'll find Cookie at the front line. She's a real fruitcake."

Now it was Marla's turn to gape. "How do you know that woman?"

"She was a senior in my high school when I was a freshman. I heard she staged a sit-in with her classmates to protest dissecting frogs in biology. Another time, she demonstrated against trash disposal policies, claiming the school didn't make enough efforts to recycle. Cookie took garbage and spread it all over the cafeteria. Then there were the palmetto bugs."

"Go on." Marla leaned forward eagerly.

"She felt they were a wasted source of protein, and every time the exterminator came, poison polluted the hallways. On Halloween, she brought in home-baked oatmeal raisin cookies. They were decorated with orange icing like a spider web, and she had enough to offer to anybody who wanted a taste. They were sweet, but a little too chewy." Nicole stopped, shuddering.

"So?"

"We thought those black things were raisins until Cookie passed out a paper giving a nutritional analysis. They were *bugs*, Marla! Ground-up palmettos. We were eating giant cockroaches."

"Lord save me!" Her stomach heaved, and she imagined what Nicole's schoolmates must have experienced.

"You want to steer clear of Cookie Calcone," Nicole warned. "She's not averse to taking physical action to prove her point." Her glance strayed to the front door. "Here comes your next client. Motor Mouth will keep you occupied."

Stifling a groan, Marla turned to greet her latest customer. The woman didn't shut up the entire time she sat in the chair. *You can talk an ear off a brass monkey,* Marla told her client silently, impatient to finish so she could mull over Nicole's words. Just how far would Cookie go to further her aims?

Gossip filled the rest of the day, including speculation about why Jolene had died.

"I think she was on dope," confided Marla's three o'clock appointment, who was a real yenta.

"Why do you say that?" Marla asked, sifting through the woman's damp strands of hair. Sheila had some perm left on the ends, but she would need another one by her next appointment.

"Jolene was always so wired. That woman had too much energy. It made me tired just watching her. She helped build that chemical company from the ground up, and I'll bet she stepped on some toes along the way. I always wondered how she managed to get a building permit for an industrial plant in our community, too. Who knows whose pocket she lined?"

"How did you meet her?" As far as Marla knew, Sheila chauffeured three kids around all day. Industrial complexes were not her normal milieu.

Sheila's luminous jade eyes met hers in the mirror. "My husband works at Stockhart Industries in the communications department. We attend their obligatory social functions. I was surprised when Jolene wasn't offered the vice presidency when there was an opening a couple of years ago, but the new CEO didn't approve of the way she was handling things. He brought in someone from the outside for the position."

"Was Jolene upset?" Marla queried, parting her client's hair with a comb.

Sheila shrugged. "Not that I could tell, but then I didn't work with the woman. No one will be able to ask her now."

"Are you talking about Jolene Myers?" snapped a customer in Nicole's chair. The slim beautician was applying coloring to the elderly lady's roots. "She was a paragon in our neighborhood. I won't hear anyone talk bad about her. If ever there was a project that needed volunteers, she would always offer her time. Jolene was a trooper, no mistake about it."

Well, there you go, Marla thought, *two different opinions. Will the real Jolene Myers please stand up?*

Not that it was any business of hers. So what if Jolene had been a client? That didn't make it her responsibility to investigate the woman's death. If she were smart, she'd heed Dalton's oft-repeated advice and keep her schnozzle out of places it didn't belong.

Nonetheless, when Sunday rolled around, eagerness made her bound out of bed. Surely people would gossip about Jolene at the sports club. She'd ask a few questions—merely to satisfy her inquisitive nature, of course—when she met Tally there later. And if she learned something juicy, she'd pass it on to the good lieutenant when they saw each other next.

"Come on, Spooks, let's go for a walk," she said, reaching for the poodle's leash, which hung on a hook in the kitchen. Hearing the familiar rattle, Spooks raced into the room and stood patiently while she fixed his restraint. She scratched his cream-colored coat before straightening her spine. Morning walks were their routine because she was often too tired after work to do much more than let him out into the backyard.

Outside, the January air was cool but bracing as they headed down the street. Green Hills was an exclusive town house community in western Broward County. Marla liked being near major shopping centers. She hunted for special outfits at Tally's boutique; otherwise, sales at Burdines drew her attention.

"Remind me to ask Tally if she got in the new spring line yet," Marla told Spooks, stopping while he sniffed the grass. It was impossible to move at a brisk pace when he halted every few feet either to do his thing or follow scents. Letting her mind wander, she wondered what Vail had learned about Jolene's death. *Whenever it is, he won't tell you. He gets closemouthed when on a case.* Besides, this may all have been a tragic accident.

"Hey, Marla," called her neighbor Goat as she rounded the corner toward her home. "How's it going?" Wearing a sheepskin vest over a plaid long-sleeved shirt and jeans, the young man crouched on the ground. He held an open jar in one hand and a fly swatter in the other. Strands of straw-colored hair stuck out from a raccoon cap on his head.

Marla's mouth quirked into a smile. "I'm just fine, Goat. What are you doing?"

"Creepy crawly into the brink, come on, little fellows, into the drink." Making kissing noises, he shook the jar, which contained a sprinkling of water.

Marla glanced at his closed front door, wondering why she didn't hear the usual sound track of animals emanating from the interior. "How's your menagerie? Are you looking to add to your collection?"

Rising to his feet, Goat undulated his body. "Come on, you lizard buggers. I'm gonna get you! Come out, come out, wherever you are. Junior has to eat today," he explained.

"Junior?"

His expression brightened. "The sweet serpent of my life," he crooned. "Would you like to see her?" Focusing on Spooks, who strained at the leash to get away, he leered. "I bet Junior would be glad to see *him.*"

"Ah, no thanks." Marla backed away, her eyes wandering to his van, emblazoned with "The Gay Groomer." Did any of his clients lose their pets during the grooming process? *No, silly.* Goat had been kind enough to retrieve Spooks when he ran away from home several months ago after the break-in. Goat had rescued her precious poodle, who had emerged unscathed from his host's lair.

"Have you seen Moss lately?" she asked, changing the subject. "His wife said he had a new limerick to tell me."

"Nope. The old guy's been out a lot. He's probably busier in his retirement than when he worked as a carpenter." Goat gave her a keen appraisal. "I could use a new holding pen for Gertrude. I should ask the codger to build one for me. You really need to meet my friends inside, Marla. Ba-a-a," he imitated, doing a sheep walk.

"No time today, sorry." Marla hastened away, feeling the cold wind bite through her clothes and chill her bones. Maybe when Dalton accompanied her, she'd venture into Goat's house. Her neighbor might be one card short in his deck, but he seemed harmless. It was his so-called friends who bothered her.

After releasing Spooks in her kitchen, she rubbed her arms to restore the circulation. Putting the heat on was an option. In south Florida, heating systems were as inefficient as air-conditioning up north: inadequate and never the right temperature. But it might take the edge off the cold in her town house, so she upped the thermostat to seventy degrees.

While she was microwaving a cup of coffee, the phone rang.

"Hi, Ma," she said upon recognizing Anita's lilting tone. "I thought you were going to a breakfast meeting at the synagogue today."

"I'm on my way out the door, but I wanted to know if you saw the local news section. Your name is mentioned."

"It is?" She'd rifled through the *Sun-Sentinel* earlier and hadn't noticed anything. "Which newspaper?"

"The *Miami Herald* reported a drowning at your health club, and it says you gave a statement to the police. Marla, you're not getting mixed up in something dreadful again, are you? Because if so, you're really meshuga. I hope your involvement has nothing to do with that good-looking detective."

Marla planted a hand on her hip. "I just happened to be there when the accident occurred."

"We'll discuss it when you come for lunch this afternoon." Anita hung up before she had a chance to retort.

Great. Now she had an interrogation to look forward to when she went to her mother's place. In the meantime, she was curious about the *Herald* article, so she bought a morning edition on her way to the Perfect Fit Sports Club.

Tucking the local section into her gym bag, she cruised into the lobby, where her eyes widened in surprise. Friday night must have been a fluke, because lively chatter filled the spacious entry. Members dressed in athletic shorts and tops milled about the juice bar. Couples sat at tables sipping hot beverages. Amy bustled behind the counter, preparing snacks and fruit shakes. Occupied with a customer, the receptionist waved at Marla.

Passing through a set of glass doors into the wet area, Marla noted the aquatics class was full. About twenty elderly women stood in the water, flapping their arms as though they were ducks, while a loud sound track played the chicken dance. Leading the troupe was a buxom brunette whose hourglass figure could have belonged to a beauty queen.

Careful not to slip on the damp tiles, Marla hastened past the whirlpool, where three gray-haired men lounged in the swirling water. She spared a quick glance in their direction, surprised the area wasn't closed off to members by yellow police tape. Didn't it matter that a woman had died there recently?

Her mood darkened when she thought about how callous society had become. Life went on routinely despite tragedy. One minute you're here, laughing and chatting with friends, and the next you're gone. *Time moves forward, stopping for nobody.* Those left behind still had their lives to live out, and who would begrudge them happiness? Yet Marla would have felt better if some respect had been shown to Jolene. The whirlpool could have been closed at least for the weekend.

Seeking solace from her friend, she sought Tally in the locker room. The tall blonde grinned broadly when she saw Marla. Always stylish, she wore a designer shorts set and Nike sneakers. Marla glanced down at her sweatsuit. It was too cold to wear shorts, so she'd opted for comfort over glamour.

"Hey, Marla! I was wondering if you'd make it. Normally, you're a late riser on Sundays." Tally's blue eyes gleamed with pleasure, as though she actually anticipated getting a workout.

"Believe it, pal. I even took Spooks for a walk already."

"I heard what happened." Tally spoke softly since the room was crowded. "Why didn't you call me Friday night?"

"I was too tired." Marla didn't admit to meeting Dalton, not caring to go into the details of their current relationship.

"You'll tell me about it later. Which class should we join, or do you want to start on the machines?" Handing Marla a yellow sheet of paper, Tally pointed to the Sunday schedule.

Squinting, Marla studied their choices. "Scratch the Step Reebok and the fab abs. Too strenuous for me. The splash class has already started, and besides, the older generation has dibs on that one."

"How about yoga? I need to stretch my muscles."

Contort them was more likely. "I don't think so."

"That leaves only pace race or Dancercize."

"Pace race isn't until eleven. Let's try Dancercize." Hadn't Keith recommended that class? Thinking of him reminded her that she wanted to have her body fat measurement recalibrated with the machine. His deductions about her weight had to be wrong.

Upstairs in a wood-floored studio, they checked in with the Dancercize instructor, a bleached blonde who managed her chin-length layered hair in an attractively tousled style. Subtle makeup highlighted emerald eyes as clear as a mountain lake and outlined thinly contoured lips. Her figure, Marla decided, was to die for. No way could I ever wear a leotard and look that good. Did all the female staff members have to resemble Barbie with hair color variations? she mused inwardly, recalling the swim coach.

"Have you taken Dancercize before?" Lindsay Trotter asked.

Marla shook her head. "Not unless it's the same thing as Jazzercize. I took that at Central Park once, but it was too time-consuming, so I quit."

The dance teacher smiled. "Dancercize is quite different. It's more fun because we use music from the big band era. You'll feel like you're dancing more than exercising. Since this is your first time, if you get out of breath or experience any discomfort, stop and watch the rest of the class. Ladies, are you ready?" she addressed the group of thirty participants.

Tally sidled to the back row, and Marla took a place beside her. "Some of these women have no shame," Marla said in a low voice, nodding at a couple of plump members in tank tops and shorts whose flab could have qualified them for ballast. "I don't want to get like them."

Her friend laughed. "What are you talking about? You look fabulous. If you've gained weight, it doesn't show."

"Oh yeah, these baggy pants really reveal my legs. Anyway, the extra pounds I gain are in the middle."

"How old are you, dear?" Tally smirked. "Getting closer to forty, I believe. Your thirty-fifth birthday is in a few weeks."

"You're not far behind, pal."

It was an ongoing joke between them that Marla was six months older than Tally, so that made her the elder but not necessarily the wiser. While Tally was happily married to Ken, Marla still struggled with her social life. Having made mistakes in her choices of men before to please her family, she was hesitant to commit herself for fear of losing her independence.

Dancercize was more fun than she'd anticipated, and Marla lasted a good thirty minutes before quitting to catch her breath. With an envious eye, she watched Lindsay sail through the hour with a continuous smile and not even a sheen on her healthy complexion.

Tally, having held out longer, staggered to join Marla, who leaned against the rear wall.

"I'm going to look for Dave," Marla said after the class finished. "He's a personal trainer who does the bioelectrical impedance test for body fat percentage."

Her hopes were dashed, however, when Dave flashed her a grin and demanded her membership card. "Not a full member? Sorry, you're not entitled to use the machine."

"Keith did some calculations with a tape measure. He said I needed a diet of ten blocks a day. That doesn't seem like enough."

"Blocks? I don't know what you mean. And I've never heard of using a tape measure. There's the caliper test to measure body fat percentage."

"Keith said he was using the circumference method."

"Never heard of it. He must have been pulling your leg. Keith can get too personal with the ladies, if you know what I mean." Dave winked. "Talk to Gloria downstairs. She'll give you a contract to sign, and then I can get you started properly."

"No, thanks." Annoyed, Marla stalked away to join Tally in the locker room, where she was changing.

"All they want in this place is your money," Marla griped, wiping her face with a paper towel from the bathroom. "If you don't sign away your life for three years, you don't count."

Tally's gaze locked with hers. "Lindsay seemed friendly and eager that everyone should have a good time."

"That's true. Unlike some of the other jerks who work here, Lindsay acts like she cares. I should ask her about Jolene."

"Why?"

"When I saw Jolene, she'd just come from Dancercize class. If she wasn't feeling up to par, Lindsay may have noticed."

"Tell me the details."

Aware that others in the room were listening, Marla lowered her decibels. "I entered the locker room and overheard Jolene arguing with someone else. When Jolene saw me, she drew me into their conversation."

"You interfering bitch!" a strident voice exclaimed behind her.

Marla whirled around, her eyes widening at the sight of Cookie Calcone shaking a fist in the air.

"That conversation was private," Cookie cried. "How dare you tell the police that I threatened Jolene."

Chapter Four

M arla stared at Cookie, unable to fathom what had provoked her verbal attack. "Excuse me? I didn't tell the police you made any threats against Jolene."

"Oh no? Then who did?" Cookie's green eyes threw fire. "I got a call from a detective who wanted to know what I was arguing about with Jolene. You were the only other one in the locker room with us."

Marla lifted her foot onto the bench so she could retie a loose shoelace. "I told Lieutenant Vail I'd met Jolene in the locker room, and she introduced you to me. I didn't mention the gist of your conversation."

A suspicious expression crossed Cookie's face. She really has good bone structure, Marla thought, glancing at her jutting chin and contoured cheekbones. Short, strawberry blond hair was styled into a side part with minimal effort put into curling the ends. Cookie's simplistic fashion statement continued with faded jeans and an Old Navy T-shirt. She wore the barest of makeup, her entire appearance telling Marla this was a woman who cared more about being active than about her looks.

"Did you leave the club right after your swim?" Marla asked.

"I wasn't here when Jolene drowned, if that's what you mean," Cookie snapped.

Finished tying her shoe, Marla straightened. Tally shot her a quizzical glance, and Marla realized she'd forgotten her manners. "I'm sorry, Tally Riggs this is Cookie Calcone. Tally and I joined for the trial membership," she explained, feeling the need to defend herself. "Look, I told the detective that you were here that day, but I also mentioned the Zelmans and Wally Ritiker. I didn't tell him about your argument with Jolene."

Cookie pouted as though wanting to disbelieve her. "Lieutenant Vail accused me of raising my voice in anger. How else would he have known I was pissed at Jolene? Someone ratted on me! What does he think, that I pushed her under water?"

That was a possibility Marla hadn't considered. Another option presented itself. "Perhaps someone entered through the rear door to the locker room and overheard us," she suggested. "Who else might have reported our conversation to the cops?"

"I figured it was you. The detective said an informant had left a tip on their hotline."

Biting her lower lip, Marla evaluated this tidbit of news. Did Dalton really have no clue who'd phoned, or did he just say that as a smoke screen? Could someone else have been quietly listening to Cookie's diatribe against Jolene? Marla made a mental determination to ask to see the member sign-in sheet for that night. Other club members might have been present that she hadn't noticed. Then again, one of the female staffers could have entered the locker room from the rear.

Aware that her mother was expecting her for lunch, Marla glanced purposefully at her watch. "If you don't mind," she said, "I need to move on. Dancercize class was fun, but I think that's enough exercise for today."

Cookie blocked her path, squeezing Tally against a row of lockers. "I do mind. What's the name of your salon?"

"Cut 'N Dye," Marla replied automatically.

"I'll be keeping an eye on you. You'd better not talk about me behind my back. If I find out that you're spreading rumors, you'll be sorry you ever met me." Her glance shot at Tally. "You work with her?"

Tally shifted uncomfortably. "No, I own a dress boutique. What's your beef, lady? Marla hasn't done anything to you. Why don't you pick on someone your size?" Tally's considerable height above the shorter woman gave her words more emphasis.

If Cookie's eyes could have spurted venom, Tally would have been dead. "Are you meaning to take me on?" Cookie snarled. "Go ahead, I've got room for the two of you. From now on, you're both on my blacklist. Watch your backs, ladies." Thrusting her chin forward, she marched out.

Tally swiped a hand across her brow. "Whew, I'm glad she's gone. What a witch! She's got a hell of a nerve talking to you like that."

Marla shrugged. "I'm not going to lose any sleep over her. Sorry to cut this short, but Ma expects me for lunch, and I've got to do some errands on the way." Pulling a cranberry sweater and black slacks from her bag, she proceeded to switch outfits. She didn't care to be seen in her sweatsuit around town.

"When shall we meet here again?" Tally asked.

"Well, let's see. Tomorrow, I'm visiting my brother and his family. Tuesday evening, I promised to take Brianna to dance class." Noting Tally's raised eyebrows, Marla offered a quick explanation. "Dalton has to work late for a few weeks, so he'll be unable to take her. I said I'd do it, but it doesn't mean we're getting more involved."

Tally snorted. "That's what you think, darling."

Pointing a finger, Marla leaned forward. "Look, I'm not a schmuck. I won't let myself get tied down on a regular basis. You know I'm not into kids and that whole routine."

"Uh-huh."

"Wipe that expression off your face, pal. Unless you want to be added to my blacklist," she mimicked with a grin.

Tally snatched up her gym bag and slung the strap over her shoulder. "What about Wednesday night? Any plans? I know you work late on Thursdays."

"Okay, Wednesday it is." She rolled her neck. "I should make a massage appointment. My shoulders have been stiff lately, and I could use a good rubdown."

"You try it first," Tally said, grinning. "I've never had a real massage, but then Ken has magic fingers. Maybe you should ask Dalton to rub your neck."

"Yeah, right." Marla wouldn't want him to stop there. The prospect of his fingers touching her skin sent tingles of delight along her nerves, as she could just imagine his caress descending lower. "What time Wednesday should we meet?" she rasped, a heated flush warming her face.

"How about seven o'clock? We can work out on the machines and try the low-impact aerobics class, unless you want to stick with Dancercize."

"We'll see. I'll make a massage appointment for nine."

She approached Sharon at the reception counter. Whoever normally staffed the massage desk was absent. "Who are your other therapists besides Slate?" she asked. "I need an appointment for Wednesday night."

Sharon's nose crinkled. "Manny Kosmo might be available, but if you want my honest opinion, he's not as good as Slate. Wait here; I'll get the appointment book."

"Did Jolene schedule a massage with Manny on Friday night?" Marla asked when Sharon had returned.

Sharon flipped a couple pages back in the calendar. "Manny's name is crossed out. He's been sick all weekend, so he must have canceled his appointments for Friday."

Leaning her elbow on the counter, Marla lowered her voice. "Does that mean Jolene switched to Slate? She didn't like him because he'd asked her for a date and got angry when she refused him. Or so she told me."

"Slate is used to getting his way," grated a harsh voice behind her.

"Amy, this conversation doesn't involve you," Sharon said in an icy tone.

Turning, Marla caught the Smoothie King attendant running stiff fingers through her bleached hair. *You need your roots done, pal*, she thought, her gaze drawn to the dark-brown layer growing in.

Amy frowned, a movement that accentuated the creases in her overly made-up face. She wore skintight jeans and a white blouse unbuttoned to mid-bosom, revealing a lacy bra. "Slate shouldn't have asked Jolene out. He knows I'm hot for him, and I can handle his moods. He gets nasty when he's crossed."

"How nasty?" Marla asked.

"Why do you care?"

"I was Jolene's hairdresser, and I'd like to understand what happened to her." She glanced at Sharon, who gazed at Amy with an unconcealed look of contempt. Animosity crackled between the two women, and Marla wondered why. Was it merely their difference in values, or was it something more?

When Sharon turned away to tend to another customer, Amy spoke. "If you're looking for someone who had a grudge against Jolene, don't bother with Slate. He's my territory, understand? Go talk to Keith Hamilton instead. That jerk is happy she's dead. So are a lot of other people around here."

"Really? I'll keep that in mind." Wishing she had time to question the girl further, Marla glanced at the wall clock and frowned. If she wanted to get her errands done, she'd better get moving. "I've got to go," she said regretfully, "but thanks for the tip."

After the girl went back to her post, Marla signaled to Sharon. "Book me with Slate for Wednesday at nine," she said. "It could prove to be an interesting session."

"Why do you think Amy said those things to you?" asked Anita Shorstein an hour later.

"Ma, please sit down. I have enough to eat, and it makes me nervous when you bustle around like that." Holding a corned-beef-on-rye sandwich, Marla sat at her mother's small kitchen table. After Anita got a cream soda and joined her, Marla answered. "It sounds like Amy has the hots for Slate, who hit on Jolene. According to Amy, Slate might have gotten nasty when Jolene rejected him."

Anita took a swallow of her drink. "Do you think he had anything to do with her death?"

"As far as I know, no one had anything to do with Jolene's accident. I'm not sure what Amy meant, but maybe Slate will tell me his version when he gives me a massage on Wednesday."

Anita waved an admonishing finger at her. "Is that wise, Marla? If you take my advice, you won't go back to the sports club. You didn't pay anything for your trial membership."

"Tally would be disappointed if I dropped out now." She chewed a bite of sandwich, relishing the salty meat. "Besides, I'm not a quitter. I didn't give up my position as chef coordinator for Taste of the World when someone sabotaged our efforts. Cynthia depended on me to do my job, just as Tally needs me to go with her now. I don't let my friends down."

"That doesn't explain why you're making a big deal out of Jolene's tragic end. Somehow I don't think it's just because she was a client." Anita's all-knowing motherly gaze met Marla's troubled glance.

Putting down her sandwich, Marla folded her hands on the table. "Okay, so I'm bored."

"Oh?"

"Taste of the World gave me a focus for the past few months. I was so busy between the fund-raiser and work that I didn't have time to think about anything else. Now the holidays are over, and I'm stuck in my everyday routine again."

"You should say a prayer every time you wake up in the morning to face another day. Be grateful for your routine." Anita hardened her gaze. "Remember when Papa died? That phone call we got?"

Marla hung her head. "Of course I do. His heart attack was totally unexpected."

"Things could be worse. Think of that when you go about your daily business. Jolene's accident had nothing to do with you. Don't make it into more than it was to liven things up."

"You're beginning to sound like Dalton."

Anita rolled her eyes. "I hate to say this, but sometimes I agree with the man. Don't take that as approval of your irregular relationship with him."

"Irregular? What does that mean?"

"You're still dating other guys, like Ralph. I know the two of you are friends, but if you felt a commitment to Detective Vail, you wouldn't want to be in anyone's company but his."

Marla kept her tone neutral. "And if that's what I decided?"

Her mother shrugged. "I've already told you my opinion. Cops make lousy husbands."

"So do arrogant lawyers who impose their will on others."

"Stan believed he was acting in your best interests."

"By keeping me from seeing my own friends and putting me down constantly? I don't think so." She chomped on another piece of sandwich. "Anyway, I didn't come here to discuss Stan or my love life."

Anita patted her hand. "I know, *bubula*. Are you going to let me take you to lunch for your birthday?"

"Ugh, don't remind me. I don't want to get older."

"You'd prefer the alternative? I doubt it."

"I'm getting fat, and the sports club receptionist asked if I dyed my hair. Do I look that bad for my age?"

"You look beautiful."

"Soon I'll be getting wrinkles."

Anita laughed, a pleasant sound like clinking crystal goblets. "Snap out of your mood, Marla. Or do you have PMS?"

Marla nearly choked on a morsel of corned beef. "Hell, no. I had that last week."

"Then you need something to focus on, so you don't think about yourself so much. Plan a dinner party. That always works when I'm depressed, because I get busy planning menus and can look forward to being with friends."

"Thanks, but it sounds like more aggravation to me." Finishing her sandwich, she fell silent. True, she'd been feeling restless lately. Was her moodiness due to a letdown after the holidays, or was she upset over her upcoming birthday? Either way, Ma was right. She needed a new goal, one that was more fun than getting into shape.

Unwilling to address her insecurities further, she wiped her mouth with a napkin and got up. "What are you doing this afternoon?" she asked her mother. "I've got some errands to run if you want to come with me."

Anita shook her head of short, white hair. "I have ballet tickets with my friend, Lil. I'm picking her up in a half hour." She glanced at a table in the hallway. "I won't have time to stop at the pharmacy. My blood pressure prescription needs to be refilled."

Marla spotted the paper with the doctor's scrawled handwriting. "Want me to drop this off? The pharmacy is on my list of errands. I need more vitamins and a few other things."

"That would be helpful. Then I could pick up the medicine on my way back from the theater." Anita embraced her in a quick hug. "Call me after you see Michael tomorrow. Your brother thought he might be coming down with a cold."

"Maybe I'll bring him some zinc lozenges." Marla grinned. "Have a good time at the ballet."

Hank Goodfellow was behind the counter at the pharmacy. After twelve years, his white-coated figure was a fixture in the community. Neighbors relied on his advice, which he dispensed with a twinkle in his blue eyes. At forty-two, his dark hair had receded considerably, but his face held enough character for him to be regarded as a handsome devil by female clients.

"How are ya, Marla?" he queried when she approached. A wide grin lit his entire face. His winged brows lifted, the deep creases beside his eyes indicating that he smiled frequently

She tipped her head in acknowledgment. "Just fine, Hank. Here's a prescription for my mother. She'll stop by later to pick up the medicine."

"Okay. You need any more of your favorite hand cream?"

"No, thanks. That stuff really works, and I've been careful not to let my hands get too dry. They're not so chapped now."

Hank glanced behind her, and his mouth tightened. "Excuse me, Marla. Here comes Wally."

Marla twisted around to see Councilman Wallace Ritiker bearing down on them, an angry scowl on his face.

"Hey, Marla," he greeted her before turning his attention to the pharmacist. "Hank, can I have a word with you?"

Marla caught the hint and drifted discreetly away. Studying a display of vitamins, she still heard every word they said.

"I understand you had a break-in a couple of days ago," Wally's voice grated in a low tone. "Why didn't you call me?"

"What for?" Hank replied.

Marla neared a corner where she could view the interchange without being in their direct line of sight.

"I expect to be informed when something like this happens that affects the town." Ritiker tugged at his navy sport coat.

Hank's face grew livid as he stared at the middle-aged politician. "Are you crazy? I'm trying to avoid publicity."

"Oh, you've done a great job. Burglars rammed a hole through the roof, lowered themselves inside, and stole prescription drugs and cash. That was splashed all over the community newspapers, including how your alarm was conveniently shut off," Ritiker said in a snide tone.

"A wire was loose, and I didn't want to trip a false alarm, so I de-activated it until the security company came out," Hank said in a curt tone that implied it was no one else's business.

"How'd the crooks get out?"

"They broke the back door lock and got away clean."

"I warned you about this sort of thing. People will be suspicious." Ritiker glowered at the pharmacist.

"It was necessary."

"Well, keep me out of it, or you'll be sorry."

Marla sauntered toward them, wanting to detain the councilman for her own purposes.

"Was there something else you wanted from the pharmacy?" Hank snapped at her.

"Not right now, thanks." Boldly lifting her chin, she addressed the councilman. "Wally, I've been meaning to thank you for voting in favor of the pool enclosure ordinance. It's too bad we didn't have enough votes for it to pass, but I appreciate your support."

Squaring his shoulders, Ritiker beamed at her. "I always support my constituents."

Marla twirled a strand of hair coyly around her finger. "I guess all your wheeling and dealing takes its toll. Eloise Zelman told me you belong to the Perfect Fit Sports Club. I just joined with my friend Tally for the free trial membership. Isn't it awful what happened to Jolene Myers?"

"That troublemaker?" His eyebrows raised. "She was a thorn in my side. Can't say I'm sorry she's gone."

An old lady shuffled to the counter. "Oh hello, Mrs. Jenkins," the pharmacist gushed, assuming his professional demeanor. "Is your ankle better? You could barely walk last week. I hope those cold compresses were helpful."

"Indeed they were, but I could use more of that pain medicine, sonny. Do you still have any available?"

"Of course." He did a quick exchange, handing her a bottle that he retrieved from a locked drawer in return for a twenty-dollar bill.

"Hank," Ritiker began, an odd glimmer in his eyes.

"Not now, Wally. I'm tending my customer."

"I see exactly what you're doing. Didn't I tell you it was time to quit?" the councilman said.

Hank shot him a dirty look. "Keep out of this."

"Or what? Listen carefully, friend, if you're smart, you'll heed my words." Turning away, he indicated Marla should accompany him. "I hope you're not on his list."

"What are you talking about?" Marla said.

Wally gave her a keen glance and shook his head. "Never mind. What were you saying about Jolene Myers?"

"Eloise Zelman said you were in the steam room with her husband Sam when all hell broke loose in the sports club that day. Was anyone else in there with you?"

"Nope. Sam and I had things to discuss in private, so we made sure no one else was around."

"How about when you entered the locker room to change?"

He stopped in the aisle by a display of household cleaning fluids. "Why are you so interested?"

She spread her hands. "I just thought I might have more information to offer to the police. Detective Vail is a friend of mine. He's not officially on the case as far as I know, but I'm sure he'd pass on anything useful."

His hazel eyes stared down at her. "We need more responsible citizens like you, Marla," he said, clapping a hand on her shoulder. "Now if you want to know who I saw skulking about that day, you might consider talking to Gloria Muñoz, the sales rep. I saw her leaving the women's locker room as I was on my way to the steamer. I remembered the look on her face. She reminded me of a cat who'd just swallowed a bird whole."

Chapter Five

Marla didn't have time to think about Councilman Ritiker's remarks. Monday was taken with visiting her brother and catching up on bookkeeping in preparation for the dreaded meeting with her tax accountant. On Tuesday, work was busier than usual, so lunch consisted of yogurt and a banana in the back room.

Waiting for her final appointment, she was brushing stray hairs off her station chair when the chime over the front door sounded. Marla glanced up, eager to do her last customer so she could leave. Tonight was Brianna's dance class, and she wanted to be on time to pick the girl up.

"Arnie, what are you doing here?" she asked as the proprietor of Bagel Buster's charged in her direction.

"Marla, you've got to help me!" The big man's mustache quivered, and his dark eyes regarded her wildly.

Aware of her staff's interest, she took his arm and gently propelled him toward an empty manicure station at the rear. He still wore an apron over a collared shirt and khakis. Beneath the fabric, she felt the rock-hardness of his biceps.

"What's wrong?" she said. "Are your kids all right?"

"Yes. That's not the problem. It's Hortense."

"Who?"

"Hortense Crone. You know."

She tapped her foot impatiently. "No, I don't. You're confusing me, Arnie. Who is this person?"

Arnie wrung his hands. "She's a former classmate. We went to high school together, and she had a crush on me. The ugliest dog in school, that was her. A real *fresser*, too. Ate everything in sight. And now she's here! *Oy vey*, what am I going to do?"

"What do you mean?" Marla glanced furtively at the reception area, hoping her next client would be delayed. Arnie needed her, making her nurturing instincts surface.

"Hortense is in town. She wants to see me. She's on her way over here!"

"So? You can exchange a few reminiscences and then she'll leave."

He leaned forward, breathing heavily. "You don't understand. She *likes* me. Hortense said she'd been sorry to learn my wife had passed away, and how difficult it must be for me to raise two kids on my own. I could tell from her tone of voice that she's still interested in me."

"Hortense never married?"

"She's divorced." His brows drew together. "I said the only thing I could think of to get rid of her. I told her I was engaged."

Marla smiled gently. "Arnie, how could you? The poor woman probably just wants an hour of your time."

"No, no. She's moving back to Palm Haven! I had to discourage her. Tell me you'll play along."

"Huh?"

"I knew you wouldn't mind, since you're such a good friend." Taking her by the elbow, he steered her into the rear storeroom. "She'll come into the salon. Tell her off for me, would you please?"

"Me?" She wrinkled her nose. "Why would she come here?"

"Oh, God," he moaned. "I remember how her second chin jiggled when she waddled down the hall. She was the only girl with frizzy black hair whose boobs were overpowered by her blubber." His eyes grew as round as bagel holes when the front door chimed.

"That may be Hortense!" he croaked. "Marla, you've got to save me. I'll give you free bagels for a year!"

"You're on," she said, laughing. How bad could this woman be to make Arnie so afraid of her? Intensely curious, Marla strode toward the reception desk.

The woman standing by the counter wasn't the ugly horse Arnie had depicted. Nor was she Marla's next client. A tall, sexy blonde, she wore a short skirt and bolero jacket with black leather heels. Wavy hair cascaded like a river down her back. A delicate lilac fragrance wafted around her. Marla approved of the woman's subtle makeup that enhanced her refined features. Envying her busty figure and shapely legs, Marla vowed to work out extra hard at the fitness club on Wednesday.

"This is Marla Shore," said the receptionist. "She owns Cut 'N Dye."

"Hi, I'm Hortense Crone." The woman grinned, displaying a row of perfectly aligned teeth. "I was told Arnie Hartman came in here. Y'all can call me Jill; I use my middle name now," she added, extending her hand.

Marla exchanged a firm handshake. *This* was Hortense? A bubble of laughter welled within her. Would Arnie be surprised to see what a looker his classmate had turned into!

"He's in the storeroom. I'll get him for you. Hey, Arnie," she called, eagerly anticipating his reaction. "Someone here to see you."

All eyes in the salon turned in their direction as Arnie marched toward the front, gaze downcast like a condemned man.

"Congratulations, Arnie," crooned Hortense. "You have a lovely fiancée."

Marla, entertained by Arnie's sudden, shocked glare as he raised his eyes, didn't catch on right away until she heard snickers from her staff.

"Don't tell me," she said to Hortense. "Arnie told you *we're* engaged?"

"Oh, yes. I hope you won't get jealous if I give him a hug. It's been so long, hasn't it, darling?" she said, crushing Arnie in a tight embrace.

"Y-yes," he stuttered, words obviously failing him.

Hortense stepped away, beaming at Marla. "We've so much news to share. Let's make a date and get together to shmooze."

"Of course," Marla said, playing her part for all it was worth. Serves the man right, she thought wickedly, tucking a possessive arm through Arnie's.

"Friday night?"

"Can't," Arnie mumbled. "Religious services."

Marla stared at him. Since when had he started celebrating the Sabbath?

"Saturday evening then. I'll meet you at the Spice Garden at seven-thirty, okay?" Hortense glanced between the two of them, her happy expression lacking any sense of guile.

Marla's heart went out to her. The woman seemed sincere in her desire to see Arnie for old times' sake. What harm could one date do?

"He's already gotten a babysitter," she said in a confidential tone to Hortense. "We were going out to dinner anyway, and it'll be a pleasure to get to know you better. Right, Arnie?" She poked him when he didn't answer. He'd been too busy studying Hortense's cleavage.

"Uh, sure. We'll be there." Arnie turned to Marla as soon as Hortense left. Before he uttered a word, the receptionist gestured Marla over.

"Grace just canceled her appointment. She's running late and is terribly sorry. She rescheduled for tomorrow morning."

"Good," Marla said, relieved that her work was finished. Now she could clean up and get ready for her duties with Brianna.

"Marla, is it true?" the girl asked. She was a temporary hire until Marla located a replacement. It wasn't easy finding a candidate who fulfilled Marla's stringent requirements for the position.

"What's that?" Marla asked, distracted by Arnie's hangdog expression.

"Are you Arnie's fiancée?" the girl persisted.

"Heck, no. It was a pretense to get Hortense off his back."

Arnie shook his head. "I don't want her off my back."

"Huh?"

"Did you see her? She's a *knockout!* Why the hell did I ever tell her I was engaged?"

"Shit, Arnie, make up your mind." Disgusted, she ignored the grins of her staff and marched to her station.

Arnie trailed after her, watching while she cleaned her counter. "Maybe we could have a fight and break off," he suggested. "Then I can tell Hortense I'm free again."

"She'll believe you're not reliable."

"So I'll get to know her first. I have an idea. Why don't we double date?"

"Ouch!" Marla felt a sharp jab of pain where she'd cut her finger on a pair of texturizing shears. "Get me a Band-Aid from that drawer, would you?" she requested, sucking on her fingertip.

Arnie complied. "Shall I kiss your hand first to make it better?" he teased, dimples appearing in his cheeks when he smiled.

"No, thanks." She applied the Band-Aid and resumed cleaning her shelf. "So tell me about your idea." Anything to get Arnie off *her* back.

"We'll invite another guy to go along with us when we meet Hortense. He can pay attention to you, and I'll focus on her."

"Won't Hortense think that's odd?"

"Not at all." Stroking his droopy mustache, he appeared thoughtful. "She'll understand I'm just interested in renewing our acquaintance. Then, when you and I have a fight, hopefully she'll be there to comfort me."

"Arnie, you're despicable." Yet his scheme appealed to her sense of adventure. Wasn't she looking for something to uplift her mood? Playing Arnie's game would serve to get him off her list, which was well and good because she'd always considered them close friends and nothing more. "Okay, who do you suggest we get to act as decoy?"

A broad grin split his face. "I know just the man: Detective Dalton Vail. He broods over you, so he'll be perfect."

Marla's jaw dropped. "Dalton! I don't think so. He'd be furious if we suggested this to him. He didn't like it when I went out with

David. Can you imagine what he'd say to pretending I'm your fiancée?"

"Ask him, Marla. Otherwise, you're stuck with me. Hortense knows a lot of people in town. I can assure you the news of our betrothal will be smeared like shmaltz all over Palm Haven by tonight."

Marla approached Vail's ranch-style house with trepidation. A dim lantern shone over the portico, but spotlights from the garage provided bright illumination. She pushed the doorbell, shifting her feet while waiting to see who responded to her summons. She'd ask Dalton now if he was home. Better to get it over with, that was her motto.

She took a step back when the door swung open, revealing Brianna's sullen face.

"Hi," the girl said. "I'll get my dance bag." Turning on her heel, Brianna retreated into the hallway without inviting Marla to enter. She wore a leotard and tights under an oversized T-shirt. A pair of white Steve Madden tennis shoes covered her feet.

"Is your Dad home?" Marla called, resisting the urge to clench her fists. This wasn't going to be a pleasant encounter.

Holding a pink sack, Brianna walked toward her. "He's still at work, and Carmen left after she fixed my dinner. I took Lucky out for a walk before getting changed," she added proudly.

"Golden retrievers need lots of exercise," Marla said approvingly as she walked beside the girl to her Toyota. "By the way, I like your bun. Did you put your hair up yourself?"

Brianna gave her a condescending look. "Of course. Do you think I'm so retarded that I can't do anything on my own?"

"I didn't mean that."

The girl's dark eyes raked her with scorn. "Let's get something straight, Miss Shore. I know you agreed to take me tonight to impress my dad. This is just temporary until I find another ride, understand?"

"I offered because I wanted to help," Marla said, holding the passenger door open.

"We don't need anyone's help." Brianna folded her arms while

Marla slid into the driver's seat and started the car. "Daddy is just being nice to you because you solved a couple of his cases. That's why he agreed to let you drive me."

"Oh, is that the reason? I'm so glad you told me. Where are we going?"

"Dance Artists Performance Studio. It's in The Fountains."

"What time do I have to pick you up?"

"Ten o'clock. Ballet class comes first, then I have jazz." The preteen turned away, staring out the window. "I just remembered, you might have to come inside. They're measuring for recital costumes, and we have to pay a deposit."

Driving down West Broward Boulevard, Marla gave her a quick glance. The girl's tightened mouth and pinched face told Marla how much it had pained Brianna to say those words.

"I'm glad I brought my checkbook," she said brightly.

Her head averted, Brianna didn't answer.

I'm trying to be nice, pal. If you can't handle that, you've got problems. "How's your dad's latest case going? Do you think he'll wrap it up soon so he can be home earlier?" she asked, her nose for news propelling the inquiry.

"Who knows?" Brianna retorted.

"Did he mention what happened to my client Jolene, by any chance?"

Brianna swiveled her head to regard Marla with a sneer. "If he did, I wouldn't tell you. Dad confides in me because I can keep secrets."

"I can, too, if he'd trust me," Marla murmured. Brianna's response was a scornful sniff.

When they arrived at the dance studio, Brianna hopped out of the car before Marla had a chance to turn off the ignition. After locking the doors, she stumbled after the girl toward a row of shops. Peals of laughter cascaded from inside the well-lit studio, where students in all age ranges bustled between classes.

"I'm supposed to pay a costume deposit," Marla said to the receptionist, peering through the crowd for Brianna, who had disappeared toward a set of classrooms.

"What's the child's name?" the woman asked with a friendly smile.

"Brianna Vail."

"Brianna is in both of my classes," crooned a voice at Marla's ear.

Marla whirled about, astonished to see Lindsay Trotter, Dancercize instructor for Perfect Fit Sports Club. "You're a teacher here, too?" she blurted.

The sleek blonde, attired in a black leotard, smiled. "It's what I do. Haven't I met you somewhere recently? You're not Brianna's mother, are you?"

Marla's face colored. "No, I'm a friend of her father. She needed a ride tonight, so I offered to take her to class. My friend Tally and I belong to the sports club where you teach Dancercize."

The green eyes widened. "Oh yes, I remember. That was your first time on Sunday. I hope you'll be back again tomorrow."

"We'll try. Brianna said I need to pay a deposit tonight."

"Judy will help you," Lindsay said, gesturing to the receptionist. "Pull Brianna Vail's card, will you?" she ordered. "I've got to get my class started. Nice seeing you." Waving at Marla, Lindsay scooted off.

From inside the nearest classroom, Marla heard the instructor's clear voice ring out: "Dip your shoes in the resin, girls, so you don't slip and slide. Come on, now! We'll start with our pliés. Take positions at the bar, please." Strains of Tchaikovsky floated through the air.

"Your deposit for each class is fifty-three dollars," said the receptionist.

"How much?" Marla's eyes bulged.

"Brianna's costumes cost a hundred and sixty dollars each including tax, so we're asking you to pay a third," the woman explained.

"That's exorbitant," Marla grumbled, retrieving her checkbook. Writing a check for $106 would deplete her account considerably. Maybe she should stop off at the police station and ask Vail for reimbursement. He might have time to take a coffee break while she was there, too.

Still shaking her head at the expense, which didn't even include the price of recital tickets, Marla approached the glass-enclosed front office of the Palm Haven Police Department.

"I'm Marla Shore, here to see Lieutenant Vail."

A few minutes later, she was given a visitor's badge and told to proceed through a door that unlatched as she approached. "I know the way," she told the female officer who greeted her.

Upstairs and to the right, she entered the detective division. Vail's private office was beside a row of cubicles where his subordinates worked. He stood up on catching sight of her and strode to her side.

"Is everything all right? Did you take Brianna to class?"

She glanced at his worried gray eyes and patted his arm. "Yes, I dropped her off and paid her costume deposit to the amount of a hundred and six dollars. I thought I'd drop by and see if you were free for coffee. I don't have to pick her up until ten."

His expression softened, and he gazed at her appreciatively. Her heart quickened at his proximity. "Thanks, Marla," he said quietly. "I knew I could count on you."

Straightening his broad shoulders, he marched to his desk and withdrew a checkbook from a drawer. "Let's settle our account before I forget." While he scribbled the check, she let her gaze roam his tall frame. He'd removed his sport coat and tie so that his dress shirt was unbuttoned at the neck. An empty coffee mug sat on his desk along with a cellophane sandwich wrapper.

"Was that your dinner?" she asked, putting his check in her purse.

"I didn't have time to go out." His glance swept her body, heating her skin.

"Can you spare a few minutes to go downstairs for a snack?" Last time he'd given her a tour, she'd spotted vending machines in the briefing room.

"Sorry, I've too much to do." Plowing a hand wearily through his peppery hair, he sighed. "Seems like I never have time at home anymore. I'm glad you were there to help out tonight, Marla." His voice deepened. "Since you dropped by, I'd like you to look at something for me. Have a seat."

"What are you working on?" she asked, claiming a chair opposite his desk.

"I'll tell you shortly." Sinking into an armchair, he shuffled through a sheaf of papers. "Here it is. This is a copy of the member sign-ins for Friday night at Perfect Fit Sports Club. Recognize any of the names?"

Marla perused the list. Wrinkling her nose, she pointed to each name in turn. "Here's Cookie Calcone. I told you about her. Apparently, she left the club before Jolene's accident. Tally and I had a run-in with her on Sunday. She's the type who looks for any excuse to pick an argument."

Marla shuddered before pushing Cookie's mental image aside.

"Wallace Ritiker was in the steam room with Sam Zelman. Sam's wife, Eloise, was changing in the locker room when she heard screams. Oh, I didn't know Hank Goodfellow was there." The pharmacist had signed in after Cookie. Where had he been during the whole debacle?

"I dropped a prescription off for my mother on Sunday," she added. "I was talking to Hank when Wally popped in. Ritiker mentioned a break-in at the pharmacy and was upset Hank hadn't notified him."

"I'm not surprised."

Vail's wry tone made her glance at him sharply. "What do you know about it?"

The detective shrugged. "Another division is investigating. It's not my jurisdiction. Hank's pharmacy has had a couple of robberies in this past year."

"Really?" Narrowing her eyes, she gave him back the piece of paper. "You didn't tell me what case you're working on. Is it related to Jolene's accident?"

He withdrew another paper from the file. "Here's a list of staff members from the club. Anything unusual that you've learned about these people?"

She smiled inwardly, gratified that he was asking for her input. "Who's this?" she asked, pointing to an unfamiliar name.

"Tesla Parr, one of the massage therapists. Nickname is Tess."

Marla tapped her chin. "Sharon told me the other therapist, Manny Kosmo, had been out sick when Jolene had her appointment Friday night. I remember Jolene saying she wouldn't go back to Slate. Maybe she'd made an appointment with Tess." Memorizing the woman's address in case she needed it later, she lifted her questioning gaze to Vail's somber face. "Dalton, what does all this mean?"

"A multi-drug screening showed sedatives in Jolene's blood. The drug would have been administered about an hour before she went into the Jacuzzi. Those capsules in her bag were gelatin, like you said. So how did she ingest a substance that made her so drowsy that she sank beneath the water and drowned?"

Chapter
Six

"Jolene was too smart to knowingly take sedatives before immersing herself in the whirlpool. It doesn't make sense," Marla said quietly.

"I agree."

"Poor thing. I would have attended her funeral if it was local." Her head lowered, she reflected upon this latest loss. Jolene had been a cheerful client, and always complimentary of Marla's efforts. She'd revealed little about her personal life. Rarely did Jolene speak about her background, and even less about her work. Yet Marla had always admired the stylish manner in which she dressed, and the solicitous way she inquired about her concerns. Usually it was the other way around with customers: Marla sounded them out, wanting her clients to leave the salon feeling that someone cared for them.

When she thought about it, Jolene had sported a more taciturn air in recent weeks. Maybe something had been bothering her. Could she have confided in that masseuse, Tesla? Harboring a sense of obligation to her former client, Marla vowed to find out. Her heartbeat accelerated at the potential for another investigation. *All right, Ma, so you were right. I've been on a downer since the holidays were over. Looking for action is better than looking for gray hairs.*

"Marla, what's on your mind?" Vail asked, while peering at her suspiciously.

Her cheeks suffused with color. What could she say to distract him? Dalton wouldn't approve of her plans regarding Jolene's case. Didn't she have another reason for stopping by besides collecting payment for Brianna's costume deposit? Oh, yes. There was that second matter to discuss with him.

Swallowing hard, she replied. "Uh, Dalton, there's a favor I have to ask you. Are you busy Saturday night?"

"Why?"

Damn his inquisitive mind. Clearing her throat, Marla twirled a section of hair. "I really hope you're free, because I'm kind of helping a friend, and we need your cooperation." She glanced away from his keen scrutiny.

"Which friend?" he demanded in a gruff tone.

"Arnie Hartman. He got himself into a situation where, you know, a former classmate thinks we're engaged." The last words gushed from her mouth, and she blanched when she saw Vail's expression.

"What?"

"Arnie was trying to get rid of Hortense. She'd been living out of town and he hadn't seen her in years. When she called, he panicked. The gal had a crush on him in high school, and he remembered her as a real hag." Her lips curved upward as she recalled Arnie's reaction to Hortense's transformation.

"I don't get it, Marla. How does Hortense believe Arnie is your—"

"Fiancé?" Marla swallowed. "He told her on the telephone. When she said she was coming over, Arnie rushed to the salon and begged me to play along. He didn't count on Hortense being a beauty, and now he wishes he'd eaten his words. His idea is for us to double date. Eventually Arnie and I will supposedly have a fight and break off our engagement. But in the meantime, you can join us ostensibly as Hortense's date. Arnie knows you'll pay attention to me, so he figures he'll win Hortense's affections."

Marla couldn't meet his reproving gaze. In the ensuing silence, she wondered how she'd gotten herself into another pickle. *If you'd stay away from men, you wouldn't have such complications*, she told herself. Was it worth the aggravation?

Risking a glance in Vail's direction, she felt her knees weaken.

Hell yes, it was worth everything to get a man to look at her that way. Now if only she could redeem herself in his eyes.

"Very well," he said, taking a ragged breath. Being with her had an effect on him, too, she noticed smugly. "Saturday night I'm to date this hag, as you called her?"

"She's very attractive," Marla reassured him. "A real looker. It won't be such a chore."

"You'll owe me. Big time."

"Arnie and I will both be very grateful."

"I don't give a shit about Arnie. Your reputation is what matters. I know how hard you've worked to establish yourself. Does anyone else know about this?"

"Arnie said word might get around. Hortense likes to talk."

He rolled his eyes. "Great. Then we'll just have to give people something else to talk about."

"We will?"

"You bet." He rose from his chair and closed the distance between them.

Marla sprang to her feet, facing him while her knees threatened to buckle. When he got near enough for her to sniff his spice cologne, her heart began a jackhammer rhythm.

"Let's start the gossip going," he said huskily. Darting a glance at the open doorway, he pulled her into his arms. His mouth descended, and he gave her a bruising, possessive kiss.

"Tongues will wag," Marla whispered against his cheek.

"Good. I don't want anyone pairing you with Hartman."

"Hortense will think I'm being unfaithful."

"It'll make her more sympathetic to your friend." He nuzzled her neck, his hot breath caressing her skin.

"Dalton, someone may be watching us."

"That's the idea."

After another quick press of his lips to hers, he stepped away. His hooded gaze raked her body. "I'll let you know if anything comes up and I can't make it Saturday."

She told him the arrangements for meeting Arnie. "I've got to pick up Brianna. Don't work too late. She needs you home."

* * *

Marla didn't have the chance that night to follow up on Tess's address. By the time she'd picked up Brianna and dropped her off at home, it was too late. Wednesday evening she was meeting Tally at the sports club anyway. Maybe Tess would be there. If not, she'd ask Slate about the female therapist.

Busy in the salon all day Wednesday, she didn't give the matter any further thought until Nicole brought her attention to a commotion outside. Excusing herself from the customer whose hair she was teasing, Marla followed Nicole toward the front.

"I couldn't believe it was her at first, but that's definitely Cookie Calcone," said Nicole, pointing. Parading back and forth like a soldier on patrol was the petite female Marla had met in the sports club. She held a sign and was exhorting passersby to listen. A small crowd had gathered, fueling her diatribe. With her animated gestures and energetic motion, she appeared to be an accomplished orator.

"Oh no," Marla groaned, torn between the need to deal with this new problem and her duty to finish the customer. "Are you waiting for your next client?" she asked Nicole. "I've got to finish Tillie. Can you see what this is about? I'm afraid Cookie has got it in for me."

Nicole complied, and a few minutes later she approached Marla at her station. "Bad news. She's kvetching about the products you use in the salon, saying cruel animal tests are performed by companies like Stockhart Industries. They and other conglomerates like them produce the ingredients for our shampoos and conditioners. Customers should protest these torturous acts by boycotting our salon."

"That's absurd." Grabbing a can of holding spray, Marla spritzed her customer.

"Sounds like you're her new crusade. What did you do, Marla? Tell her to change her hairstyle?"

"To the contrary, that strawberry blond color is perfect for her complexion, and her layers have the proper lift. No, this is something else entirely. Cookie believes I told the police she argued with

Jolene before the woman died. It's true I overheard their conversation, but I didn't reveal what they said. I wonder who did," she ended, biting her lower lip. She might have to get to the bottom of this if only to get Cookie off her back.

"Thanks, Marla," Tillie said, rising from the chair after Marla removed her cape. She was a gray-haired lady active in the Jewish Federation. "Don't worry about your loyal customers. We'll always stick by you. It'll take more than one woman's slander to keep us from our favorite stylist." She gave a crinkly grin, showing a row of capped teeth.

"Maybe you should check with a lawyer, Marla," Nicole suggested, wiping the counter with a clean cloth. "Cookie is defaming your reputation. You could sue her."

Marla scribbled Tillie's bill and handed it to her. "Bless my bones, I don't need that kind of *tsuris*. I hope my dear ex-husband, Stan, doesn't get wind of this, or he'll embrace the situation. He might even take on Cookie's cause just to throw me off balance."

Primed for battle, Marla marched outside. "Cookie, this has to stop. You're not welcome here." She waved at the sign. "These are false accusations. You haven't even been inside the salon to see what products we use."

The diminutive woman glared up at her. "I'm a member of SETA. You need to be aware of the crimes you're committing."

"SETA? What's that?"

"Society for the Ethical Treatment of Animals. You're promoting cruelty by supporting those companies."

"We use only quality professional products. Rusk, Sebastian, Paul Mitchell, and Nexxus, for example. Biolage, Joico, and Redken are other well-known names. Most, if not all, claim to protect the rights of animals. Many of these companies are benefactors to groups like yours." Marla couldn't help her strident tone. Onlookers were watching them, and she hoped to show that Cookie was an uninformed troublemaker.

"Not Stockhart Industries." Cookie's eyes narrowed. "They produce the chemicals that go into many of those hair care products. Sure, your companies claim they don't do animal testing, but they neglect to mention where they obtain their ingredients. I know for a fact that Jolene's division was responsible for the deaths of hundreds of animals. I have ways of finding out things."

"Oh, yeah? Then what have you heard about Jolene's death?" According to what Vail said, Jolene had ingested sedatives about an hour before entering the whirlpool. That's when she was in the locker room with Cookie.

Cookie's expression hardened. "The woman drowned. She should have suffered more cruelly, like those poor creatures she tortured."

"Maybe you hastened Jolene on her way. How badly did you want revenge?"

"Meaning?"

"Never mind." Marla's nostrils flared. People walked away, not wishing to get embroiled in a personal conflict. At least she'd succeeded in taking the heat off her salon.

Cookie rested her placard against a wall. Green eyes blazing with hatred, she faced Marla. "Jolene ruined my life. She took away every chance at happiness I'd had."

"I'm sorry to hear you say that," Marla responded softly, hoping to encourage confidences.

"She came to your salon, was *your* friend. Maybe Jolene confided in you. Women like to tell their hairdressers things. Did she tell you about the falsified reports?"

"What do you mean?"

Cookie's eyes glittered. "You'd like to know, wouldn't you? You do favors for me, I'll be more accommodating."

Trembling with anger, Marla gave up on being civil. She whirled around and stormed through the door to her salon. The chutzpah of the woman! *Maybe I should take up boxing instead of Dancercize*, she thought, visualizing a match between herself and Cookie.

Tense and irritable, she greeted Tally with a snarl that evening at the sports club. "Thank goodness that woman isn't here," Marla muttered, stuffing her street clothes into the gym bag she'd brought. They were in the locker room, changing before their group class began. Marla had spotted Lindsay on her way out just as they came in. Apparently, the dance instructor used the same facilities. Had Lindsay changed back into her street clothes the night Jolene died? Marla wondered. Jolene had mentioned taking her class; then she'd eaten a snack at the refreshment bar. Lindsay could have changed and left before Jolene reentered the locker room and encountered Cookie.

Tally finished tying her shoelace. "Why do you have such a gloomy face? We're here to relieve stress, remember?" Using a hairbrush from her sack, Tally proceeded to fix her thick hair into a ponytail.

Marla filled her in on events of the week. "I'm glad Cookie isn't here. I don't think I could have tolerated her tonight."

"She's a royal pain in the butt," Tally agreed. "I hope she doesn't find an excuse to picket Dressed to Kill Boutique!" Her blue eyes twinkled playfully. "By the way, did you ever make a massage appointment for later?"

"I've got one with Slate. Manny is still out sick, and I just found out about Tesla. I'm hoping she's here so I can talk to her about Jolene."

Tally straightened. With her statuesque body and clear complexion, she could have been a model. "Marla, why are you pursuing this? Jolene's drowning was tragic, but in all likelihood it was an accident. Are you feeling responsible for another one of your clients?"

Dalton's revelation poised on her tongue, but she didn't mention the sedatives. "This isn't a clear-cut case like Bertha Kravitz's death, so I'm curious, that's all. Let's go upstairs."

On the way, she eyed the sleek, athletic bodies of their fellow members, and a moue of disgust formed on her face. How did they stay so slim? They probably subsisted on grapefruit diets. With all the jewelry on their arms, they didn't need to lift weights. So this was where the yuppie crowd hung out. Viewing the men, she noted a preponderance of paunches and graying temples. Were they trying to keep up with their mates?

She supposed one could really get into this culture and turn physical fitness into a personal crusade. Maintaining health was important for everyone, but she preferred other social venues than talking while treadmilling. After their trial membership was over, she'd rather meet Tally for dinner than Dancercize.

Not that it wasn't fun. While she was skipping to a big band beat, her worries flew out the door. Concentrating on following Lindsay's steps took her full attention. Blood surged through her taut muscles, energizing her body and eliminating fatigue. What galled her was the effortless grace with which Lindsay bounced through the routines. *If only I were as young as that again, I'd be fitter, too, especially if I taught dance classes all week.*

Keith Hamilton waylaid her outside the door. "Hi, Marla. How's it going? Are you enjoying the club?" His nut brown eyes swept her in a practiced once-over.

She introduced him to Tally. "We've been taking Lindsay's class," she responded, her gaze flickering over his muscled torso. He wore the club logo shirt and shorts, leaving the rest of his hairy body exposed.

His eyebrows rose. "I hope you're having a better time than when we first met."

"Oh, yes. That was awful. Poor Jolene."

"Marla," Tally interrupted, "I'm going to try the cycle machine. Come join me when you're ready." Flicking a meaningful glance in Keith's direction, she walked off.

"Amy isn't too upset," Keith responded, his mouth curving downward. "Now she's got a clear field to Slate."

"You don't seem too happy about that."

"I'm not, man. We've gone out a few times, and I know she likes me. But whenever Mr. Smooth Talk is around, she forgets I exist. It's not just him. She hangs at the scene down by the beach." His gaze narrowed. "I'm not worried as long as I keep tabs on her. That way, I can see she doesn't lose sight of who really matters."

"Like you, I suppose?" Marla shifted her weight to her other foot. After Lindsay's class, her body was beginning to ache in places she hadn't known existed. Thigh muscles in particular were getting a rude awakening.

From the corner of her eye, Marla noticed Lindsay waving

farewell to a lingering member of their class and then stooping to brush the remaining vestiges of resin off her jazz shoes. Lindsay had advised her class to use the powdery substance, normally provided for dancers *en pointe,* to reduce slippage on the polished wood floor.

"What are you trying next?" Keith asked, his expression reverting to one of open friendliness. "Want to take a turn on the treadmill? I'll show you how to set the controls."

Marla glanced at the row of treadmill terrorists. Eloise and Sam Zelman were going at a furious pace. She wouldn't want to compete with them. "No, thanks, I've got a massage scheduled. Say, do you know Tesla, the masseuse? I was wondering if Jolene had arranged an appointment with her."

An odd light sprang into his eyes. "Yeah, I know Tess. She doesn't come in too often. Don't know if Jolene ever used her."

"Well, I've got to go. I'll see you again, Keith." She whirled around to find herself facing Lindsay. "Oh, I enjoyed your class today," Marla told the lithe blonde, whose makeup wasn't even smudged one whit after the strenuous workout.

Lindsay's blue eyes twinkled. "Thanks. I heard you talking about Jolene. She was your customer, wasn't she?"

Marla studied her, wondering why the girl's inflection sounded so insincere. "Yes," she admitted. "Jolene recommended your class to me. Had you known her well?"

"Not as well as you, I'm sure. Don't women confide in their hairdressers? I'll bet she told you all her secrets."

"Secrets?" screeched a voice from the stairs. "Wait for me!" Cookie scrambled into view. A red-and-black bandanna circled her head, and she wore a Spandex top with bike shorts that made her look like a wide version of a rubber band.

"I've got to go," Lindsay said, smiling apologetically at Marla. "See you later."

Marla decided to take the offensive. "You know, Cookie, I was thinking about Jolene and her work. Maybe someone in her laboratory wasn't happy with the way she handled things. Didn't you say something about falsified reports?"

Cookie glared at her. "Why should you care? I thought you

weren't interested. Or maybe Jolene had told you everything like *she* suggested." Cookie nodded at Lindsay, who'd paused on the steps. At her accusing tone, Lindsay hastily proceeded downward.

"Jolene didn't talk much about herself," Marla admitted. Hesitating, she wished it was possible to reveal what she knew about Jolene's death. The woman had obtained sedatives somewhere, but no other similar drugs were found in her purse. An alternate explanation was that she'd obtained them from someone present at the club.

She glanced at Keith, ostensibly filling out a form at the trainer desk. Vail must be obtaining background information on these people, she surmised. That wasn't her job, but it wouldn't hurt to learn all she could by casually questioning them.

"I'd be interested in hearing more about animal testing," she said sweetly. "I'm not really familiar with the topic, and you can help to educate me. Certainly, I don't want to carry products in my salon that derive from such cruel techniques." *That's right, Marla, lay it on thick. Butting heads with Cookie will only make things worse. Playing her tune might get better results.*

A smug grin lit Cookie's elfin face. "Okay. Where are you off to now?"

"I'm getting a massage. Want to go out for coffee later?"

Cookie grimaced. "You drink that poison? Hell, no. Let's get some yogurt ice cream. You can eat a sundae while I give you the scoop on Jolene."

Chapter
Seven

"Do you want to come with me when I meet Cookie?" Marla asked Tally. Having her friend along as moral support would make the interview easier.

"I'd love to hear what that witch has to say," Tally said, giving Marla a sideways glance, "but Ken is expecting me home by ten. You go ahead. Call me tomorrow and fill me in."

"Okay. Maybe Slate will be talkative. I'd like to get some information to pass on to Dalton. The sooner he solves this case, the sooner he can resume taking Brianna to dance class. Oh, my God. I forgot to tell you about Arnie!"

Cycling at a steady pace, Tally gestured to the adjacent machine. "You've still got extra time before your massage. Try this while you're talking."

Marla eyed the row of Tectrix VR bikes. At the end was a young guy wearing earphones, swaying his head, and smiling. Presumably, she wouldn't have to worry about him listening in.

"All right, I can do this." Straddling the seat next to Tally's, she placed her feet on the pedals. "Now what?"

"See that blue handle on your right?" Tally instructed. "Use the plus and minus signs to select your scene on the monitor."

Glancing at Tally's screen, Marla saw her friend cycling through a virtual town. "What are you doing?"

"This one takes place in New England. You can pick Penguin Peak, which is a winter adventure; Tank, a military game; Aztec 2000, which is a futuristic competition; or a Caribbean island."

"That's for me." Marla made her selection, then set the speed with the controls on the left handle. She set the timer for ten minutes. Any longer and she'd be late for her massage appointment. Soon she was pedaling along a path lined with tropical flowers. Steel drum music played from speakers built into the chair at head level. Pulling on the handles tilted the machine and let her steer around trees.

"Hey, this is fun," she cried, adding pressure to push her bike up a virtual hill. Over the horizon was a beautiful expanse of azure ocean. It wasn't long before her thigh muscles ached in protest and her heart raced. A panel display showed the time elapsed, miles ridden, difficulty level, and calories burned.

While she zoomed down the hillside, Marla proceeded to inform Tally about her plans with Arnie.

Tally's face broke into a wide grin. At the end, she laughed aloud. "I wish I could be there to watch Dalton pretending to be this girl's date. You've got to call me the next day! Oh, Marla, you do get yourself into the strangest situations."

"Help! I'm cycling into the ocean!" Unable to steer around a sand dune, Marla ended up in the sea. Afraid she'd virtually drown, she was relieved when a vast underwater vista opened before her eyes. She'd barely had time to study the iridescent fish when the timer went off.

Strange didn't adequately describe her encounter with Slate. After rushing into the locker room for a quick shower, she changed into jeans and a cotton blouse before heading for the massage suite. No one was present at the sign-in desk, which seemed to be a normal occurrence, so she knocked on the nearest open doorway and strolled inside.

Slate whipped around, his matinee-idol face sporting an embarrassed grin as she spied him stuffing a pair of pantyhose into a drawer. His light-brown hair was cut short and gelled away from his face in a spiky style. Amber eyes widened in recognition. "Miss Shore?"

"Call me Marla. This is my first time having a massage, so I'm not sure what to do. Shall I lay down on that table?" She nodded to a treatment table covered with a clean white cloth. It had a hole where her head would rest.

"Not yet. You need to remove your clothing and wrap this sheet around yourself, then lie down on your back. I'll give you a few minutes."

"Wait! I, uh, only need my back and shoulders done." Damned if she was going to completely disrobe.

Slate didn't change his expression. "Well, then, just take off your shirt and bra, honey."

Bless my bones, the things I do to gather information, she thought wryly as she lay face-up on the table, her nude upper body wrapped in a sheet. She'd found a closet to hang her clothes in, although it appeared as though another woman had left her outfits there. A couple of dresses, heels in an awkwardly large size, and various undergarments took up most of the tiny space.

After a brief interval during which she counted dots on the ceiling, Slate reentered. He'd donned a white jacket to make himself look more professional.

That won't help, pal. You still look like you belong on a marquee. Embarrassed by her half-naked state, albeit covered by a cloth, she gritted her teeth. *He probably regards female bodies like a gynecologist does*, she told herself reassuringly. Merely a day's work.

Slate advanced to a panel on the wall and turned a dial. Soothing New Age music filtered into the air. He flipped another switch, and Marla could swear she smelled orange blossoms. Her heart quickened when he approached. Pulling out a stool, Slate sat himself at her head and put his thumbs on the base of her neck.

"Relax, honey, you're here to relieve tension. Do you have any physical problems we need to work on?" he said. His low voice rippled over her, buoying her like a wave. She felt his fingers press on a tender area at her nape.

"I feel knotty after a long day at work," she confessed. His thumbs began a gentle massage, and she could feel the coil of tension dissolving. This wasn't so bad. If she weren't careful, she'd get too relaxed and then she wouldn't accomplish anything.

"Slate, I understand there's another therapist whose name is Tess. When does she come in?"

His hands paused, then resumed their motion. "She works during my off-hours. I don't see her much."

Marla detected a strain in his voice. "Jolene had an appointment for a massage the night she died. She'd scheduled it with Manny, but he was out sick. Do you know if Jolene switched to Tess?"

His fingers stretched to stroke her neck. They pressed lightly on her carotids, making Marla imagine how easily he could encircle her throat. "Tess wasn't here. I took Jolene's appointment."

She squirmed uncomfortably, suddenly uneasy. "I thought Jolene and you, uh, were not on the best of terms."

"There wasn't any hassle. Jolene agreed to let me do it. She stayed for her session and then left to change into a swimsuit. That's what I told the cops when they asked me."

"I see." She didn't understand the reticence in his tone. Was there something more he was leaving out? "Did Jolene feel all right when she was here?"

Again his hands paused. "Sure. Why wouldn't she? What do you know about her accident, anyway?" he asked suspiciously.

"Oh, no more than you do. Tell me, how would you describe your relationship with Amy?"

"Who told you about us?"

"Amy did. Apparently, she considers you her territory. Do you think she was jealous of your interest in Jolene?"

"There was nothing for her to be jealous about. Jolene thought she was too hot for me." His voice rose. "She didn't realize she was turning down the best jock in town. Babes usually ask *me* out."

Stepping away, he flexed an arm muscle to prove his point. "Now turn onto your stomach, please. You'll see how good I am."

He waited while she flipped over and resettled her position. It felt peculiar to hang her face through the hole in the table.

"If you want to see who's really the jealous type, check out Keith upstairs," Slate said. "You won't believe the lengths that guy will go to protect his turf." Shifting his position, he kneaded her shoulders. Her muscles relaxed as he dug into the sensitive areas below her clavicle. Immersed in the process, she closed her eyes and enjoyed the sensations.

Gloria had a different take on matters when Marla ran into her outside the massage suite a half hour later. "What time did I leave on Friday? Let me see." The sales associate tapped a manicured fingernail to her chin. "After you left my office, I stayed to finish some work on my computer. Jolene must have been at her appointment with Slate, because I heard them arguing."

Marla's ears perked up. "Could you make out what they were saying?" she shamelessly asked.

"No, they were inside one of the massage suites. What's it to you, anyway?"

She smiled as though it didn't matter. "Just curious. How did you know they weren't getting along if you were unable to hear them?"

Gloria raised a supercilious eyebrow. "Do you think I'd make things up just because Jolene found out about my—" She broke off what she'd been about to say, her cheeks flaming. "Their voices were raised, and I heard a slapping sound. Slate probably made a move on her, and Jolene retaliated. You should've seen the look on Amy's face."

"Amy could hear all the way from the snack bar?"

"Hell, no. She was standing right outside the suite. She'd seen Slate show Jolene into a treatment room."

"Did you see Jolene leave?"

"No, Lindsay wanted me to check on one of the customer records."

"I didn't know Lindsay was still here." During her conversation with Jolene in the locker room, Marla had understood that the Dancercize class was over about a half hour before, because Jolene had gone after class to get a snack. Lindsay hadn't been upstairs when Marla met Keith. So how long had she hung around?

Eloise was in the club, Marla remembered. Maybe she had noticed staff members playing musical chairs. Putting Eloise, as well as Amy, on the list to interview, Marla thanked Gloria for the information.

"You want to thank me properly? Sign up for a full club membership. I need to make my quota this month."

That's not my problem, pal. "I'll think about it," she hedged.

Gloria followed her as she headed for the front door. "I'll get the papers ready. You can sign next time you're here."

Muttering under her breath about obnoxious salespeople, Marla hurried to her car. She didn't want to be late for her talk with Cookie. It was dark out, and she walked with her keys in hand. The parking lot was fairly full, but no one else was around. A chilly breeze ruffled her skin.

She barely heard the revving engine before twisting her head. A car, headlights off, charged straight at her. With a shriek, she threw herself to the side just as the vehicle whizzed past. Banging against a parked SUV, she experienced a sharp pain in her side, but that was the least of her worries. Screeching tires grazed the pavement, and she saw the car rushing back, aiming to crush her against the sport utility vehicle.

Heart thumping, Marla ran between cars. She'd parked her Toyota Camry near the end of the row. Gasping for breath, she reached the driver's side and halted. Her mouth dropped open. One of the tires had a flat. *Damn.*

Wildly, she glanced over her shoulder, confused by the sudden silence. The car's engine had cut off, which might mean one of two things. Either the driver had left the parking area, or he'd cut his ignition and was proceeding on foot. Since she hadn't noticed a vehicle burning rubber to leave the lot, the latter seemed more probable.

With trembling fingers, she fit her key into the lock and twisted it just as a body hurtled out of the darkness. Moonlight gleamed off the jagged edge of a broken bottle aimed at her face. She couldn't identify her assailant, who wore a mask over his head. Dodging the makeshift weapon, she jerked sideways, twirled around, and lashed out with her foot. She was satisfied to hear a grunt of pain when she hit his shinbone.

Using the distraction to her advantage, she threw open her car door and slid inside. Slamming the door and pushing the lock, she started the engine. Her assailant pounded on the window, looming like a ghoul in the night. Curse the flat tire. She'd ruin the wheel if necessary to get out of there!

Lurching into reverse, the car halted while she shifted gears. Her eyes darted to the rearview mirror. Would the man follow in his vehicle? She careened from the parking lot, her pulse racing as she drove to the nearest gas station.

While a service attendant jacked up her wheel, she succumbed to an attack of nerves. Chills racked her body. She'd nearly had her face slashed, or worse! Knowing she should notify the police, Marla hesitated. Vail's disapproving frown surfaced in her mind, and she decided against it. What could anyone prove? That she'd been attacked and was a fool for setting herself up? Thankfully, she hadn't been harmed. Now that she'd been forewarned, she would be extra cautious.

As she steered toward the ice cream parlor where she was overdue to meet Cookie, Marla wondered what she might have done to provoke an assault. Had someone at the health club been angered by one of her conversations? Or did this relate back to the episode between Hank Goodfellow and Wallace Ritiker at the pharmacy? They'd been on Vail's member sign-in list along with the Zelmans. Then again, Sam and Eloise could easily have eavesdropped on her conversation with Cookie outside the dance studio. Keith was in the vicinity as well. Or had it been something she'd said to Slate? He could have grabbed that pair of pantyhose in his drawer, yanked it over his head, and run outside to nab her.

If there had been any notions in her mind that Jolene's death was purely an accidental drowning, tonight had dispelled them.

Turning into the parking lot at The Fountains shopping center, Marla was glad to see a crowd hanging out at TCBY. Cookie was smart to have chosen such a public venue for their meeting.

Her knees wobbled when she approached the brightly lit store, where she glimpsed Cookie pacing inside. Drawing a deep breath, she attempted to put a benign expression on her face. It wasn't easy with her heart still beating at a fast rhythm, but she didn't want Cookie to notice her distress.

No such luck. As soon as she spotted Marla, the activist marched over, a determined gleam in her eyes. "You're late. I thought you'd stood me up." Cookie peered closer. "What happened to you? You're white as a sheet."

"My car had a flat tire."

"Your voice is shaking. Are you sure you're okay?"

"Too much exercise tonight. Guess I need to get in shape."

Cookie gave a snort of disbelief. "Whatever. Do you want to order? I'm going to get a cone."

Marla decided to splurge on a high-calorie dessert and ordered a hot fudge sundae. The sugar dose would help restore her composure. Cookie stuck to a traditional scoop of vanilla. With her short stature, capri pants, and animal-print top with the ends tied at her midriff, she almost blended in with the teen crowd. She'd applied more makeup than usual, as though wanting to impress Marla with her professionalism. *You look good when you dress up, pal*, Marla admitted silently. With her tousled hairstyle, Cookie could be stunning in the proper wardrobe. The dog hairs on her shirt would have to go, though.

"I'm glad you've decided to let me help you," Cookie began, seated across from Marla. A dribble of ice cream rolled down her chin, and she dabbed at it with a napkin.

Savoring a mouthful of rich fudge sauce, Marla sought a diplomatic reply. "You've awakened me to the issue of animal testing. I've really never thought about it before."

"Neither have most people. You don't consider how the cosmetics and household products you use are the source of suffering and death for thousands of laboratory animals."

"Aren't those tests necessary to make certain the chemicals are safe on people?"

"Not necessarily. Even when tests show that a product is dangerous, it may not be kept off the market. It'll simply bear a warning label telling you to call a doctor if you ingest the product or if it splashes on your skin."

"I don't see how that relates to the hair care products I use in my salon."

Cookie leaned forward, her gaze intent. "Besides shampoos, your cosmetics, toiletries, and household products involve animal tests at some stage in their development. You clean counters and wash towels at the salon, don't you? Detergents, bleach, and soaps derive from animal experiments. So even if all your hair care products are botanicals, you can't escape culpability."

Marla's shoulders stiffened. "Botanicals can cause problems in people, too. Herbal components may cause sensitivity reactions if customers are allergic. As for other products, surely not all companies use the techniques you mention."

"You have to learn the difference. Firms that label their products as not having been tested on animals may still use ingredients from other suppliers who do these tests. Or they'll contract other laboratories to do the tests, and then they can claim their company doesn't perform animal testing. There's a difference between companies that have made a real commitment to ending such cruelty and those who continue to use ingredients tested by torturing helpless creatures."

"What about medical research?" Marla asked. "Isn't it necessary to perform animal tests to discover new treatments for diseases? How else are scientists to find therapies that are effective and safe on humans?"

Cookie jabbed a finger in the air. "I'm talking about product tests that treat animals as expendable beings with no lives of their own. It subjugates their existence to serve humans merely to produce a new lipstick, shampoo, or toothpaste. Let me tell you about some of the tests."

"Go ahead." Marla ate a spoonful of ice cream, wondering how she could turn the direction of their conversation to Jolene.

Cookie's sea green eyes glowed with fervor. Turning her ice-cream cone upside down in a dish, she ignored the melting mess.

"In the Draize Irritancy Test, potentially harmful products are dripped into the eyes of rabbits, who don't produce tears to flush them away. The substances remain on the cornea, causing burning and ulceration, while the animals are restrained.

"Then there's the Lethal Dose Fifty Percent test. The toxicity level of a product is assessed by force-feeding it through a syringe directly into the animal's stomach. A number of animals are treated until fifty percent of them die. Death comes slowly, often after seizures, pain, and loss of balance. Animals left alive at the end may be killed and autopsied. What does this prove? In many cases, nothing. The animals die because of the volume forced into them."

Cookie's gaze misted, and her voice choked with emotion. "Finally, there's the skin test. A patch of skin is shaved and scratched, then the test substance is applied while the animals are restrained. They receive no pain relief as the substance burns through their skin. These cruel tests don't make the products any safer. If you use compounds derived this way, you're just as guilty as the researchers."

Marla's stomach churned. "What's the alternative?"

"Computer programs can predict toxicity using structural analysis. Cells can be grown in cultures and products tested on them. Other methods are being developed. The point is that these tests can be conducted differently."

"I remember hearing you accuse Jolene's company of conducting animal tests. How do you know so much?"

A pinched look came over Cookie's face. "I have a lot of friends in SETA. Jolene's reports minimized her department's use of animal experiments, but she was getting data from another source and claiming it as her own. Those test results were more favorable, although that lab does animal tests, too."

"So you're saying Jolene falsified her documents to reflect this other material. Where did she get it?"

"I suspect from someone over at Listwood Pharmaceuticals," Cookie said. "They're the only other chemical plant in town."

"I see why you were upset with Jolene about the animal testing, but this other place conducts experiments, too. So why did you target just her?"

Cookie's fists clenched. "Jolene destroyed my life."

Understanding dawned. "You used animal rights as a smoke-screen. Your vendetta against Jolene was personal. Tell me, why did you hate her so much?" *Did you hate her enough to kill her, pal?*

In a rare show of vulnerability, Cookie's lower lip trembled. "My husband worked at Stockhart Industries until Jolene fired him. We ended up getting a divorce. Now I'll never have a family, and it's her fault."

No wonder Cookie rambled on sounding so scientific. She'd learned the lingo from her ex-spouse. "You might still meet someone worthwhile," Marla said gently, taking a sip of water from a plastic cup. The noise level in the ice cream parlor dropped as patrons began to leave. Uneasy about driving home on her spare tire, she didn't want to leave too late.

"I'm not sorry about Jolene's accident."

Cookie's comment jolted her. "Oh?"

"She was immoral. Do you know I saw her meet Sam Zelman a few times on the sly? I wonder what they had going."

"Jolene wasn't involved with your husband, was she?"

Cookie's expression darkened. "If she had been, she'd have been dead a lot sooner."

"Detective Vail suspects there may be more to her death than an accidental drowning. Do you remember those gelatin capsules she took in the locker room?"

"Yes, I do. I warned her about them."

Marla sat up straighter. "Meaning?"

"Almost all capsules are made from animal sources. She just insisted on abusing those poor creatures any way she could. And her foolish practice of taking gelatin to harden her nails! I told Jolene that gelatin is an animal protein. It's extracted from beef and pork skin and bones."

Marla wrinkled her nose. Gelatin was widely used in the food industry. Already she was learning more about animal products and testing than she'd ever wanted to know. She bit her lower lip, focusing her thoughts. "If someone wanted to do Jolene harm, who would be the first person you'd suspect?"

"Other than me?" Cookie snickered. "There are too many candidates. Maybe whoever had been selling her the better test results got spooked they'd be discovered. Or Eloise found out Sam was fooling around with Jolene. Amy at the club was angry at her for taking Slate's attention away. Even Gloria complained about her. As I said, Jolene got what she deserved."

Chapter Eight

"Will you let me know if you learn anything more about Jolene's affairs, business or otherwise?" Marla asked Cookie.

"Why should I?" Rising, Cookie tossed her sticky dish into a
trash can.

Marla discarded her sundae cup. "If you keep me informed, I'll
check my inventory at the salon to see if our products comply with
SETA's recommendations."

Cookie gave her a considering look. "I didn't realize Jolene was
such a close friend." Her tone implied the woman couldn't possibly
have had anyone who cared so much about her.

"I don't believe she drowned accidentally. Jolene was a mensch,
you know what I mean? She had a good head on her shoulders.
Jolene wouldn't have taken something that made her sleepy when
she still had to drive home."

Cookie's eyes narrowed. "Cough it up, Marla."

Marla sighed. "Jolene had sedatives in her blood. She ingested a
drug about an hour before she died."

Cookie didn't answer immediately. "I'll call you," she promised
quietly, making Marla believe Cookie might have some redeeming
qualities after all.

Her next action refuted that thought. Reaching forward, Cookie
grabbed the glass sugar container from their table and loosened the

metal lid. "The next person who puts sugar in his coffee will get a surprise," Cookie said, a mischievous grin on her face. "Something I learned in high school. Refined sugar is bad for you anyway."

Marla was unable to follow up on any of the loose ends nagging at her until later in the week. Work and chores kept her occupied, including buying a new tire for the Camry.

Friday after work, she put aside time to accomplish one task. Fortunately, she remembered the address for Tesla, the massage therapist, thanks to Vail, who had shown her the list of sports club staff members in his office. Now she could at least check this trail to see if it led to Jolene. Vail might have already investigated this angle, but she had an advantage over him. A woman was more likely to confide in a hairdresser than in a cop.

Her car's clock read six-thirty, meaning she had less than an hour before Eddie, Nicole's boyfriend, started barbecuing jerk chicken for a get-together at his house. Hopefully, Tess would be home if she hadn't yet gone out for the weekend.

Driving through an older section of Plantation near Fig Tree Lane, Marla admired the spreading banyan trees that shaded the streets. The lots extended well away from the road. From the house numbers, she surmised Tesla's place was the lemon yellow cottage with white shutters just ahead. She'd pulled along the curb and put her hand on the gear shift when a movement caught her attention. Someone was leaving the yellow house. Tall, broad-shouldered, and dressed in a vibrantly colored kerchief dress, the lady wobbled on high heels toward a dark-green Buick parked in the short driveway. Squinting, Marla tried to get a better view in the encroaching darkness.

Two choices confronted her. She could approach the house and knock on the door. If Tess was inside, her patience would be rewarded. But if this person leaving was Tess, maybe Marla should follow her.

Have some *saichel*, she told herself. Good sense mandated that she continue with her original plan. Waiting until the visitor left, Marla studied the house. Weeds had overgrown the front lawn. A sodden newspaper in a plastic bag lay on the swale, victim of an early-morning sprinkler shower.

As she got out of the car and walked along the cracked sidewalk, her nostrils inhaled a sweet, fruity scent. Old Florida, she thought fondly, veering around a spreading bird of paradise plant.

The front door swung open, and a thin woman wearing rollers and a housecoat confronted Marla. "Do I know you?"

Marla mustered a smile. It was difficult to ignore the woman's red-rimmed eyes and trembling lower lip, but she managed a cheerful demeanor. "I'm looking for Tesla Parr. My name is Marla Shore."

"You just missed her. She left a few minutes ago."

"Oh. Isn't this her place?"

The woman gave a harsh laugh. "Hell, no. Who are you and where did you get that information?"

"From the sports club where she works. I'm a member there, and I wanted to know if she gave private appointments. As a hairdresser, I'm on my feet all day. I really need someone to come to my house and give me a massage after work. I can afford whatever fee Tess charges."

"Oh, yeah?" The woman's blue eyes glinted with avarice. "Wait just a minute, honey. I'll write down an address where you can find her."

"Are you her friend?"

"Sorry, I'm Betsy. We're . . . more than friends."

Betsy grinned, showing surprisingly even teeth. With a smile, her expression lost its haunted look and transformed her features. She was a pretty woman, Marla thought, when she wasn't crying. Now what did she mean by that remark? Were she and Tess on intimate terms?

Clutching the piece of paper in her hand, Marla returned to her car. Temperatures ranged in the seventies, and humidity was low, making it a delightful evening for a barbecue. Her rumbling stomach heralded dinnertime. One more stop, then she'd proceed to Eddie's house, where the rest of her staff had probably finished their first round of drinks.

Traffic was heavy with rush-hour commuters, so it took her longer than normal to travel to Davie, the nearest town to the south. The directions took her to a community with speed bumps, which she cursed each time the Camry jolted over one. Whoever voted them into the development should grow like an onion, with his head in the ground. All they did was ruin the tires.

Hungry and annoyed, she wasn't in a good mood when she rapped on the door at 501 Fairlawn Court. It hadn't escaped her notice that the dark-green Buick she'd seen Tess leave in earlier now sat in this driveway. Expecting the woman to open the door to her house, she received an unexpected shock when a man responded to her summons.

"Slate! What are you doing here?" she asked as soon as she could speak. From his matted dark hair, freshly scrubbed face, and bare chest, she surmised Slate wasn't prepared for visitors. His exposed feet bore strange marks and looked swollen.

"I'm going to ask you this same thing," he snapped, eyes flashing dangerously.

"I was looking for Tess."

"Why? And who told you to come here?"

She shifted her position. "Betsy said I had the wrong address, and she gave me this location. Is this where Tess lives?"

"Yes and no."

Resisting the urge to crane her neck and peer inside the house, she gave him a determined stare. "I need to talk to her."

Slate pursed his lips, which, Marla realized, bore faint traces of lipstick. Did he and Tess have a relationship? If so, what was Tess doing over at Betsy's house? And why did Tess list her girlfriend's address as her own?

"She's not available," Slate told her. "But if you want to come in, just give me a minute to straighten things up." He raised his eyebrows suggestively. "You probably wanted to ask Tess where I lived anyway."

"Oh . . . right. So are you two very close?"

He slicked a lock of hair off his forehead. "Not in the way you mean, sweetheart. Come in and I'll prove it."

"Okay." Her foot shot forward, but he wedged the door against her.

"Wait." A look of panic flickered behind his expression. "I have to put some things away."

"You just said I should come inside."

"Not yet. Maybe we should make it another time." His biceps bulged as he held the door in place. Hooded eyes raked over her. "I can give you a private massage."

Holy highlights, just what I need! "Ah, sure, Slate. That sounds interesting. Let's schedule a time when Tess will be here. I'd really like to meet her, but it's hard to catch her at the club."

"Sorry, I can't guarantee when she'll be around." A flush crept over his skin. "She keeps irregular hours."

Marla puzzled over their relationship, but Slate wasn't going to give any easy answers. Strange how Tess was so elusive.

Maybe she'd stake out the place another time and wait for her to show. "I'll see you at the club, and perhaps then we'll make a date for my private session."

Winking, he grinned. "You bet. I guarantee you'll never have it better. Some of the ladies take this stuff to heart, but I don't think you're the type. You know the score. We'll have a good time."

You wish, pal.

Wondering how Amy would feel if she knew about her heart-throb's philandering, Marla decided to sound out the Smoothie King attendant at the first opportunity. Amy had overheard Slate arguing with Jolene and had admitted to being jealous. Playing upon Amy's emotions might be a technique Marla could use to get her to talk about Slate.

She decided to confide her suspicions to Vail on their double date the following night. The only difficulty she foresaw was getting him away from Hortense.

It was a good thing they'd all decided to meet at the restaurant, or an awkward situation would have ensued. She waited for Arnie after work, and they drove together. She'd never seen him so excited.

"Do I look all right? Is my hair okay? I used a new cologne the kids got me for Chanukah." Stroking his mustache, he guided the wheel with his other hand. His dark eyes glanced anxiously in her direction.

Seated on the passenger side of his Chevrolet, she smiled gently. "You're fine, Arnie. Just relax. You're supposed to be my date, remember?"

Sweat beaded his brow, and it wasn't from the Florida heat. A mild cold front had swept through the area, bringing temperatures in the sixties. "How did Vail react? I swear that guy doesn't seem as though he has a sense of humor."

"He agreed to come along, more likely to keep an eye on me. I think he's jealous of you."

Arnie gave a disarming grin. "He might have had reason to be, if you'd ever given me a second look."

"We're friends, pal. That means a lot to me."

"I know." Shaking his head, Arnie focused on his driving. "Hortense bowled me over. Never in a million years would I have expected her to show such a *shayna punim.*"

"Ugly ducklings can turn into beautiful swans."

"Yeah, and what a shlemiehl I was for telling her we were engaged! What a tight tush she has, too. Did you see her—"

"Arnie, please concentrate on where we're going. You just passed a stop sign."

"Oh, sorry. Anyway, it was a real good *chochmeh* of mine to ask Vail to join us. He'll pay attention to you, so I can focus on Hortense. She'll have to like me."

"She already does. That's why she called you when she came back to town."

Arnie's face glowed with happiness. "That's true, isn't it? So everything will work out when you and I have our supposed fight. Maybe we should break up tonight."

"Let's see how things progress. The best-laid plans go oft astray," she quoted.

How prophetic were those words, she realized later. The Spice

Garden was located west of Nob Hill Road in Palm Haven, on a corner beside an office complex. Weekend evenings brought out the singles crowd, whose boisterous chatter extended beyond the walls. Lacking early-bird specials, the restaurant appealed to a young, professional group of upscale patrons.

Marla scanned the crowd milling outside the lushly landscaped entrance. Her gaze alighted on a tall, masculine figure. *Bless my bones, Dalton is already chatting with Hortense.* No shyness there, she noted cattily. Wondering who had recognized whom first, she was glad introductions weren't required. "I see you've met," she remarked idly.

Dalton, who looked smashing in a herringbone sport coat, grinned at her broadly. "Hi Marla. How are ya, Arnie? Jill and I were just getting acquainted."

The subject of his attention leaned forward, giving Marla a view of her substantial cleavage. "Dalton is such a hunk, isn't he? I've never dated a police officer before!" Simpering under his gaze, Hortense patted the bleached blond hair piled atop her head, its delicate tendrils framing her face.

Marla glanced approvingly at the fancy updo. Either the woman was skilled with a curling iron, or she'd seen a hairdresser earlier. Hortense knew how to apply makeup artfully as well. Marla couldn't fault her taste, but Hortense's appearance seemed too perfect. How much of it was real, and how much was artifice? Would Dalton know the difference? Or Arnie, for that matter? And did they care?

She surveyed the woman's low-cut sapphire cashmere sweater, skimpy black leather skirt, and strapped heels. No matter what Hortense wore, she exuded sex appeal. Any man would be a fool not to look twice at her.

Marla's own outfit consisted of a silk tangerine-and-black dress that clung to her curves. Sensible pumps covered her stockinged feet. Standing all day in the salon made her careful about footwear. Comfort came first, saving a visit to the podiatrist.

Dalton poked her on the shoulder. "This was such a great idea. Jill has some fascinating stories about when she grew up here. I'm glad you included me."

Arnie, hovering beside Marla, frowned. "But we used to call her Hortense, and she—"

Marla kicked his ankle. "Be careful," she warned him under her breath. "You're trying to snow her, remember? Don't bring up ugliness from the past."

Their number was called and they went inside to be seated. Marla wasn't too happy when Dalton preceded her with Hortense. In fact, she wasn't happy at all. He seemed to have forgotten their scheme and was being far too attentive to the newcomer.

"Your job is so exciting," Hortense said to him. Winding her arm through his elbow, she sashayed forward.

Strolling beside Marla, Arnie panted like a puppy. Staring at the woman's swaying derriere, he smacked his lips. In another minute, he'll be drooling, Marla thought.

"Arnie, stop that," she ordered. "Now who's acting like a dog?"

"*Oy vey*, I can't help it. She really turns me on." He tugged on his knit shirt tucked into a pair of Dockers slacks.

"Oh, so what did I do to you that you kept trying to get a date? Reminded you of a pot roast while she's the dessert?"

"Marla, you're a *shayna madel* and a beautiful person, but no one can compare to Hortense's uh . . ."

"Good taste? Cultured upbringing? Give me a break."

She waited until they were seated at a table overlooking an artificial brook and tropical greenery before throwing a wrench into their conversation. "So who's babysitting for Brianna tonight?" she asked Vail in a honeyed tone. She and Arnie sat together facing the other couple. "I don't imagine she goes out on dates yet. Your daughter is too young."

To her annoyance, Vail seemed unperturbed by her comments. "She's got a friend staying over. They rented a movie from Blockbuster." He turned to Hortense. "I have a twelve-year-old daughter. She'll turn thirteen in the Spring. How are you at planning birthday parties?"

Hortense thrust out her bosom. "I just love parties, sugar. I can help you arrange something for the sweet little girl."

Sweet little girl, my ass. You've never met Brianna, lady. "I'm good at planning parties, too! We have them all the time for our salon staff. Boosts morale, you know."

Vail's smoky gaze fixed on her. "I'll keep that in mind. When the time comes, I may call on you."

Great, now I'll get stuck planning a teen shindig. Lord save me, this conversation is veering way off course.

"It's Marla's birthday next month," Arnie interrupted. He'd been too occupied gawking at Hortense to speak since they'd been seated. "She'll be thirty-five on Valentine's Day."

"Arnie!" Marla nudged him angrily.

"How romantic," Hortense crooned, beaming at them. "Are you planning a special celebration?"

Marla and Arnie glanced at each other. "Well, we hadn't thought about it," Arnie confessed, a bewildered look on his face. He seemed confused by the turn of events, too.

"You'll have to include us," Hortense suggested, lowering her lashes coyly at Vail. "I'm so thrilled you introduced Dalton to me that I feel I owe you. Let us take you out to dinner for your birthday."

Us? Who the hell did this woman think she was? *Dalton belongs to me, you twit.*

She glanced at him and caught the twinge of amusement before his normally implacable expression took over. *Bless my bones, is he playing mating games?* Marla hadn't thought him the type. He seemed too somber, too rooted to the truth. Thus far in their relationship, he'd laid all the cards on the table. So why was he being so devious now?

His angular face gave nothing away. Shifting in her chair, she admitted that his unpredictability set her pulse thrumming. He'd been singularly interested in her, and maybe she'd taken him for granted. But it appeared that two could play the same game.

Patting Arnie's arm affectionately, she answered Hortense's offer. "We'd be delighted. I was getting depressed about my birthday, and now I'll look forward to it. So tell me, Dalton, anything new on the case you're working on? You've been so busy, keeping those late hours and hardly ever being home. Poor Brianna. She needs someone besides your housekeeper to watch over her."

"You're right, she does."

His intense stare took her breath away. *Not me, Buster. I don't want that shtick.* Unfortunately, his daughter was part of the package. She was saved from a reply by the waitress, who came to take their beverage order. Arnie expansively offered to pay for a bottle of wine, doubtless hoping to impress the newcomer.

"I spoke to a few of the staff members at the club," Marla blurted when Vail's attention was again distracted by Hortense.

"Go on," he said, his lips quirking upward while his leisurely gaze perused her.

Heat coursed through Marla's veins. Tamping her reaction, she went on. "Slate gave Jolene a massage the night she died. He said he didn't notice anything unusual about her behavior. But Gloria told me she'd heard them arguing. Amy was nearby and overheard also. She warned me about Keith."

Hortense placed her hand over Vail's. "Must you talk business, sugar? We're here to enjoy ourselves."

Arnie jumped in. "Marla is helping Dalton with his case. Maybe we should get our own table and let them talk in private. You and I have a lot of catching up to do, Hortense."

"Don't be absurd, you need to keep your fiancée company. And my name is Jill now."

"Can't I call you Hortense? It brings back such sweet memories."

Marla rolled her eyes, but Hortense seemed taken in. "I suppose so," Hortense conceded. "You know, Arnie, you're looking quite spiffy."

He preened happily. "You're quite a sight yourself."

Hortense leaned forward, engaging him in conversation, and Marla took this as an opportunity to snag Dalton.

Lowering her voice, she asked, "Don't you want to hear what else I learned? Cookie and I had a long discussion. She indicated Jolene was falsifying lab reports."

"Hmm." Vail regarded her with an unreadable expression.

Maybe he already knows about Jolene's work. "Cookie revealed another interesting tidbit: Jolene had met Sam Zelman on the sly a couple of times."

He raised an eyebrow. "Is that so? You might want to ask his wife about it. I believe that's Eloise on her way to the restroom."

Marla twisted her neck in the direction of his pointed finger. Sure enough, Eloise's plump figure was headed for the ladies' room. What good fortune that she was here tonight! Delayed by the waitress, who had returned with their drinks, Marla hastily gave her dinner order and then rose.

"I'll be right back."

Turning, she was dismayed to feel a rap on her shoulder. "I'm coming too," Hortense said, giggling. "I'm dying to hear the intimate details about you and Arnie."

Chapter
Nine

Marla's heart sank. The last thing she needed was Hortense accompanying her to the ladies' room when she spoke with Eloise. "I need to talk to that lady," Marla indicated.

"No problem." Hortense strolled beside her. "I'll just fix my lipstick while you're grilling the suspect."

When Marla glanced questioningly at her, she frowned. "What is it? You think I'm not smart? Just because I look like a bimbo doesn't mean I'm a ditz. Do you know how much it cost me to change my appearance? First I lost thirty pounds, then I had a boob job." Lifting her breasts, she grinned. "They look great, don't they? All through college, I worked hard to change my image. I bleached my hair, wore braces for two years, got contact lenses, and started an exercise regimen. Nobody calls me 'Horrible Hortense' anymore."

"I guess not," Marla mumbled. "You look terrific." A wave of sympathy mixed with admiration rippled through her. The poor girl must have had a difficult adolescence. Through fortitude and determination, she'd conquered her problems. Understanding didn't assuage Marla's jealousy, however.

She pushed open the door to the lavatory. A row of sinks and closed stalls met her gaze.

"Eloise, are you in here? It's Marla Shore."

"Hi, Marla," called Eloise's voice from behind a partition. "Where did you come from?"

"I'm at the restaurant with friends, and I just spotted you heading this way. I need to talk to you."

After using the facilities, she washed her hands beside Eloise, who peered disconsolately into the mirror. She needed to come in for a wash and blow dry, Marla thought, giving a quick glance to the woman's unkempt hairstyle. Dark shadows under her eyes and minimal makeup gave her face a sallow hue. Surely she could do better with her appearance. Eloise hadn't looked so bad the other day. What was wrong with her? Hortense stood by, watching them with a curious expression. Marla wished the girl would leave so she could talk privately to Eloise.

"Eloise Zelman, this is Hortense Crone," Marla said, feeling obliged to introduce them. "Hortense used to live in Palm Haven. She's moving back to town."

Eloise's expression brightened. "Really? I work as a realtor if you need help finding a place. What's your situation?" Withdrawing a lipstick from her handbag, she applied a light-pink coat. It wasn't the right color for her skin and only made her look worse.

Hortense regarded her coolly. "I'm renting an apartment."

"For how long? If you're planning to stay here permanently, maybe you're interested in a condo. Or are you just on a fishing trip for now?"

Hortense's chin lifted. "I got a job in public relations at Stockhart Industries."

Marla stared at her. "That's where Jolene used to work!"

Eloise snapped her purse shut. "Don't mention that woman's name."

Hortense exchanged a meaningful glance with Marla. "What did you have against her, sugar?"

"Ask my dear husband, Sam. Ask him why he told me he was going to the library one day, but when I followed him, I saw him meet Jolene at the Holiday Inn. To this day, he denies being there." She narrowed her gaze. "That slut was asking for trouble."

"She paid a heavy price," Hortense murmured.

"Why do you suppose Sam was meeting her?" Marla inquired, pretending innocence.

"What do you think? His head is turned by every pretty face that walks by. No matter how hard I work out to lose weight, or get my nails done or fix my hair, it doesn't matter." Her hazel eyes glistened. "You get to my age, and you'll see what I mean."

Heck, the A-word was creeping up on all of them! Marla resisted the impulse to search her roots for telltale gray. "Eloise, you know that isn't true. Sam is devoted to you. You need to come into the salon, that's all. We'll do some highlights, spruce things up. You could use more lift on the bottom, too. A different style will make you feel better."

Anger ignited the woman's features. "I've been coming to you for two months, and that's when things started to get worse. I don't think Sam likes this new tint. It's too coppery. He says I can't hide what I am."

"Nonsense, Eloise, you're overreacting. The two of you have a successful business partnership. I'm sure he appreciates your contribution. With age comes experience, and that makes a woman more attractive to a man."

At the mention of their business, Eloise's expression closed. "Marla, did you notice Hank at the bar?" she asked, effectively diverting their conversation.

"No, I didn't. What's he doing here?"

"Who knows? Maybe he's meeting someone. I'd better get back out there. I don't want Sam to get impatient and walk out on me."

"Well, you got an earful," Marla said to Hortense once Eloise had left.

Hortense leaned against the wall, arms crossed. "Eloise doesn't seem too happy with herself."

"I don't understand it. She comes to the salon every week, and she never said a word."

"Secrets have a way of surfacing when there's a crisis," Hortense said cryptically.

"We should be going, or the men will think we fell in," Marla remarked. Glancing into the mirror, she noted her mahogany hair still held its bob without any stray ends. Large toffee eyes glared back at her under lashes tipped in mascara. She didn't need another application of apricot lipstick; it stayed smooth and matched her tawny powder blush.

Eloise hovered outside the door to the ladies' room, giving Marla pause. Had she pried the door open to listen?

"I see that detective is here," Eloise commented, moistening her lips. "I didn't tell him anything about Sam meeting Jolene. You won't reveal what I told you, will you?"

"Uh, he already knows."

Eloise clenched her arm. "What?"

Marla couldn't meet her eyes. "Cookie told me about Sam meeting Jolene, and I'm afraid I passed that information along to Detective Vail. I was only trying to help," she added defensively.

"How the hell did Cookie find out?"

"I'm not really sure."

"Did Cookie tell you anything else about . . . about my husband's liaison?"

"I'd gotten the impression she just spotted them together, maybe more than once. She didn't . . . offer any judgment on their behavior." Her expression softened. "Maybe it's not what you think, Eloise. Maybe Sam had a perfectly legitimate reason to meet Jolene."

"At the Holiday Inn?" Eloise scoffed. "Look, ladies, I'd appreciate it if you kept our conversation confidential. You're right, Marla. I may just be imagining things. On the other hand . . ." Her voice trailed off as her gaze wandered the room. "You're here with that detective, aren't you, Marla?"

"Actually, Dalton is *my* date," Hortense boasted. "We're doubling with Marla and Arnie, her fiancé."

"What?" Eloise's eyes widened. "Marla, you've been holding back on me! Congratulations."

Marla groaned inwardly. Now Eloise would spread the news that Hortense apparently hadn't broadcast yet. "Thanks," she muttered ungratefully.

Both men stood as the ladies approached. Eloise veered off toward her husband's table; Hank was nowhere in sight. Marla wondered what Vail had been discussing with Arnie, because his quicksilver eyes alighted on her in a bemused fashion.

"What did Eloise say?" Vail prompted.

Marla sniffed, disliking how Hortense slid into the booth beside him while jiggling her bosom. "She just confirmed what Cookie said about Sam meeting Jolene."

"That doesn't prove anything," Arnie contributed, his dark gaze fixed on Hortense.

Their wine had been poured, and a spinach dip appetizer was on the table. Marla helped herself. "Hank Goodfellow was here earlier," she mentioned, biting into a crunchy corn chip. "Maybe the pharmacist spoke to Sam while Eloise was in the ladies' room. Did you guys notice anything?"

"No, we were too busy talking about you," Arnie blurted.

"Is that so? Did I miss anything important?"

Vail gulped a sip of wine, then grinned broadly. "Arnie was telling me the plans for your wedding. Sounds like a grand affair. I hope I'll be invited."

Rising to the bait, Marla raised an eyebrow. "Oh yes, along with your lovely daughter. What time should I pick her up for dance class next week?"

"Does the young lady need a ride?" Hortense cut in. "I'd be happy to oblige. Surely you have more important things to do." She emphasized her last sentence as though to say, *you belong to Arnie, so what are you doing with Vail's daughter?*

"I promised to take Brianna. It's no trouble," Marla said sweetly. "By the way, when do you start your new job at Stockhart Industries?" Across from her, Vail straightened his shoulders.

"I report in on Monday, but I'm not sure what hours I'll be working yet," Hortense replied.

"If you, uh, hear any gossip about Jolene, will you pass it on to me?"

"Sure will, sugar. Why is everyone so hung up on that woman's death? It was an accident, wasn't it?"

Marla and Dalton exchanged a quick glance. "Maybe, maybe not," Dalton said. "We're investigating the possibilities."

She gave him an appraising look. "Such as?"

"Jolene ingested a sedative before she went into the whirlpool."

"So? She must have been stressed out. That's probably why she went to the club in the first place."

Vail shook his head. "It wasn't the type of sedative you can buy over the counter."

"You didn't tell me that!" Marla exclaimed.

"Oh, I didn't? It must have slipped my mind."

Like hell it did. He was revealing that little tidbit now on purpose. Why? Their entrees arrived, and Marla put aside further questions while they made small talk.

"Tell me, I've always been curious about police officers," Hortense said between bites of grilled salmon. "Do you carry a gun when you're off duty?"

"Depends," Vail answered in a noncommittal tone.

"How did you get into this line of work?"

"I've always liked puzzles, so being a detective seemed a natural direction for me to take."

Arnie, who'd been watching Hortense with a lovesick expression, finally found his voice. "I used to admire firefighters, but I'm afraid of heights. Putting *on* a fire in the oven is more my speed. I make the best bagels in town."

"Of course you do," Hortense said patronizingly.

"Where did you work before you moved back to Palm Haven?" Marla asked, wondering if it was coincidence that Hortense had showed up right when problems with Jolene developed. Come to think of it, Hortense had jumped into their conversation as though she already knew what was going on. Could be she'd just heard the gossip. Or maybe she was more involved than she let on.

Hortense's glance flickered toward the entrance. "Up north. Wait here, and I'll get something from my car to show you."

While she was gone, Arnie excused himself to attend the men's room. Marla was grateful for the interval alone with Dalton.

"You don't have to be so nice to Hortense," she gritted. "I thought you were going to pay attention to me."

"What's the matter, Marla? Is your little scheme backfiring? It doesn't always work out when you attempt to manipulate people." His frank gaze made her flush with guilt.

"We're supposed to be doing Arnie a favor, but the way things are working out, Hortense barely notices him."

The corners of his mouth quirked upward. "Do I detect a hint of the green-eyed monster?"

"The hell you do. Arnie wants to score with Hortense, so please keep your hands off."

Raising his palms in supplication, he leaned across the table. "Where would you like me to place them instead? On your shoulders, perhaps?" His gaze intensified. "Or elsewhere. I'd be happy to provide . . . satisfaction."

Marla's breath hitched. "I—I don't know what I want," she stammered.

"You'd better make up your mind. I'm a patient man, but I can't wait forever."

Arnie returned, frowning when he saw the empty seat beside Vail. "What's taking Hortense so long?" he said, glancing at the door. The waitress had cleared the table, and while they sat in awkward silence, she brought over a dessert menu.

"Maybe I should see if anything is wrong," Marla began, but just then Hortense breezed through the entrance.

Her face looked flushed as she swung into the seat beside Vail. "This is what I've been doing part-time," the buxom blonde said, withdrawing a sheaf of papers from a portfolio. Spreading them out on the table, she pointed at two large black-and-white photographs. "My headshots, see? This is my résumé, and this is the last script I worked on. In my spare time I'm an actress."

"Hortense, that's wonderful!" Arnie gushed, fascinated by the sexy pose in one of the photos.

She smiled at him. "You think so? I figured, why let this beautiful body go to waste? I worked hard enough to look this way."

"You're absolutely right," Marla said firmly. She held up one of the dessert menus. "Sweets, anyone?"

* * *

"You heard her," Marla said to Arnie later in the parking lot on the way to his car. "She's an actress. Maybe Hortense returned to town at this particular time for a reason she isn't sharing with us. She could be cozying up to Dalton to sound him out."

"On what subject?" Arnie's shoulders slumped, and his stride lacked its usual spring.

"She seemed almost to know about Jolene. From the things she said to Eloise, I got the feeling Hortense was interested in the case."

"She might have known Jolene. Most of us went to the same high school." He gave a long sigh. "Maybe that's the problem. Now that Hortense has seen me, I've disappointed her."

Guests no longer waited outside the restaurant. The shadows of trees fell across the road, strange shapes that crowded the dim street lights. An eerie orange glow from downtown pierced the darkness to the east. Marla's pumps clacked on the asphalt as they proceeded through the parking lot. Her recent experience outside Perfect Fit Sports Club came back to haunt her, and the hair on her neck prickled. Was that same person lurking here?

Glancing back for reassurance, she caught the low murmur of voices. Hortense and Dalton hovered beside his car, making jealousy rear inside her.

"Don't feel bad," she said to Arnie. "Dalton is only paying attention to her to get back at me."

Giving her a forlorn look, he said, "I wouldn't count on that if I were you. Her bazongas are enough to make a man drool."

"Yeah, and she paid enough for them! Arnie, looks are only skin deep. If she doesn't like you just because you're not so young anymore, she isn't worth your energy." As a stylist, Marla strove to make her clients look their best, because creating an image of beauty was important for a person's self-esteem. But when it came to making character judgments, she relied on intuition and not just appearances alone.

Anger brought spirit back into his expression. "What do you mean, I'm not so young anymore? I don't vegetate in front of the TV like a lot of other schmucks my age. I work out at home and watch my diet." Patting his lengthening forehead, he glared at her. "I can't help my hair, but least I've still got some!"

Marla stopped in her tracks. "Arnie, I love you, and any girl who doesn't has blinders in front of her. You're a sweet man, and I've always found you attractive."

"You have?"

She chuckled. "Don't look at me that way. We're good friends, and let's leave it there."

"At least you're honest. So if you like Vail, why don't you go after him?"

Glancing in Dalton's direction, she was glad to note Hortense heading for her own car. "I'm not ready," she confessed, wrapping her arms around herself. It was cool out, and she'd forgotten to bring a sweater. Darkness surrounded them, encouraging confidences. "He might try to control me, like Stan did."

"Come on, Marla, you don't believe that. Vail is used to taking charge, but he strikes me as a decent guy. Stan was a putz who needed to dominate you."

She shivered. "I know, but I'm scared to get that deeply involved again."

"You're not getting any younger either, babe. You're still a looker, but do you really want to be alone the rest of your life?"

"I'm happy being alone," she retorted, stung by his words.

"No, you're not. You keep yourself so busy that you don't have time to think about it. What Jewish girl isn't raised with home and family ingrained in her mind?"

She resumed a quick stride to his car. "A family is the last thing I want."

"A husband, then. You won't have to run around solving murders if you have someone at home waiting for you."

"Dammit, Arnie, don't tell me what I need."

"*Shayna madel*, I just want you to be happy." He kept pace beside her, dark eyes gleaming in the faint moonlight. "You're a rare find, a woman who is beautiful and sincere. You care about others, but you don't let anyone care for you."

I don't need anyone! an inner voice shouted. "There's my mother," she offered. "Ma is always telling me what to do."

"Anita is a sweetheart." Arnie paused before opening the passenger door for her. "If you like Vail, don't let him get sidetracked by a pretty skirt."

"Oh, so now you're not bowled over by Hortense? Your eyes bulged out when you first caught sight of her at my salon."

"Maybe I was too hasty. I should get to know her better. She could be all frosting and no cake."

He reached over to unlock her door when a loud concussion ripped the air.

The ground under her feet shook, and a wave of heat blasted the left side of her face. Stumbling, Marla felt Arnie's arm steady her around the waist.

"What the hell was that?" he cried, the keys in his hand forgotten.

Together, they peered in the direction of the explosion, where several vehicles had ignited in a fiery conflagration. Vail, apparently knocked off his feet, stirred on the pavement.

"It wasn't his car, thank God," Arnie rasped, as they hastened toward him. Patrons, responding to the disaster, flew out the doors of the restaurant to see what had happened. Cries of horror mingled with the crackle of flames.

Vail stood and brushed himself off, his face paler than she'd ever seen it. His mouth set in a grim line, he yanked a cell phone from his belt.

"Where's Hortense?" Marla said, suddenly noticing the girl's absence. "I hope she wasn't . . . oh, Lord save me. No, it can't be." She trembled violently.

"Detective, what happened?" Arnie asked urgently. "Where's Hortense?"

Vail's eyes were hard as nails. "She went toward her car. I couldn't quite see . . ." His mouth tightened. "No one could have survived that blast. You can't even get near; it's too hot."

"It's not your fault," Marla said hastily.

"I should've gone with her. Maybe I would have noticed something."

She didn't understand what he meant. Stunned, she stared at the blazing vehicles. "How do you know for certain it was her car that blew up?"

"You don't see her anywhere, do you? All right, everyone, out of the way." His training took over. Creating an imaginary line, he kept onlookers at a distance until rescue personnel arrived.

"I don't believe it," Arnie repeated several times, shaking his head.

They watched firefighters attack the smoldering ruins while Vail directed his backup team. There would be witnesses to interview, detailed reports to file. He could be stuck here for hours. Questions plagued her, but she wouldn't bother Vail with them now. Foremost in her mind were the ones regarding Jolene's death. And now this. What, if anything, connected the two events?

Chapter
Ten

Her face reflecting the glow from the emergency lights, Marla clutched Arnie's arm. "Look, over there!"

A familiar figure staggered into view from the edge of the spectacle. A bedraggled and dazed Hortense stumbled toward them.

"Hey, guys!" she called in a trembling voice.

Vail whirled around, did a double take, then marched in her direction.

Arnie reached her first. "Are you okay, babe? We thought it was *your* car."

Hortense ran a shaky hand through her hair, which had tumbled from its upsweep onto her shoulders. "I—I'd unlocked my door. Then I got slammed to the ground. I don't know what happened." Her gaze darted like that of a trapped animal.

"Bless my bones, you're bleeding," Marla said, pointing to Hortense's skinned knees. "Maybe you should see the medics."

"N-no. I'll be all right."

Vail reached her side, a concerned expression on his face. "Did you see anything unusual?" he asked in a quiet tone.

"Isn't that *your* job?" Marla retorted, shaken by Hortense's near miss. "You're a detective. Didn't you record every detail while the two of you walked to your car?" He'd probably noted every contour of Hortense's outfit, she thought shrewishly. If Vail hadn't detained her so long, Hortense might have driven away before the explosion.

Hortense lifted her glazed eyes. "Well, now that you mention it, Sam was just starting his car, which was a row ahead of mine."

"Sam?" Marla queried in a high-pitched voice. "Do you mean Sam Zelman?"

"Yes," Hortense whispered.

How would Hortense recognize Sam unless they'd met earlier? Maybe she'd spotted him at Eloise's table, Marla surmised.

"Hortense needs to go home," Arnie stated, taking Hortense's arm. "She's shaken up."

"I'll have to get a statement," Vail told the shaken blonde, "but I can catch you later after this mess is cleaned up. Did you see anyone else in the vicinity?"

"No, I didn't. Sorry." Hortense stared at her shredded hosiery. "I didn't expect this to be dangerous."

"Stick around Marla, and trouble will find you," Vail muttered, exchanging a knowing look with Arnie.

Arnie grinned, dimples creasing his cheeks. "Look, Hortense needs a ride. I'll take her home. You can keep each other company."

Marla stared after them as they walked away, arm in arm. "Dear Lord, if Sam was in that car, then where's Eloise?"

"Good question," Vail told her. "Let's see if any witnesses saw them both leave the restaurant."

"Eloise can't be dead." She shook her head in disbelief. Vaguely, it occurred to her that Arnie's plan had worked. He'd gone off with Hortense while she remained with Vail. Except this disaster hadn't been part of their scheme. So who had orchestrated the blast?

"Was it a car bomb?" she asked Vail, walking fast to keep up with his long-legged stride. His stern profile revealed nothing of his feelings. She had no way of knowing whether this was just routine to him, or if he cared about the victims. His mouth was pinched into a tight line; his eyes were flat as a metal plate. From the determined set of his shoulders, she understood he meant to get answers, but that was his job. Actually, investigating this accident might not be in his jurisdiction. But since at least one of the casualties was a suspect in his case, she supposed that authorized involvement.

"You don't think this had anything to do with Jolene's death, do you?" she ventured.

"I have no theories at this point—only questions."

"How can you tell if Eloise was in that car?"

He paused, glaring at her. "Normally, a wife leaves a restaurant with her husband. Did Eloise say anything to you to indicate they'd arrived here separately?"

"Not really."

The firefighters were putting away their equipment. Tow trucks would need to clear away the rest. She waited while Vail rattled off orders to his team. A nauseating smell permeated the air: burning tires, gasoline fumes, and something else that reminded her of barbecued meat.

Her dinner rose in her stomach. Going home seemed like a good idea for her, too. "Dalton, could they tell how many people were in the car?" she asked him when he had a free moment. "Was anyone else hurt?"

He gave an exasperated snort. "If you'd let me get my job done, maybe I can find out."

Thanks, pal. That's just what I needed to hear. No one wanted her—not Arnie, and now Vail. She knew when to leave. "Fine, I'll call a friend to pick me up. I left my car at the salon, remember?"

Remorse flickered briefly in his eyes. "That's right, you drove with Arnie. If you'll wait—"

"No, I can see you're busy. Tally doesn't live far from here. She'll come get me."

Fortunately, Tally was home when Marla called from inside the restaurant. Within fifteen minutes, Marla had settled onto the seat cushions in her friend's black BMW.

"I'm so grateful," she said, shooting Tally a weary glance. The tall blonde had been watching a movie with her husband. Her casual slacks outfit fit as elegantly as on a mannequin. In contrast, Marla's clothes felt rumpled and grimy. A hot shower and a cup of coffee seemed like a piece of heaven.

Tally drove steadily, hands on the wheel. "What happened at the restaurant? And why were you and Vail there?"

Folding her hands in her lap, Marla related the course of events. "I didn't know Sam all that well, but I'll feel awful if Eloise was in their car."

"Why wouldn't she have been?"

"I don't know. I just have a feeling."

"Uh-oh."

"Eloise suspected Sam was having an affair with Jolene. Maybe she confronted him over dinner. If he was nasty or evasive, she could've walked out on him."

"Or maybe she planted the bomb herself. It fits, doesn't it? Knock off Jolene who is screwing hubby, then do in the old man? Maybe even disappear afterward so everyone believes you were in that car."

"I can't picture Eloise putting together a bomb. She's a realtor, not a mechanic."

"Anyone can learn. I'll bet they have lessons on the Internet."

Marla shuddered. "How awful. Learn to blow up people in ten easy steps? What is this world coming to?"

Tally maneuvered into the right lane. "Eloise never had evidence Sam's meetings with Jolene were for amorous purposes. What if they met over a matter of business?"

"Like what?"

"He was a realtor also. Was Jolene interested in changing her residence? Or investing in property?"

"Good point. Maybe I'll stop in at their office Monday. Dalton should have word on Eloise by then."

They pulled into the parking lot where the Cut 'N Dye was located. Tally found a spot near Marla's Toyota and idled the engine. Another deserted, dark avenue for muggers, Marla thought with a shiver. Or mad bombers. How could she tell if her car was wired?

"Are you still meeting me at the club tomorrow morning?" Tally asked. "Ken has a golf game, so I've got a few hours free."

"Yeah, I'll be there. I want to talk to Amy, so maybe we can have a snack before our workout. Is there a Dancercize class scheduled?"

"I think so. Eight o'clock too early?"

"On Sunday? Hell, yes. Let's make it at nine."

"Nine-killer. That's another name for the butcher bird, or shrike, which supposedly kills nine birds a day," Amy said while Marla perused the food choices at the juice bar.

"Is that so?"

"Three down. More to go. If you don't watch out, you'll ruin the show."

"Huh?" Now Amy sounded like Marla's neighbor Goat, who often spoke in obscure phrases.

Amy's turquoise eyes bored into hers. "I heard about the Zelmans. Mr. Goodfellow is here with Wallace Ritiker. He told me."

"Hank? I thought he'd left the restaurant already. We didn't see him later on."

Amy shrugged. "It must have been a blast."

Marla winced at the girl's bad attempt at humor. She'd arrived early, hoping Amy would be on duty. Funny how the prospect of questioning a suspect propelled her out of bed in the morning. Maybe Ma was right, and she needed some spice in her life. So what if an amour wasn't the direction Marla wanted to go? Solving a murder served the same purpose: cozy up to the opposition; learn his secrets; eliminate conflicting viewpoints; and get to the climax. As simple as a haircut. Snip away those dead ends; blend the different layers; finish off the style. Real life wasn't so easy, though. Relationships required constant work, and murders didn't always offer simple solutions.

Tally breezed in, and the next few minutes were spent exchanging greetings and ordering snacks. Marla was relieved to see coffee on the menu. Amy gave her a paper cup, and she served herself from a large metal urn. Brown sugar was the only sweetener available. Tally ordered a raspberry sunrise fruit drink and chose a Clif Bar from a selection of packaged goods.

"It's similar to a granola bar," she said. "This tastes better and is loaded with protein and antioxidants."

"I'll have a bagel," Marla said to Amy. Breakfast was an important meal; she needed something substantial. "I was hoping to make an appointment with Tess, the massage therapist. Have you met her?"

Amy leaned on the counter, her straight hair falling forward. "Several times. Tess hangs at the same club I do, down by the Strip."

"Are you two friends?"

She wrinkled her nose. "I wouldn't go that far. We've only exchanged a few words, and she doesn't come in here that often."

Marla took a sip of coffee, aware that Tally could overhear them from her seat at the table. "What about Slate? Don't they ever share the same time slot in the massage suite?"

"Nah, Tess comes in during off hours."

"He seems reluctant to talk about her. I was wondering if they had anything going on."

Amy's expression grew stony. "He'd better not be seeing her, but I wouldn't put it past him. He chases after every skirt that walks through this door."

"I figured that was Keith's act. He put the moves on me the first day I met him. I think he really likes you, though."

"He can stuff it. Slate's the man for me, except he's too blind to see it."

"What would you say if I told you Slate not only knows Tess well, but she might be living with him?"

No wonder Tess had given Betsy's address. If Amy happened to see the staff roster, she'd notice Slate's street number. So Tess had given the address of her friend Betsy, instead.

"I don't believe you."

"I wanted to talk to Tess. She was at Slate's house, but I just missed her."

"There has to be a reason why she was there. Slate's a hormonal drone, but he wouldn't do it with that broad. Have you seen her? She's huge!" Her eyes narrowed, and she lowered her voice. "The jerk tried to hit on Jolene. I heard them. She told him off, but I don't think she meant it. Like she was playing hard to get, you know."

"Gloria told me you overheard Slate and Jolene arguing inside one of the massage rooms. Did Jolene stay for the full hour of her appointment?"

A smug smile curved the girl's ruby lips. "No, she left early. I meant to follow her into the locker room to make sure she had no real interest in Slate, but Lindsay was just leaving and I needed to ask her something."

"So you didn't consider Jolene to be a rival at that point?"

"Honey, I consider everyone a rival who wears a dress, yourself included. You heed my warning, and stay away from Slate." Her gaze lifted. "There's Gloria. She's a first-class bitch if ever you met one."

"Tell me about it."

"She was standing outside the door trying to hear what Jolene said to Slate. I could tell she was worried. Jolene knew things about Gloria that she doesn't want to get around."

A beefy man wearing denim shorts and a gray muscle shirt plopped his gym bag on a table and approached the counter. "Gimme a lemon twist, luv," he demanded, winking at Marla.

Raising an eyebrow, Marla turned away and joined Tally. Spreading cream cheese on her bagel, she related what she'd learned and brought her friend up to speed about Hortense.

"I'm concerned that Arnie might get hurt," she told Tally. "He's awed by her, but I know how deceiving appearances can be, having learned my own lesson the hard way. I'd rather know more about Hortense before he gets too involved."

"I thought you said she was attracted to Dalton."

"She played up to him, at least while we were discussing Jolene's case. Don't forget, she thinks Arnie is my fiancé."

Tally's azure eyes danced with delight. "Man, I wish I'd been there!"

"I hope Ma doesn't hear the news. She's always liked Arnie. She'd be disappointed to learn it's a pretense. Would you believe I was afraid Eloise would tell people? I can't accept that she's missing. First Jolene dies, then Mrs. Zelman disappears. I never told you what happened in the parking lot the other night." Speaking rapidly, she related the incident.

Tally finished her Clif Bar. "Holy smokes, you don't suppose someone is knocking off your clients and having a swing at you because you make women look good, do you?"

"Who'd do that? A jealous wife?"

"Maybe an aging woman whose spouse won't look twice at her anymore because his head is distracted by other pretty faces."

"That's absurd."

"Yeah, but it's something to think about."

"Eloise fits that bill, but she's one of the victims."

"Were her remains found in that car?"

"I don't know. Dalton won't tell me anything."

"Well, what else have you got?"

"I want to know why Hortense seems interested in this case. She appeared out of nowhere and latched herself onto Arnie. When Vail came along, suddenly she liked him. Perhaps she's on the level, but I want to find out before she screws Arnie." *Or takes Dalton away from me,* she added silently.

"How are you going to pursue that angle?"

"Arnie might know where she was located before she moved here. She wasn't that far away; I know that much. I'll take a ride and see what I can learn."

"Call me if it's one of my days off, and I'll go with you—oh, I didn't tell you about the guy who came into my boutique." Her face creased into a smile. "He said he wanted to look at some outfits for his girlfriend, but after he selected several dresses, he tried them on!"

Marla chuckled. "Did he buy anything?"

"Yes, two items plus matching accessories. Very weird. He was a hunky-looking guy, too."

"It takes all kinds." She fell silent to finish her bagel. Revved up from the coffee, she rose and tossed her empty containers into the trash. "Let's get changed. How much time before Dancercize?"

Tally stretched, then checked her watch. "It starts at ten. We've got fifteen minutes."

"If we hurry, we'll have time to talk to Hank. I'd like to ask him how he found out about the incident last night. Was he still at the restaurant, and if so, did he see anyone else around the cars that got blown up?"

Tally placed a warning hand on her arm. "Don't look now, but here comes Cookie."

"Hi, gals." Cookie bounced in, looking chipper in a sweatshirt and shorts. "So Marla, I hear the Zelmans got bumped off last night."

"Who told you?" Marla demanded.

Cookie smirked. "One of my SETA colleagues. Her brother owns the tow-truck company that does accident cleanups. The Zelmans screwed a lot of people. It's no secret they made money off other people's misfortunes. Something to do with mortgage foreclosures."

"I was in the restaurant last night," Marla confided. "I talked to Eloise in the ladies' room. She believed Sam was having an affair with Jolene. Why else would they have been meeting at the Holiday Inn? It's not your usual business location."

"You tell me, doll. Jolene acted strange in many ways. Must've been those chemicals she worked with every day. Affected her brain. Or else guilt afflicted her from all the suffering she caused those captive animals."

Pushing open the door to the locker room, Cookie preceded the others inside and marched directly toward an unoccupied bench. The room wasn't crowded yet, but it was bound to fill later when all the Sunday snoozers woke up. Marla, trailing after Cookie, chose an empty cubbyhole and took out the combination lock she'd brought in her bag. She motioned Tally to the space beside hers.

"Did you discover anything new about Jolene's work or those lab reports you'd mentioned?" Marla asked Cookie, determined to squeeze every bit of information from the woman.

"Did you rid your salon of products from companies that use animal testing?"

"I haven't had a chance."

"Well, I won't tell you anything else until you do." Cookie's expression hardened. "Someone has to stand up for those poor creatures. Too much of our society is based on animal abuse. Drugs, cosmetics, and industrial products all require liability and safety tests, but they can be done in a more humane manner. You're the ones who influence those industries. If you boycott their products, you won't be held personally responsible for the deaths of animals. Otherwise, you're nothing more than murderers."

Plopping onto the bench, she slid her feet from a pair of scuffed sandals and took out a can of antifungal powder from her backpack. Sprinkling the yellow substance on her feet, she then pulled on a pair of white cotton socks and stuck her feet into sneakers.

Marla stared at the sprinkling of yellow dust on the floor, but she had no time to consider Cookie's inconsiderate habits because a cough sounded from around the bend. Who had been listening in on their conversation?

Lindsay's grinning face popped into view. "Sorry, guys. I was changing into my leotard when I heard you come in, and I wasn't exactly presentable. Are you joining my dance class?"

"Sure thing," Tally responded, beating Marla to the punch. Engaging Lindsay in small talk, she changed into a black-and-silver combo that reminded Marla of a Victoria's Secret window fashion.

By comparison, her own shorts and tank top seemed overly conservative. It didn't help that Lindsay looked like Barbie with her swinging ponytail, leggy pink tights, and glowing complexion. Where were all the overweight patrons who really needed the class?

Probably upstairs, she told herself as they followed Lindsay to the second level. Two people were missing from her group today, Marla realized with dismay. First Jolene met her demise, then Eloise vanished in a puff of smoke. Who was next?

"Hello, it's me!" trilled a voice from inside the studio.

Marla's jaw dropped open. Dressed in a two-piece outfit that showed more skin than fabric, Hortense grinned at them.

Chapter
Eleven

"What are you doing here?" Marla asked Hortense, determined to find out why the woman popped up at the most opportune times.

"I decided to take advantage of the three-month trial membership." Whipping back a stray hair from her face, she glanced pointedly at Tally.

Marla introduced them as Lindsay stepped forward. "This is my friend Tally Riggs, and here's Lindsay Trotter, the dance teacher. Are you joining her class?"

"I was hoping there'd be enough room."

"Wow, the place is full," Tally commented, noting the crowded studio.

Lindsay bounced on her heels. "We always get a good group on Sundays. Come on inside, ladies. Don't forget to rub your shoes in the resin so you don't slip," she advised Hortense. "It's not necessary for sneakers, but I recommend it for jazz shoes or ballet slippers on a polished floor." Beaming a toothpaste-advertisement smile, she strutted inside the room.

Marla studied Hortense's smiling expression. Her eyes were wary, unlike her upward-curved mouth. *If that gal doesn't have an ulterior agenda, I'll eat beet borscht every day for a month*, Marla thought.

"Are you fully recovered from last night?" she asked with pretended concern.

Hortense waved a hand in dismissal. "I'm fine. Arnie was such a dear. You're really lucky to have hooked him, you know."

Tally chuckled. "That's what I keep telling her. She and Arnie make such a sweet couple."

Throwing her friend a dirty look, Marla said, "Lindsay's about to start the class. Come on."

She got into the swing doing warmups with big band music blasting from the speakers. Starting out with "In the Mood," they picked up the pace with "Chattanooga Choo Choo" and then moved to "Boogie Woogie Bugle Boy." By then her Danskin Spandex tank top was stuck to her sweaty back, and her bike shorts felt molded to her thighs. She enjoyed learning the Charleston and the Lindy Hop, if that was what you called it. Occasionally, she'd tuned into those ballroom dancing competitions on TV and was amazed at how strenuous a form of exercise it could be. This was a lot more fun than doing sit-ups or power boxing, although that last one wasn't a bad idea for self defense.

"Thin is in!" Lindsay chanted during the cool-down period, rotating her arms in a graceful port de bras.

"Great session," Marla said afterward while the others filed out. "I wish I had time to continue when my trial membership is over, but I've got too many other things to do. Can you recommend an instructional tape that I can use at home?"

Lindsay's steady gaze assessed her. "There's one with Denise Austin that you might like. It's a low-impact workout with some of the same tunes."

"Okay, thanks. I'll see you again on Tuesday when I bring Brianna to ballet class."

"Sure. Too bad her dad is busy. Is he still working up Jolene's case? I thought her tragic drowning was an accident."

"He said Jolene took sedatives before going into the whirlpool, and it wasn't a drug you can buy over the counter." She watched Lindsay for her reaction.

A smooth eyebrow rose. "Really? Meaning what?"

"Maybe Jolene was murdered."

"Murdered?" Her pink lips gaped.

Marla glanced around the empty classroom. Tally was chatting with Hortense outside the glass wall. They could start on the machines without her.

"The drug made Jolene drowsy enough to sink underwater, so it must've been fairly quick-acting," she confided.

"But why would Jolene take it if she knew that?"

"Maybe she didn't. She'd swallowed gelatin capsules in the locker room when I was there with Cookie, so that's one possible route. She'd gotten a manicure earlier that day and was in the habit of biting her nails, because I caught a glimpse of Bite No More in her bag. So maybe the sedative was painted on her nails. Then again, she had a snack after your dance class. Could someone have slipped a Mickey Finn into her drink? Somebody got to Sam Zelman last night, which makes me think their deaths were related. I guess Detective Vail concurs because he's still investigating."

"Why are you so interested, Marla?"

"Jolene was my client. She shouldn't have died that day. It won't make any difference now, but I want to understand what happened."

Stooping over, Lindsay reached for her dance bag and slung the strap over her shoulder. Her short-sleeved leotard allowed Marla a glimpse of sculpted arm muscles. She must work out with weights, Marla figured with a twinge of envy.

"I noticed Eloise wasn't here today," Lindsay commented as they strolled toward the exit. "I heard about the disaster last night. It's such a shame. We'll all miss them."

"I'm not so sure Eloise was in the car. Although it's a natural assumption, we're not even sure they arrived together. Hortense only caught a glimpse of Sam sitting in the vehicle."

Lindsay's eyes widened. "You were there?"

She gave a wry smile. "Hortense and I were double-dating. We went with our guys to dinner at the restaurant."

"And you didn't invite me?" Keith clucked his tongue as he approached the cluster of people outside the dance studio.

Hortense had apparently been holding court by dramatizing last night's incident. Since many of the people knew the Zelmans, she had gathered quite an audience. Keith hastened to introduce himself to her and Tally before sidling back to Marla.

"So, babe, want a fitness consult today? We still need to review your diet." His chocolate brown eyes swept her body.

"Haven't you heard the news?" Hortense cried. "She's engaged to Arnie Hartman."

Marla groaned inwardly as others heard the announcement and came over to congratulate her. When the circle of acquaintances finally dispersed, she gestured to Tally. "Let's do fifteen minutes on the Virtual Reality bike. That's all the time I can spare. I have things to do at home."

While they were cycling, Marla's gaze followed Keith. He flirted with Hortense, showing her the equipment and apparently finding reasons to put his hands on her. When he headed downstairs, Marla decided it might be a good opportunity to catch him alone. If she must endure his sexual advances in order to gain information, so be it. She left Tally after arranging to meet her friend in the lobby.

On the lower level, she rounded a corner just as Keith emerged from the massage suite. His eyes were stormy as he conversed with Slate. "You're not keeping close enough tabs on her," Keith muttered, jabbing a finger in the air.

Marla paused by the partially open door to Gloria's office, staying just out of either man's visual range.

"You're crazy; I can't be on the chick every minute. Besides, Amy doesn't want you, man. She has the hots for me."

"When I tell her what I know, she'll drop you like a rock."

Slate made a growling noise. "You'd better not, or I won't follow your orders anymore."

Keith cursed. "Don't worry, your secret is safe with me as long as you do what you're told. Just make sure she doesn't end up like Jolene."

"What does that mean?" Slate snarled.

"Amy overheard you arguing with Jolene. What'd you do, slip something into her glass of water?"

"That's ridiculous."

"Oh yeah? Remember how you smashed Jolene's headlights after she refused to go out with you? I'm surprised she let you give her a massage."

"She had something to tell me about Gloria and wanted to know if you were involved. I told her you're too dumb to even know what's going on."

They strode away, giving Marla a moment to consider what she'd heard. Slate, as well as Gloria, had something to hide. Before she reached any conclusions, a cough sounded from inside Gloria's office, and she backed away. *I wonder if Vail has checked the personnel files,* she thought. *Imagine the wealth of information that must be in Gloria's records!* If only she could get into that office when no one else was around. Gloria probably had profiles on all the customers as well.

"Marla, I thought you were getting changed," said Tally from behind her.

Marla swirled to face her friend. "I just overheard an interesting conversation," she said in a hushed voice. "I'll tell you about it when we're outside." Gesturing toward Gloria's office, she indicated they should hasten past.

In the locker room, Hortense stood by a bench, conversing with Cookie. The shorter woman had pulled an oversized T-shirt over her Jockey zip-front sports bra and black capri pants. Her strawberry blond hair, in disarray after class, looked as though she'd been in a windstorm. Despite her dislike of Cookie, Marla's fingers itched for a hairbrush to tame the unruly locks.

"Marla, we were just talking about you," Hortense stated.

"Oh?" She walked toward her locker.

"Cookie was telling me you use bad products in your salon."

Grasping a clean towel, Marla spun to face the troublemaker. "Are you spreading false rumors about me? If you slander my salon, I'll take legal action."

Cookie's emerald eyes gleamed defiantly. "You promised to weed undesirable items from your stock, but you haven't done anything!"

Marla gritted her teeth. "I told you earlier that I haven't had a chance to take inventory regarding which products comply with

SETA standards. It's not the highest thing on my priority list. I'm worried about Eloise."

Cookie's gaze hardened. "She's not my problem. You are."

Tally butted in. "Leave my friend alone, or you'll answer to me. Marla isn't doing anything to offend you. You're the type of person who picks a fight because you don't know how to get close to someone. You could be attractive, but your sour attitude puts people off."

"It's a *shandah,*" Marla said to Tally on their way out later. "Cookie is a driven woman. What a shame she's misusing her talents by being so aggressive."

"She attacks people verbally because it alienates them. By latching onto different causes, she reminds me of a lost child who lacks a sense of self-direction."

"Since when are you a psychologist?" Marla paused in front of a Dodge minivan, thinking that the parking lot could qualify for a foreign car show. Down one aisle alone, she noted two Mercedeses, two Jaguars, a gold Lexus RX-300, three Toyotas, and a Honda Odyssey. Typical of upscale west Broward County.

"Cookie irritates me. I'm just trying to understand what makes her tick," Tally said, squinting in the morning sunlight. "She strikes me as a lonely person."

"Well, I don't feel sorry for her."

"Do you have time to stop for coffee? You didn't tell me what you learned from Keith after following him downstairs. I'd like to hear more about Dalton, too. Ken and I should double-date with you guys one night. That is, after your engagement to Arnie breaks off." A wide grin split her face. "I can see why he'd be floored by Hortense. She's got equipment in all the right places."

"Dalton noticed that, too." Marla glanced at her watch. "I have to go directly home. This afternoon is the West Regional Fair, and my Child Drowning Prevention Coalition is handing out leaflets supporting a proposed bill in the state legislature. If passed, it'll mandate safety measures on all new pools and hot tubs built in Florida after the law goes into effect. If you've got nothing else to do, maybe you'd like to join us. Volunteers get a potluck supper."

Tally's lips compressed. "I saw the article in the newspaper this morning about the two-year-old who drowned in his family pool. You'd think people would keep their doors locked."

"I know," she said sadly. "Child-proof locks are readily available. Alarms can be set to go off when anybody opens a door. People just don't think about the most basic safety measures until something bad happens."

And even then, tragedies still occurred. Hadn't she lived through one herself? Drowning wasn't the only danger. She'd seen the statistics. For every ten children who drowned in Broward County, 36 were admitted to hospitals, and 140 were treated in emergency rooms after near-drownings. Some children suffered aftereffects as serious as brain damage. It was a tragedy that could be prevented through education, and that was why she'd gotten involved. If only someone had educated her when she was nineteen years old, little Tammy might still be alive. Drowning was still the main cause of death for children under four years of age in South Florida.

"What time do you have to be there?" Tally asked.

"It's at Central Park. I have to check in by one, and I promised to bring noodle kugel for the supper. Lord save me, I have so many things to do! I never took Spooks for his walk this morning because I was in a rush to get here, and I need to call my mother. Oh, and I told Goat I'd let him plant impatiens in front of my house. You know I have a brown thumb, and he's been nagging the neighbors to put more flowers in. He's going to do Moss and Emma's house next door, too."

"That's generous of him." They strolled toward Marla's white Camry.

"Goat may be one socket short in the lightbulb department, but I believe he's got a good heart. Even if weird animal noises do come from his house. Look, why don't you meet me at my place? I'll put on a pot of coffee, and we can have an early lunch. Then you can decide if you want to come with me to the park later."

* * *

Spooks greeted Marla with wild barking when she entered the town house through her garage. Tally trailed along, having parked in the driveway behind her. Throwing down her purse on the kitchen table, Marla bent to pet the poodle. His cream-colored hair felt springy and soft, but it was also growing too long over his eyes. *Call the groomer next week*, she noted mentally, scratching behind the dog's ears.

Goat ran a pet-grooming business out of his van, but Marla was satisfied with the woman who came to her house. Besides, Goat claimed to have a big snake among his menagerie, and she wouldn't want Spooks near if the creature got hungry.

After Spooks finished sniffing Tally, Marla let him out into the backyard. Tally seated herself at the kitchen table and read the newspaper while Marla set a pot of coffee to brew. When it was percolating, she picked up the phone to call Anita.

Her mother answered on the second ring. "There you are! I called you earlier, but you weren't home. What's this I hear about you and Arnie Hartman?"

Marla cringed. "It's nothing, Ma. We're pretending to be engaged so Arnie's former classmate doesn't bug him, except now Arnie likes Hortense. We got Dalton to double-date with us, figuring he'd be attentive to me so Arnie could snow her. But things didn't work out that way—at least not at first."

"Whoa, slow down, you're losing me."

Marla heard Tally's snicker. "Don't talk about our engagement to anyone, okay?" she pleaded to her mother.

"People have already started congratulating me. I always said Arnie was right for you. Such a sweet man. He'd make a stable husband, Marla. Not to mention that he's Jewish, unlike this Lieutenant Vail who's taken your fancy. Maybe you should take advantage of this situation and claim Arnie for your own."

"I don't think so."

"So why continue the pretense if Arnie likes the woman?"

"We're planning to have a fight and break up. He took Hortense home after the excitement at the restaurant last night, but apparently he didn't have the guts to confess the truth."

"Restaurant? Were you at that place where the cars blew up? Marla, if I didn't already have white hairs on my head, you'd be causing them!"

"I gotta go, Ma. Tally is here. Are Michael and his family coming for dinner tonight?" she asked about her brother.

"Yes, and you're still invited. We need to talk about your birthday next month."

"Thanks, but I have a date with Lance."

A snort of exasperation followed. "Is he the man who works in the body shop?"

"No, that's Ralph. He's been busy with night school, so I haven't seen him in a while. Lance is my computer friend. I called him after I got home last night and asked him to look up car bombs on the Internet to see if a normal person could figure out how to make one. I'm invited to his place later; he's barbecuing chicken."

"Is that kosher when you're going steady with Lieutenant Vail and are engaged to Arnie?"

"I'm not attached to anyone, Ma. Now I've got to hang up. Give my love to Michael, Charlene, and the kids. Love you, bye."

She turned to Tally. "Bless my bones, our conversations always turn to my love life."

Tally's eyes twinkled. "Doesn't Lance usually ask you over to view his favorite web sites?"

Marla pursed her lips. "Don't worry. I'll tell him Arnie and I are engaged. Being taken does have its advantages!"

Spooks scratched at the door, so she let him back in. He headed for his water dish while she made tuna sandwiches and poured their coffee. Marla tossed the poodle a biscuit before sitting opposite Tally. Her body sagged as she delved into lunch. She hadn't realized how tense being at the sports club made her feel. Wasn't that the place where she was supposed to relax?

"I was hoping Dalton would call," she began. "He might have found out more information about the explosion last night, or if Eloise was there. I wonder if anyone has tried calling her house."

"Did the Zelmans have any kids?"

Marla swallowed a piece of sandwich. "Two grown children.

Eloise talked about them when she came into the salon." Her eyes misted. "I'll have to see when she made her next appointment. Guess I'll have to cancel it."

They finished eating in silence. Marla brought the dishes to the sink, then turned to Tally in dismay. "Oh, no, I forgot to make the noodle dish! Would you mind if we talk while I work around the kitchen?" Already she'd found an apron and donned it before Tally responded.

"Can I help?" Tally jumped from her seat.

Marla crouched to withdraw a soup pot from the cabinet. "No, thanks. It'll take me longer to do the dishes than to make the kugel." Filling the pot halfway with water, she set it on the electric burner to boil.

"Do you really think Jolene's death was not an accident?" Tally asked, watching Marla stride to the pantry.

Marla grabbed a sixteen-ounce bag of wide egg noodles, a tall can of crushed pineapple, and a jar of cinnamon. Placing them on the counter, she turned to face her friend.

"Vail is suspicious, and so am I. He's never said outright that he's investigating a murder, but that must be why he's on the case. Lab tests detected sedatives in Jolene's blood. Why would she take something that would make her drowsy when she still had to drive home? It doesn't make sense."

"So the alternative is that someone drugged her."

"Tell me about it. But how? She'd swallowed two gelatin capsules, but Vail said the rest of the capsules in her bottle were genuine. Could it have been in the nail-biting solution?"

When the water boiled, Marla tossed in the egg noodles and set her kitchen timer for eight minutes. Next up was to melt a stick of margarine in the microwave. Spooks followed at her heels, eager for any particles she might drop on the floor. His nose worked overtime sniffing the different aromas.

"It's also possible the guilty party slipped a drug into Jolene's drink at the snack bar," Tally said, snatching up a clean dish towel. "Anyone walking by could have done it if her attention was diverted."

Rummaging in the fridge, Marla selected four eggs. She brought them to a bowl beside the kitchen sink. Cracking each one, she beat them together until blended.

Tally regarded her steadily. "So who do you suspect?"

Marla grinned wryly. "Everyone we've encountered at Perfect Fit Sports Club."

Chapter
Twelve

"Gloria must be doing something crooked," Marla said to Tally, draining the hot noodles in a colander. "According to Slate, Jolene informed him about Gloria's activities that Friday night during her massage. She'd wanted to know if Keith was involved. If I could get into Gloria's office, I might learn more." She poured the noodles into a large bowl after rinsing them in cold water.

Putting aside her damp dish towel, Tally opened the microwave and retrieved the dish holding the melted margarine. "Gloria might have wanted to get rid of Jolene to shut her up."

"That's one possibility." Marla stirred a couple of hot noodles into the beaten eggs, then added all the eggs to the noodles. A half cup of sugar went in the bowl next, followed by the margarine and quarter teaspoon cinnamon. "Meanwhile, Keith is forcing Slate to follow his orders in return for his silence. That means Slate is involved in some dirty business. Jolene could have found out what he's hiding."

"Don't forget Amy, who was jealous of Slate's attention to Jolene," Tally contributed.

"Maybe they're all in it together!" Marla tossed the drained crushed pineapple into the mixture along with the juice from a fresh lemon.

"Don't you add raisins?" Tally asked, peering over her shoulder.

"That's an option. You can add a half cup of raisins, or cut the butter to a quarter pound and add a pint of sour cream. Or you can put in one teaspoon of vanilla instead of lemon juice. I'm using the ingredients I have available." She spread the mixture in a greased rectangular pan, sprinkled two tablespoons of corn-flake crumbs and cinnamon-sugar over the top, then put it in the oven at 350 degrees to bake for one hour.

The phone rang, and Marla resolved for the umpteenth time to get Caller ID.

"Hi, Marla. It's Stan."

Lord save me. She threw Tally an annoyed glance. "Yeah, what's up?" Her ex-spouse was the last person she wanted to talk to on her day off.

"Kim and I are going to be in your area this afternoon. How about we drop in to say hello?" His smooth tone oozed oil.

"Sorry, I won't be home."

"We'll come now, then. We've had a new offer on our rental property. It's a good deal, Marla. A good deal. Let's unload the place before values go down."

"I'm not stupid. Property values in that area have been rising. I'm not going to sign, so you'd be wasting your time coming here."

"You're not as adept in financial matters as I am, dear heart. That's why you have to work for a living these days. You know you need my advice."

"Go to hell." Slamming the receiver down, she faced Tally, who'd been idly thumbing through a *Modern Salon* magazine. "That louse. He'll never give up trying to get me to sign those papers. Kimberly is probably nagging him to get the money so they can move to the beach. Well, wife number three isn't going to gain anything from me."

Tally nodded. "Don't let him get to you. He can't stand it because you've made something of your life without him."

Marla's heart rate, which had accelerated at the sound of Stan's condescending tone, calmed. "At least Dalton respects me for what

I do. I'm going to call him and see what he's learned," she decided, picking up the phone.

He didn't answer either at his home or at the station, so she left a voice message.

"I hope he isn't out with Hortense," she grumbled, sinking into a seat at the kitchen table.

"What makes you think Dalton's interest in her goes beyond being professional?"

Marla gave her a considering glance. "You know, I got taken in by her looks myself. I just assumed Dalton was attracted to Hortense, because he was paying her more attention than me. But you may be right. That detective can be very subtle when he wants to interrogate a suspect. When he thought I might be guilty of Mrs. Kravitz's murder, he pretended to be interested in me. I knew it was a ploy to get me to talk, so hopefully that's all he's doing with Hortense." *Except he did become involved with you, girl. He'd even said he didn't know if he should arrest you or date you. He couldn't possibly feel the same way for the blonde bombshell.*

Restless, she called Arnie next.

"Bagel Busters, Arnie speaking."

"Hi, it's Marla. Hortense showed up at the sports club this morning. Why didn't you tell her the truth about us when you took her home last night?"

"Because if I confess I lied, she'll run in the other direction. We'll follow through with our original plan to break off our engagement."

"But Arnie, word is spreading around town!"

"Don't worry, it'll work out."

His reassuring tone did nothing to ease her concerns. "Did Hortense say where she lived before moving back to Palm Haven?"

She heard voices in the background, and Arnie didn't answer right away, until he had dealt with the customers at the cash register.

"She'd been in Vero Beach. She liked the town, but there weren't enough opportunities for her acting career. Living in Fort Lauderdale, she can easily commute to Miami, and plenty of casting agents have offices in the area."

"If she's an actress, why does she have a job at Stockhart Industries?"

"Since when has acting been a full-time profession? She still has to earn the rent."

"Speaking of real estate, have you heard anything new about the Zelmans?"

His voice lowered. "No, but Vail was in here earlier asking me questions about Hortense."

Her ears perked up. "Why?"

She sensed Arnie's silent shrug. "Beats me. You know the detective, he doesn't give anything away. Could be he's interested in her from a purely male viewpoint, or could be he suspects there's a link to his case. I made it clear Hortense is my target, and you're his domain."

"Gee, thanks, pal. I knew I could count on you. So what's our next move?"

"You and I should definitely be seen together. It'll make Hortense jealous. I think she still likes me."

"She was impressed by your kindness last night, so I'd say you're right." Hortense had flirted with Keith earlier, Marla recalled. Was it true she played up to men to pry information from their loosened lips? If so, who was she really, and what did she want? "I'll talk to you later," she promised before disconnecting.

Tally patted Spooks, who'd been begging for attention. "Any news worth reporting?" her friend inquired.

"Arnie said Hortense used to live in Vero Beach. Tomorrow I'll stop by Eloise's office in the morning, then I'll take a ride north to see what I can learn. If I gain nothing else, there's a great outlet mall off I-95."

"I wish I could go with you, but I'll be at work."

"That's okay. It'll give me a chance to think things through regarding my relationship with Dalton. I'm not sure where I want to go with him."

"Are you ready to stake a claim?"

"Not yet, but if I don't, he might lose patience and find someone else."

"What about his daughter?"

"Brianna would be happy keeping things status quo. When we saw *Rent* together, she warned me that Vail quickly lost interest in his lady friends, but she was just trying to scare me off."

"She probably misses her mother, poor thing. I'd expect her to resent any woman who insinuates herself into Vail's life. She must be afraid of losing her father's attention or of being disloyal to her mom's memory."

"Yeah, but if I go a step farther with the lieutenant, it would mean accepting Brianna with her multitude of problems, whatever their cause." A stormy road would surely follow. "Come on, let's get some fresh air," she suggested, anxious to change the topic.

They took Spooks for a short walk. Old man Moss and his wife, Emma, were outside chatting with Goat.

"Hey, mate," Moss called, his weathered face crinkling into a smile. "How ya doing? Hi, Tally, good to see you."

"Tally, I don't think you've met Goat before. Goat, this is my friend, Tally Riggs." She felt silly calling him Goat, but she didn't know his real name—if he had one. He wore a sheepskin vest over a Hawaiian shirt, a raccoon cap, and shorts over his skinny knees.

Moss pulled a piece of paper from his pants pocket. "I wanted you to take a look at this new limerick," he told Marla.

"He's too shy to show it to his poetry group," his wife remarked. Emma wore a wide-brimmed straw hat over her gray head, a faded housecoat, and slip-on shoes so worn they could have been a dog's chew toy.

Her sickly complexion would benefit from the sun, Marla observed with a critical eye. Normally, she advised clients to avoid basking in sunlight to protect their skin and to keep their hair coloring from fading. The strong Florida sun could damage skin cells easily, but Emma might benefit from exposure to fresh air to restore her healthy glow.

Aware that Moss was anxiously waiting for her opinion, she took the paper from his outstretched hand. "Can I read it aloud?"

His face flushed, but he nodded his agreement, so Marla read in a clear tone:

A woman named McGuire
Once lit a fire
She meant to cook a steak
But her oven did break
So she ended up building a pyre.

Goat danced a little jig. "Light a fire under my pyre. We'll toast some marshmallows, roast a swallow, and rub on the Aloe. Give it to me, babe. Ugamaka, ugamaka, stew me a brew." The tail on his raccoon cap swung with each jerky movement.

"Is he always like that?" Tally murmured.

Marla grinned. "You got it. He keeps a whole zoo in his house, although I've never been brave enough to step inside."

He heard her last sentence. "You babes want to tour my humble abode? I promise I'll keep Junior in her cage."

"No thanks. We're working at the fair this afternoon, and we have to leave soon." She gave Moss back his poem. "Show this to your writing group," she urged him. "They'll be able to advise you where to send your collection."

"I'm not quite ready, but thanks for your comments, mate." Moss winked. "Y'all have a good time this afternoon."

Central Park was crowded with citizens when they arrived. Marla parked near the community center; then they walked past the lake to the field beyond, where artisans' booths mingled with exhibits by local businesses. The aisles were clogged with fair-goers. Feeling warmed by the sun, Marla adjusted her cardigan sweater. Her low-heeled pumps sank into the soft earth as she trotted toward her volunteer group.

After introducing Tally to her colleagues, she handed over her noodle kugel dish. "This is for the volunteer supper," she explained.

"Thanks," said the coordinator. "Marla, you can help Wally pass out leaflets. Tally, if you wouldn't mind, we need an extra person in the booth."

"How's it going?" Marla asked Councilman Wallace Ritiker after grabbing a stack of pamphlets from a nearby table.

He smiled, showing a row of even teeth. "We've had a good turnout, and a lot of folks have signed our petition supporting the pool safety bill. It's been approved by three committees in the legislature so far. Only one more to go." His face was ruddy from the heat, and he yanked a handkerchief from his pocket and wiped his wide brow.

"Yeah, but then it has to get through the senate. The measure failed twice already."

"It's been modified to offer more choices to homeowners."

"How many choices do you need to save lives?" Marla said vehemently. Her body shook with outrage. How many children had to drown before legislators put safety measures into effect?

"You can't force people to put up pool fences. An exit alarm or self-latching locks on doors with pool access can be just as effective."

"Those are better than nothing," she agreed. "People who move here from up north aren't aware of the dangers. They should give their kids swimming lessons as soon as they're out of diapers. Not everyone knows that the city offers free instruction."

"You're right. There's a lot for us to do."

Marla glanced inside the booth, where Tally was explaining a pictorial display to a family lost in clouds of cotton candy. Her friend had joined the cause with alacrity, she noted with a surge of affection.

Speaking of causes, if Cookie created more trouble for the salon, perhaps Wally could help her out. "Are you familiar with Cookie Calcone?" she asked him. "Half the town seems to know her."

An uneasy expression crossed his face. "I've run into her a couple of times, and I can't say they were pleasurable occasions. Are you her friend?"

"Hell, no. She was at the health club the day Jolene died. I understand you were in the steam room with Sam Zelman."

He stepped off the grass and into the relative shade of the booth's awning. "So I was. It's hard to believe he isn't around anymore. We played poker together, you know."

"What do you think happened to him? Have you heard anything about Eloise?"

"I don't know much more than was on the news."

"Hank was at the restaurant Saturday night. I noticed his name was on the sign-in list at the club when Jolene had her accident. Do you think he's involved?"

Wally snorted. "That fool is up to his ears in his own troubles. He won't listen to my advice."

"What do you mean?"

He glowered at her. "That break-in was a stupid move. It only brought Hank the kind of attention he didn't need. If Jolene were around, she would've blown the whistle on him."

Apparently, Ritiker believed she had insider knowledge about Hank's activities, whatever they were. "Are you saying he wanted Jolene out of the way?"

"Let's just say it was convenient for him when Jolene kicked the bucket."

"Detective Vail believes Jolene was murdered."

"I'm not surprised." Nor did the councilman appeared blown away by the news, except for the tensing of his jaw muscle.

"Did you notice anything on your way to the steam room? Was Jolene already in the whirlpool?"

"I didn't see her if she was there. The pool area appeared vacant. Sam and I went directly from the men's locker room into the steamer. The entrances are right next to each other, and we were talking."

"And you were both still inside when the police came?"

"That's right."

"Had you seen Hank earlier?"

"Maybe." His shoulders hunched. "You're asking a lot of questions, Marla. Seems to me it would be safer if you kept your mouth shut. Jolene is gone, and if anything is amiss, let the cops figure it out."

He strode back to their booth while Marla continued to hand out leaflets and mull their conversation in her head. Maybe Wally hadn't seen anything, but was it possible that Sam had? It would have given the killer a reason to get rid of him. One piece of important information eluded her: exactly how had Jolene ingested the sedative? Timing was the factor here, and Vail must know the answer.

While she was home getting ready for her date with Lance, the detective returned her phone call.

"Sorry I didn't get back to you earlier," he said in a gruff tone. "Brianna's friend from camp visited us for the weekend, and I took them to Beach Place today. Then there were a couple of things I had to check at the office."

"You don't have any time to rest, do you? Did you get in very late last night?"

He grunted affirmation. "You'll be happy to know Eloise was not in the car."

"Oh, thank God. Then where is she?"

"That's what I'm trying to find out. We've been in touch with her children, and they haven't heard from her. Sam's funeral arrangements were already made, so that's no problem. Both he and Eloise had pre-need plans. Her daughter needs to arrange for the memorial service, though, so she's hoping her mother will be in touch."

A frightening thought loomed like a specter. "What if the person who set the car bomb has Eloise?"

"I'd say that's a faint possibility. Eloise believed her husband was having an affair with Jolene. First Jolene meets an untimely death, then Sam. It's more likely Eloise is hiding because she's culpable."

Marla's blood pressure rocketed. "You can't believe my client is guilty! I know you mistrust everyone, but that's absurd. How could Eloise construct a bomb? She's a realtor, for God's sake." *So why are you having Lance research the Internet to see if a layperson could build an explosive device?*

"Maybe she hired someone else to do the deed. Until we find her, Mrs. Zelman remains a possible suspect."

Her temples throbbed. "What if Eloise is in trouble?" Marla persisted, knowing from past experience that she shouldn't be so trusting herself but unable to visualize Eloise as the killer.

"Then she'll show up, one way or another."

Marla shuddered, not wishing to imagine what the word *another* represented. "I've been meaning to ask you, what was the sedative that Jolene took, and in what form?"

A pause followed. "It was a variation of Flunitrazepam. You may recognize the street name: roofies. It's a sedative that's ten times more potent than Valium."

"Isn't that the date-rape drug?"

"Right. The drug's effects begin within thirty minutes and are strengthened when taken with alcohol. It has no taste or odor and can render a person unconscious with no memories of what happened. The substance is very dangerous for two reasons: the cost is low, less than five dollars per tablet; and high schoolers take it for recreation without realizing it can cause dependence with withdrawal symptoms, not to mention impaired judgment."

"I thought roofies were illegal here." She had read articles in the newspaper about girls who'd been raped after being unknowingly drugged. It was a horrible commentary on society, that women had to be careful at social events to get their own refreshments. Thank God she didn't have any daughters to worry about. Another reason not to have children, Marla thought. She could imagine the lectures Brianna was in for when she matured, and she pitied the girl.

"Abuse is more widespread in Florida and Texas, because the stuff is smuggled in from Mexico or through Miami from Colombia. It's distributed legally as a sleeping pill in other countries," Vail explained.

"So did someone dissolve a tablet in Jolene's drink?" she asked, thinking about Amy at the snack stand.

"No," Vail said in a grim tone. "It was in those gelatin capsules she took in the locker room while you spoke to Cookie Calcone."

Chapter Thirteen

"Funny thing is, none of the other capsules in the bottle contained the drug," Vail continued.

"Meaning?"

"The killer may have switched bottles after Jolene took a dose."

"How? No one else was around. I went upstairs and met Keith. Cookie had left the club, or so she claimed. It was unusually quiet because of that competition at the other gym."

"Eloise was in the sauna. And don't forget the female staff members, who also had access to the locker room."

"What was the purpose? To make Jolene sleepy?"

"Sure. Didn't you tell me Jolene always took gelatin before going into the whirlpool?"

"Well, yes. In fact, she'd had a manicure that morning. She wanted to protect her nails."

"The killer must be somebody who was familiar with her habits, and who had access to her bag."

"When would the tainted capsules have been put there?"

"My guess would be while she was in Dancercize. I toyed with the notion that the capsules might have been substituted earlier—when Jolene was at work, for example. But then the killer would have had no control over when she took the drug, nor could the bottle be switched afterward. Probably the perp didn't realize the drug would be traceable."

Marla nodded. "Next time I see Cookie, I'll ask her if anyone left in the middle of dance class. How about when Jolene went for a snack? That would've given the killer another opportunity to plant the drug."

Vail cleared his throat. "It would depend upon how closely she followed Jolene's movements."

"She?"

"It seems more logical, considering the circumstances."

"Unless the killer is a *he* with a female collaborator. Personally, my bet rides on one of the staff workers at the sports club. I wouldn't overlook all the possibilities if I were you." She thought about Eloise and Sam. "Do you have an alert out for Eloise?"

"Not officially, but I want her for questioning."

"I hope she turns up soon."

"What are you doing for dinner tonight?" he asked, as though deliberately changing the subject. "Brianna and I are going out for pizza. You could join us."

"Thanks, but my mother invited me for a meal." That was true; Marla didn't tell Vail she'd declined Anita's invitation because of her date with Lance. Even though the computer guru was an old friend, Dalton would probably get upset if he knew her plans.

Lance Pearson lived on the east side of Fort Lauderdale in an older section with willowy bottlebrush trees and melaleucas shading the streets. His three-bedroom home was sand-colored with white shutters, a popular combination in Broward County's sunny climate. The bright pastels that were popular in the Caribbean were scorned here. Beige tones ruled, with occasional deviations by brave souls who wanted more color in their lives.

Marla parked in the circular driveway overrun with dead leaves from a black olive tree, scourge of the region. For motives unknown to her, people planted them for their height and shady canopy, but the leaves that shed periodically could stain the paint on the sturdiest car. Split nuts from a mahogany crunched underfoot as she strode to the front door. It was only 6:30 but already dark. Insects buzzed by the hanging lantern that illuminated the entrance. A sweet scent of orange blossoms permeated the air. Were they starting to bloom so early? February was nearly here, she reminded herself. Soon it would be her birthday. She didn't want to think that far in advance.

Her hands patted the pair of black slacks and rose hooded sweater she'd picked up at Macy's latest Karen Kane sale. Tonight was casual; she expected a pleasant evening with a good friend. A smile curved her lips as she remembered how they'd met. Lance had sold her the first computer she'd ever owned. Those were the days when he worked in an electronics store before branching out on his own as a systems analyst. Freelancing as a consultant suited his lifestyle and improved his budget. Calling upon him for computer advice had become a habit. Somewhere along the way, he'd stopped charging her and asked her out instead. Marla liked him but not in a romantic way. Keeping him at arm's length would be the challenge of the night.

He opened the door right after she pressed the doorbell, as though he'd been loitering in the foyer. His acorn eyes, round as an owl's, peered at her with delight. He'd spiffed up for the occasion, wearing a checkered collar shirt and tan Dockers. His mud brown hair, frizzy as always, inspired her to offer an anti-humectant product, but she bit her tongue and smiled.

"Come in, love," he said in a deep voice that could have belonged to a radio announcer. "The computer's turned on. If you're not starving, we can take care of business first."

Any other guy might have complimented her on her appearance, Marla thought in bemusement as she followed him into his home office. Maybe he was just too eager to show her his favorite web sites.

She sat in the chair he'd motioned to beside the desk. Lance scrunched into a seat beside her and moved the mouse to get rid of the screen saver. Interested by what popped up on the screen, she leaned forward. It was some kind of anarchy site listing weapons you could construct at home.

"Bless my bones, is this for real?" she gasped. Militant anarchism seemed to be the aim, with choices for drugs and bombs, news reports on racism issues, and claims of American war crimes in developing countries. Lance clicked on the "drugs and bombs" button. Her blood chilled as she viewed selections for malicious chemistry, a terrorists' handbook, a classic must-have for America's youth known as the school stoppers' textbook, and dangerous drugs. Explosive devices included not only pipe bombs, but also chemical fire bottles, dry-ice bombs, antifreeze-gelatin explosive, and aspirin plastique, among others.

"Look," Lance said, clicking on pipe bombs. "These seem too complicated for your average Joe to construct. So I found this other site called 'Ways to Send a Car to Hell.' " The screen changed, and up came a site describing a substance you could buy in specialty hardware stores, an extremely explosive chemical called Solidox.

Marla read the instructions, confused by the chemistry. "I don't get it. The active ingredient is potassium chlorate, but you still need an energy source to cause an explosion."

Lance's eyes lit with excitement. "Household sugar serves that purpose. All you do is grind up the Solidox sticks, mix in some sugar, and you've got a bomb. It's probably not that easy, and I wouldn't know how to detonate the thing, but techno-wizards could figure it out."

Marla frowned. "Who has that kind of knowledge? Jolene was the only one who worked in a chemical plant."

"There are simpler methods. You can also stuff gasoline-soaked rags up the exhaust pipe. I'm not sure what effect those would produce, but you don't need any technical expertise." His questioning gaze caught hers. "Why don't you tell me what you're working on over dinner?"

Shoving his chair back, he stood. "I mixed a carafe of sangria. Come into the kitchen. The chicken's marinating in the refrigerator. I'll get the grill ready, and we can munch on appetizers." He lowered his voice. "I'm really happy you're here tonight, love. We don't get the chance to be alone that often."

She swallowed at the predatory gleam in his eyes, and a forced smile cracked her face. "I appreciate your efforts to get me the right information all the time."

In the kitchen, he took out the pitcher of sangria and poured them each a glass. Facing her, he raised his hand for a toast. Just under five feet seven, he was less than an inch taller than she. Close up, his nose looked broader, and his lips fuller than she preferred on a man.

"To our friendship," he announced, sipping his drink.

Marla followed suit, enjoying the fruity flavor despite the strong liquor he'd added. When his amber gaze dropped to her mouth, she swallowed apprehensively.

"I can get the grill ready or give you a tour of my house. I don't believe you've seen the renovations to my bedroom."

Her hand waved in dismissal. "That's okay, maybe later. I'm getting hungry. Did you say there were appetizers?"

Putting his glass on the counter, he stepped closer and placed his hands on her shoulders. She got a whiff of Old Spice cologne and tried to ignore the view of golden chest hairs below his open collar.

"I know what you really came for, so you can quit the shy act. I'm hungry too, but not for the food." His eyes glittered meaningfully.

Marla endured his kiss, wanting to be kind to him. Poor guy was married to his computer instead of a real woman.

"That was for old times' sake," she said after disentangling herself. "You know I value our friendship, but we need to keep things at this level because I have news. You know Arnie Hartman, owner of Bagel Busters? Well, we're engaged."

Dismay and surprise warred in his expression. "Is that right? I guess I should be happy for you, then."

She touched his arm gently. "I hope you understand. You'll always be special to me, but not in that way."

His foot kicked an imaginary spot on the tile floor. "Sure. So I guess this is a celebration dinner."

"Yes, it is. Next time, you can come to my place and chat with Arnie. Maybe you'll even bring a date." *Or I'll fix you up with one*, she thought, considering Hortense as a candidate. Not a bad idea. It would get her out of Vail's range.

Lance's mood shifted, and he grinned at her. "What are we waiting for? Let's chow down. Tell me what's been going on while I start the grill."

Arnie's mustache quivered with delight when he spotted Marla entering his deli on Monday morning. The place was crowded, but he left his post by the cash register to greet her with a warm embrace.

"Marla, darling," he said in a loud enough voice for most of the patrons to hear. "How nice of you to drop by on your day off. Guess you couldn't keep away from your fiancé!"

"This has got to stop, pal," Marla replied in a hushed voice. "Any word from Hortense?"

His face sagged. "Not since Friday night. She's supposed to start her new job today, so maybe she was getting ready. Have you talked to Vail?"

She strolled with him back to the checkout point. "He called me yesterday. He's still trying to locate Eloise. I thought I'd stop by her office to see if her staff knows anything. Oh yes, and I believe she has a hair appointment for this week. I wish she'd show up!" Worry gnawed at her. What if the killer's target had been Sam, and Eloise had walked toward the car at the moment when the bomber was planting the device? Eloise might have been taken captive. Or maybe she'd been frightened into hiding, especially if it was a person she'd known. Marla didn't subscribe to the theory that Eloise had schemed to do in her husband. No, it had to be someone else.

"Josh and Lisa have been about asking about you," Arnie said after a customer paid his bill.

"They're good kids. Have they heard the rumors?"

His dark eyes gleamed. "About us? Not yet, although they'd be happy if it were true."

She bopped his shoulder. "I thought you liked Hortense."

"I do, but only because you turned me down. Are you changing your mind?" Dimples creased his cheeks as he gave her a teasing smile.

"I love you, Arnie, but as a dear friend."

"Aw, shucks. I thought of getting hair plugs just for you."

Glancing at his receding hairline, she grinned. "Bald is sexy, don't you know?"

He rang up another bill. "I wonder how Hortense feels about me. She looks so young."

"Yeah, thanks to various cosmetic alterations. Look, Arnie, be careful where she's concerned. Did Hortense tell you where she used to work in Vero Beach?"

"Nope. She mentioned a breakfast bar, though, when we were talking about how I got started in the restaurant business."

While he was distracted by still another patron, Marla debated how to coax more information from him. For some reason, Hortense's motives didn't ring true, and Marla didn't want Arnie to get hurt if his relationship with her developed any further. *Thanks, Dalton. Your suspicious nature rubbed off on me.* Come on, she thought, that wasn't fair. After her recent fling with David had ended in disaster, she'd learned to be cautious. It wouldn't be right to let Arnie fall into the same pit.

Are you sure you're not jealous, bubula? she asked herself. *Before Hortense arrived, Arnie was interested in you. Suddenly another woman comes along, and you immediately think she's here under false pretenses.*

Arnie's attention turned back to her. "I like Vero Beach," she said quickly before he changed topics. "It's good for a quick weekend getaway, and there's a great outlet mall off I-95. What's the name of Hortense's breakfast place? I'll have to stop in next time I visit the area."

"Seagulls & Saucers. It's on the beach strip. So what are you doing the rest of today?"

She played with a pen on the counter. "I've got a lot of errands to run."

Ruth, one of the waitresses, stopped on her way to the kitchen with an order. "Congratulations, honey. We're pleased as pie for y'all."

"Oh. Thanks." Marla stuck out her tongue at Ruth's retreating back. "Look what a monster you've created, pal. We'll never live this one down!"

"It's Vail's loss. He should have nailed you first."

"He's more ready than I am." Her mouth watered as the aroma of garlic bagels and coffee wafted to her nostrils.

"Baloney. You're just afraid of getting involved again. You tested the waters with David and came up dry. Mr. Perfect turned out to be a dud."

"Tell me about it. The same thing happened with Stan, my delightful ex-spouse. So why should I risk a third round?"

"Life is a risk, *shayna madel*. You might dive in this time and find you can swim like a dolphin. Vail cares about you. You can tell by the way his attention always wanders in your direction. If he seems overbearing, it's because he wants to protect you. It must frustrate him when you won't listen."

She pursed her lips. "I can take care of myself, thank you. Witness the two killers that I subdued."

"Ha! You were lucky those times. As your friend, I'll defend your right to forge your own path in life, but not when you endanger yourself."

Men! They're all alike. Gritting her teeth, she changed the subject. "Did Hortense give you her phone number?"

"Of course. I'll call her later to see how her first day on the job went. Maybe she's heard gossip about Jolene."

"Let me know," Marla said. "I'll talk to you later."

Jolene was the topic of conversation when Marla entered the Zelmans' realty office. She'd half-hoped Eloise would be sitting at her desk and was disappointed when her familiar figure wasn't evident. Approaching the woman at the front, she waited until the agent finished her telephone conversation.

"No, Miss Myers's house isn't for sale yet. Her relatives contacted me, but it will be a while before things get settled. Wasn't Sam handling your account? I thought you just signed a lease for an apartment."

Marla's gaze wandered the area while the agent listened through a set of earphones. Three desks stood on each side of the room like double columns. In the rear, a man sat behind a desk talking to an elderly couple. The other spots were vacant, making Marla wonder how successful the venture was, or if those agents just worked alternate hours. She didn't suppose that Monday mornings were a great time for showing properties. Posters with listings lined the walls. It was a utilitarian setting, functional more than aesthetic.

"Certainly, Miss Crone, I'll tag your account and let you know as soon as the place is available. Bye, now."

She hung up while Marla stared at her in bewilderment. Was that Hortense Crone who'd just called? If so, Hortense must be acquainted with Sam if she'd rented an apartment through him. Funny how she'd never mentioned that during their conversation with Eloise. Hortense knew a lot more than she let everyone believe. Why else would she be interested in Jolene's residence?

"Hello, I'm looking for Eloise," she told the agent.

"Mrs. Zelman isn't here today. Can I help you? My name is Judy Sherman."

Nice shag cut, pal, but you could use less makeup. The woman, in her sixties, was a medium ash blonde with a pasty complexion made worse by a heavy application of foundation. Her ebony eyeliner skewed outward at the corners of her eyes. Besides lipstick that was too red for current styles, she wore a turquoise suit with silver studs that completed her garish appearance.

Marla managed a distressed smile. "I really need to consult Eloise. You see, I gave her my key because I wanted her to evaluate my property over the weekend. She said to stop in this morning and she'd return it."

Judy pulled a pad of paper in front of her with an impatient gesture. "I'll notify her to contact you as soon as she comes in. It may be a while. Her husband was in an accident, and I fear . . . she's very upset."

Marla grew hopeful. "Has she called you since then?"

"None of us have heard from her."

"Isn't that unusual? I don't mean to pry, but I'm her hairstylist. She has an appointment with me later this week."

"Oh." Judy gave her an appraising stare. "You don't look like a hairdresser."

Get your eyes fixed, pal. If you could see straight, your eyeliner wouldn't be so crooked. Withdrawing a business card from her purse, Marla handed it over. "I couldn't help overhearing your telephone conversation when I walked in. Such a pity about the Myers woman. I belong to that athletic club where she drowned. It's scary since Jolene and Sam died, and now Eloise is missing." Marla was well aware that she could have become another victim that night in the parking lot.

"Sam handled Jolene's property transaction several years ago," Judy confided.

"Eloise wasn't too fond of her. Jolene and Sam had been meeting behind her back. Do you know why?"

Judy gave her a shrewd glance. "I have my theories, but I'm not going to tell you. The Zelmans aren't here now, so that leaves me in charge. Unlike Sam, I play things straight."

"What happens to the business if they're both dead?"

Judy appeared startled. "Why do you ask that? Eloise will show up."

"I hope you're right."

"In any event, I suppose it passes to their children. I'm sure they'll keep me on as manager."

"Well, I might be interested in making a move if Jolene's house goes up for sale," Marla lied, shifting in her chair. "Was that Hortense Crone making an inquiry about it earlier?"

The real estate agent's brow crinkled. "Yes, but I don't understand. She's just rented an apartment and has a six-month lease. Although if I recall, Miss Crone wanted to find an apartment on a month-to-month basis."

"I've met Hortense at the club. Does that mean she isn't planning to stay in town?"

"She may be more interested in purchasing a permanent residence. Now if you'll excuse me, I have to get back to work." Shuffling through a stack of papers, she generated an air of dismissal.

Rising, Marla grabbed her handbag and flung the strap over her shoulder.

"A word of advice," Judy said as Marla strode toward the exit. Marla wheeled around, her thoughts jumbled.

"If the police look more closely into Sam's background, they'll find plenty of folks who had cause to harm him. Maybe that's why Eloise is staying away. She's afraid she'll share the blame, but he was the bad egg, not her. I just wanted you to know."

Chapter Fourteen

Heading north on the Florida turnpike, Marla grimaced when the foul smell of decaying garbage invaded the Camry. She zoomed past a hill with grass growing on its sides and pipes sticking out like spiked hairs—a mountain by South Florida standards, even though it was composed entirely of refuse. The rest of the landscape was as flat as its swampy origins, but this way, one could avoid the heavy truck traffic on I-95.

Once a flat expanse of road stretched ahead, she let her thoughts drift. According to Judy, Sam's demise might have been related to his nefarious past, and Eloise could be running scared as a result. Judy believed Mrs. Zelman would turn up eventually. If she were right, did Sam's prior dealings have anything to do with Jolene? It was too powerful a coincidence for two Perfect Fit Sports Club members to die within a couple weeks of each other. Sam's murder must be connected to Jolene's. In that case, they were not crimes of passion committed by Eloise, as Vail believed. Instead, there was some connection to Sam's business practices.

Feeling she was viewing different parts of a puzzle, Marla couldn't conceive how they fit together. Sam and Jolene were meeting secretly at the Holiday Inn. Cookie knew about them, and so did Sam's wife. But was it an illicit affair that brought them together, or was it a matter of professional interest—legal or otherwise? Could

Jolene have been blackmailing Sam about his past? Had he bumped her off to shut her up when she threatened to talk? Or had Eloise done it to protect her husband? Then who had killed Sam, and why?

Jolene knew secrets about staff members at the club as well. Jolene had asked Slate if Keith was involved in the same thing as Gloria. Marla resolved to sneak into Gloria's office to find out what the girl was mixed up in. She couldn't forget Amy's jealousy, and Slate's resentment that Jolene had turned him down. And hadn't Wallace Ritiker remarked at how Hank seemed glad Jolene was out of the way? But what would those people have against poor Sam?

By the time she drove off the turnpike exit at Fort Pierce to switch to I-95, her temples throbbed. More pondering wouldn't provide the answers. Hopefully, this visit would be fruitful and steer her in the right direction.

Ignoring the temptation to spend the afternoon shopping at Vero Beach Prime Outlets, Marla headed east toward the ocean. Indian River Mall provided another distraction, but she resisted her urge to stop and stretch her legs. She'd spent a weekend here once at Disney's Vero Beach Resort, touring Harbor Branch Oceanographic Institution, the historic downtown, and Heathcote Botanical Gardens. If time permitted, she'd like to stop at Hale Groves on the way home to buy some tropical fruit preserves for her mother.

Route 60 heading east dead-ended at Ocean Drive. Halting at a red light, Marla admired the beach straight ahead, between the Holiday Inn Beachside on the left and the Ocean Grill on the right. That restaurant alone was worth a drive up here, she remembered fondly from her previous visit.

As soon as the light changed, she turned right and cruised along Ocean Drive until she spotted Seagulls & Saucers, located between a resort clothier and an art gallery. She pulled into a free parking space a few doors down.

Half afraid the restaurant would be closed after lunch, Marla was relieved to push the door open and enter a brightly lit interior. Gleaming metal stools faced a high counter that zigzagged to the rear in a wave design. Booths lined the opposite wall. The two women who were the sole patrons looked like bored socialites,

Marla decided after glancing at their jewelry-bedecked necks and tanned faces.

She slid onto a counter stool and beckoned to a waitress whose name tag identified her as Sherry. Hunger took precedence over work, and Marla ordered a quarter-pound burger with french fries and a Coke. Forget the diet food, she told herself as she sniffed the aroma of freshly baked bread.

"This is a neat place," she said when the waitress delivered her meal.

"Yeah, it's popular with the tourists." Sherry stuck a wad of chewing gum in her mouth. "Nine o'clock in the morning, this place is full. You should see the line out front."

"I'm visiting the area," Marla went on in casual tone, "but my friend, Hortense Crone, recently moved to my neighborhood in Fort Lauderdale. She told me how much she missed this restaurant, so I thought I'd stop by while I'm in town."

The girl's face crinkled into a frown. "Huh? Hortense came in here as usual this morning. She ain't moved nowhere. Who are you talking about?"

Marla stared at her. "A tall blonde, sexy figure, wears tight tops and short skirts."

"She moved south about two weeks ago?" At Marla's nod, a knowing look sprang into Sherry's hazel eyes. "Oh, that was Jill. She got a boob job. Big hair and big tits. She thinks they'll get her more acting stints."

Hortense said we should call her Jill. "I don't understand. The girl I met said *she* was Hortense."

Sherry scraped a lock of listless bluish-black hair off her wide forehead. "Beats me, lady. Maybe you should talk to Hortense while you're here. She had a heavy conversation with Jill last time they both came by."

"Really? This keeps getting more curious. Where can I find your Hortense?"

"Dr. Crone works down at the Marine Annex. She's one of them ocean scientists. If you go into the gift shop, one of the volunteers can put you in touch with her."

* * *

Fortunately, Marla didn't need an appointment, and her befuddled brain didn't have to wait long for clarification. As soon as a volunteer connected her via telephone to Dr. Crone's office, and she mentioned the names Arnie and Jill in the same breath, a garbled background conversation followed.

"You can come right now, and Dr. Crone will see you," said a woman's controlled voice at the other end. She rattled off directions and then hung up abruptly.

Feeling as though she were rousing a hornet's nest, Marla followed the road signs until she reached the area indicated. It was near a huge vat that held swimming sea creatures of indeterminate origins. A strong fishy odor permeated the place, which was outdoors but protected from the sun by a canvas awning.

A white-coated brunette carrying a clipboard strode in her direction when she emerged from her car. Steel-rimmed glasses shielded a pair of intelligent cocoa brown eyes. Emitting an aura of competence, she wore her hair in a business-like bob.

"You're Marla Shore?" the woman asked in a firm voice.

"Yes, I am," Marla said, smiling hesitantly.

"Nice to meet you. My name is Dr. Hortense Crone."

Feeling the heat on her back, Marla stepped inside the shaded portion. "I thought I met Hortense in Palm Haven, but she doesn't look anything like you."

Dr. Crone's shoulders slumped. "No, that's Jill. I suppose I should explain."

"Please do." *This better be good, or I've come a long way for nothing.*

"Let's sit down." The woman indicated a concrete bench.

Marla sank onto the hard surface. Dr. Crone sat beside her and regarded her with a frank stare.

"You're Arnie's fiancée, aren't you? I heard all about your exploits."

Marla's eyebrow shot up. "Oh?"

"Jill calls me every day. You see, I thought of approaching Arnie because I had a special fondness for him since high school. I couldn't go to Fort Lauderdale myself, and Jill seemed the perfect type to catch his eye. I hadn't realized he was engaged. Silly me, I heard he'd been widowed, but it never occurred to me that Arnie might have found someone else."

Marla squirmed uncomfortably. Their engagement was a deception, but apparently, so was Dr. Crone's sending Jill to pose as herself. She kept silent, putting aside until later the decision whether or not to reveal her own truth.

"Who is Jill?" she demanded, seeking the scientist's confession first.

"She's an actress I met at Seagulls and Saucers. Jill wasn't happy working as a publicity manager for a local company. In her spare time, she traveled to Orlando for acting jobs. Miami is a bigger market, and she was thinking of moving there. I knew right away she'd be perfect for the role I had in mind."

Marla had an inkling where Hortense was going next. "What role was that?" she asked, unable to keep the sarcasm from her voice.

"Arnie always admired tall, slender women. We hadn't seen each other in so many years—not that he'd ever noticed me before. But let me start from the beginning." Her soft brown eyes captured Marla's. "I'm Jolene Myers's cousin. We weren't terribly close, but we did see each other at family holidays. A couple of months ago, Jolene mailed me a manila envelope with a note that said not to open it unless something happened to her."

Swatting away a buzzing insect, Marla leaned forward. "Did you speak to her and ask why she sent it to you?"

"Yes, but she wouldn't explain. She said something very strange, though." Her voice lowered. *"I'm doing something I'll probably regret later. In case anything happens, you can set things right.* Guess how I felt when I heard about her death?"

"She must've known something was wrong."

"Damn right. Jolene wouldn't drown in a whirlpool. She was too disciplined, always in control."

Marla studied an ant crawling along the ground. A fallen leaf obstructed its path. At first, it tried to climb up and over, but the height was too great. Instinct moved the creature along the obstacle's edge.

Jolene hadn't seemed terribly in control that day in the locker room. She'd admitted to being stressed, and Cookie had made things worse. She appeared rattled when she downed the two capsules. Did she regard Cookie merely as a mild interference? Or did the issues between them go deeper, making it more difficult for Jolene to find the right path? Instinct hadn't helped her; she'd chosen the way to death.

"Detective Vail mentioned that Jolene had taken sedatives," said Dr. Crone. "I told him my cousin subscribed mostly to homeopathic remedies. Gelatin is a natural substance, you know, derived from animals."

Ah, so Vail knew Jill's true identity. She felt a momentary irritation that he hadn't shared that knowledge with her. "Did you give Vail the envelope Jolene had sent you?"

Hortense stood. "I didn't mention it to him. After opening the package, I understood why she'd mailed it to me. We're both in the science field, you see. Come to my office; I have the papers there. I know you've been trying to help."

She pointed to a squat building in the distance. "We can take my buggie," Dr. Crone said, indicating a golf cart, "or you can drive us. You're not really supposed to park here."

"Let's take my car." Marla was glad to get away from the fishy smell. She'd been afraid it might linger in her car, but the air-conditioning soon dispelled any briny odors.

"I hope Jill hasn't interfered in your relationship with Arnie," Hortense said after they emerged from Marla's car a few minutes later. "She was only supposed to use him as a jumping-off point to meet other contacts who knew Jolene. From our conversations, I surmised that Jill likes him."

"You could fool me. She was doing a good job on Detective Vail when we all went to dinner together."

"You're right; she was doing her job—for me. It was a lucky break that brought you all together. Meeting the homicide detective in charge of Jolene's case gave Jill an excuse to question *him*. She learned quite a bit at dinner that night, listening to y'all and meeting Mrs. Zelman."

Marla suppressed a retort as they approached the building. Dr.

Crone pushed open a double set of white doors leading into a concrete structure that looked more like a bunker than an administrative wing. Nodding at a receptionist who waved in return, she walked ahead to a corridor lined with cubicles occupied by clerks and research assistants. Apparently, the large private offices with picture windows overlooking the grounds had been appropriated by the upper echelon. Marla was impressed by the size of Dr. Crone's allotment, but she smirked at the mess inside. Boxes and papers were strewn across the floor and piled a foot high on the counters.

"My laboratory is a lot better organized than this," Hortense said, gesturing toward her desk. Marla hesitated just inside the door while Dr. Crone strode straight ahead to a tall four-drawer file cabinet.

"I'm still unclear on why you hired that actress," Marla said. "What's her real name anyway?"

The scientist whirled around. "Jillian Barlow, or at least that's her stage name. Promise me you won't expose her identity until she finishes what I sent her there to do." Anxiety radiated from her intense gaze.

Marla planted her hands on her hips. "Give me a good reason why I shouldn't tell the whole town who she really is."

The real Hortense pursed her lips. "As I said, I sent Jill to investigate Jolene's death by playing my part. As a former classmate of Arnie's, I figured this would be a good means of inserting Jill into the company of those who'd known my cousin. Arnie would introduce her around, and she'd question anyone who'd been close to Jolene. As it turned out, many of those people disliked my cousin. I can't say that I blame them. What she did in her lab goes beyond the pale."

Turning back to the file cabinet, Dr. Crone retrieved a sheaf of papers from one of the drawers. She handed them to Marla, who examined the various graphs and numbers with puzzlement. They might as well have been Egyptian hieroglyphics from her viewpoint.

"Would you care to interpret?" Marla asked dryly.

A fatigued expression transformed the scientist's face. "They're product test results . . . from another company."

"Not Stockhart Industries where Jolene worked?" She felt as though her mind were slogging through mud.

Hortense nodded, gesturing for Marla to have a seat. Before continuing, she sank into a plush armchair behind the desk. "These results supposedly came from Jolene's laboratory, but as you can see, that's not the true source."

"I still don't get it."

"Jolene was buying data from somewhere else and passing it off as her own. See these other sheets?" Dr. Crone waved a cluster of papers in the air. "These are the real stats, and they show a much more dangerous toxicity level."

Realization dawned. "Your cousin was falsifying statistics, using results gained from another company." Cookie had been right, then. Possibilities tumbled through her head as she reviewed the animal activist's accusations. "Do you know where this other data originated?"

"Unfortunately, no. Is there another chemical company in the vicinity?"

"There's a place called Listwood Pharmaceuticals." Marla moistened her lips. "Now I have a confession to make. Arnie and I are not engaged. He, uh, prevaricated to avoid an entanglement with Jill when he thought she was you. I mean, when she first called him to say she was moving back to town, he panicked." A blush stole over her features. This wasn't coming out right.

Dr. Crone laughed, a pleasant, infectious sound that made Marla smile despite her embarrassment. "I gather Arnie wasn't too pleased. It's no wonder. Other kids used to call me Horrible Hortense in high school. Short and fat was not a great combination in those years. Add to that clunky eyeglasses, dowdy clothes, and a shy personality, and you've got a teenage tribble: something to avoid before it multiplies."

Marla's eyes sparked with admiration. "You've certainly changed," she commented, realizing the scientist's charisma reached beyond her improved appearance.

Hortense's eyebrow lifted. "Self-confidence made all the difference. I love my work, and once I realized public speaking would be required, my views shifted. I've always been very goal oriented.

During high school, aiming for the career I wanted was my main focus. Guess I was a late developer sexually, too. College was where I started to care about how I looked."

"Well, as a hairstylist, I can say that your cut is great for the shape of your face. It's very flattering."

"Thanks, Marla. Coming from you, that's a real compliment. Now tell me, are you going to keep my secret?"

"You mean Jillian's secret? I don't know. Arnie likes her, but I don't know how he'll feel when he learns the truth. I just don't want him to get hurt."

"He's a dear man." Hortense's eyes glowed with affection, but then she frowned. "Jill thinks you're engaged to him. Even if she likes him, she wouldn't encroach on your territory. It might seem that way because she's trying to get information, but Jill is a decent character. I made sure about that before I hired her. So what is your relationship to Arnie?"

"We're good friends. I love the guy, but I'm more interested in Dalton Vail."

"I see."

Marla struggled with her conscience. She should tell Arnie so he wouldn't fall for Jill's allure. But then again, if Jill sincerely cared for Arnie, how would she feel about their deception? The situation appeared to be a catch-22. And what about Vail? Jill was perfectly placed at a position inside Stockhart Industries. If either of them blew her cover, would the girl be dismissed?

"How did Jill get a job at Stockhart Industries if she was pretending to be you?" Marla asked, trying to understand the different angles.

"She obtained the position under her own credentials," Dr. Crone replied, picking up a Mont Blanc pen. "Jillian Barlow graduated college as a communications major. She worked for a few years in Orlando while doing acting jobs on the side; then she accepted an offer for a better position here in Vero Beach. The girl might look like a bimbo, but she has brains."

"I suppose she does, especially when she's playing the role of undercover detective. You must be paying her well."

Hortense didn't answer right away, doodling instead on a scratch pad. "She'd intended to move to south Florida anyway. I found out about the opening at Stockhart Industries and figured she'd be perfect for a job in public relations. My influence helped to land her the position. She's happy enough about that much, but I also offered to supplement her moving expenses and apartment costs until she could manage on her own."

"That's very generous of you."

Her gaze hardened. "Make no mistake about it, I intend to find out what happened to my cousin. She meant for me to air the truth about those lab tests, but I don't want to tip my hand until Jill discovers who killed her. Now that you're in on the game, will you help us?"

Biting her lower lip, Marla considered her response. If she continued to play along, she'd be deceiving everyone except Vail, and they'd have a better chance of unmasking a murderer. Perhaps that was why Vail had kept his lips sealed up to this point.

"All right, I'll join your scheme for now. But I'm going to warn Jill not to play false with Arnie. I won't let him get hurt." She looked at Hortense speculatively. "When this is over, I hope you'll meet him. I don't think he'd be so disappointed in you now."

Dr. Crone's face eased into a grin. "I may have had a crush on Arnie during high school, but that was a long time ago. If Jill wants him and you have no claim, she can have him."

Holding up her left hand, she let a low chuckle escape her throat. "I don't wear rings because of my laboratory work; otherwise you'd see my gold band. I've no interest in Arnie because I'm married."

Chapter
Fifteen

Marla drove straight home so she could let Spooks out and grab a bite to eat before deciding her next move. The message light blinked on her answering machine, so after a quick trip to the bathroom, she spent a few minutes in her home office. Anita had called, and so had Tally and Dalton Vail. Maybe she wouldn't have to take Brianna to dance class tomorrow night.

Aware that it was past six and that he might be in the middle of dinner, Marla dialed Vail's home number first.

"Hello," Brianna responded.

"Hi, this is Marla. Is your father there?"

"Nope, he's still at work." Chewing sounds emanated from the phone receiver.

"Oh. I guess I'll give him a call at the office, then."

"Is it about the case he's working on? Because if not, you shouldn't bother Dad at his job."

Marla wondered if those were his actual instructions to his daughter. "I don't think he'll mind. Am I taking you to dance class tomorrow night, or will your father be free?"

"I dunno. Guess you'll have to drive me again, unless you're busy."

"I'm never too busy for you, honey." *Lord save me, where did those words come from?* "I'll pick you up the same time as last week, okay?"

"Sure."

"Are you home alone? Because if you want company, I can—"

"No. I don't need anyone else."

Stung by the abrupt refusal, Marla stuttered. "W-well, I won't disturb you further."

A pause. "Lucky is here. He's my friend."

"Of course. I'll see you Tuesday evening, then. Bye." Gritting her teeth, Marla hung up. That girl persisted in getting on her nerves, but Marla felt sorry for her. She had no mother to guide her, nor any close relatives in the area, a father who was away from home more than half the time, and only a golden retriever for company. Approaching the harrowing years of puberty, how would the child cope?

It's not your business, girl. No, it wasn't, but she couldn't help her feelings of empathy. After Tammy's drowning, she'd been vulnerable herself and had only survived thanks to a strong support system. It would grieve her to see Brianna going down the wrong path because no one was available to advise her. Dalton knew he needed help as a parent. That scared her as much as it drew her closer to him. Mothering was a role she'd avoided intentionally, because she couldn't stand the pain if something bad happened to someone she loved. If getting more involved with Dalton meant accepting his daughter as part of the package, was she really interested? And did he want her for herself, or because he needed a mother for his child?

God, it was so complicated. All she knew was that her blood surged whenever he looked at her. His smoky gaze melted her resistance so that none of this mattered in his presence. Maybe she should just go with the flow and see where it led. She was only taking the girl to dance class, for heaven's sake. That didn't warrant a commitment on her part, although Dalton preferred she didn't go out with anyone else. He'd made his feelings clear on that score. She was afraid the detective would lose patience and find someone

else who'd give him her full attention. Someone like Hortense, perhaps.

Shlemiehl, you mean Jillian Barlow.

Deciding to call him later, she stalked into the kitchen to pre-
pare dinner. She was savoring a meal of eggplant parmesan and
garlic bread when the phone rang. Now what? Couldn't she eat in
peace?

"Where have you been all day?" Tally demanded. "That guy
came into my boutique again."

"What guy?"

"The man who buys clothes for his girlfriend but tries them on
first." Her voice lowered. "I think he's weird."

"You mean he's gay?"

"No, but I can't explain it. I wish you could see him."

"So call me next time he comes into your store. If I'm free, I'll
rush over while he's still in the dressing room."

"You've got a deal. So what's up?"

Marla discussed the morning's events but skimmed over her afternoon session. "I've got a few leads about Jolene's activities at
work, but I'll wait to see how they pan out. Are you doing anything
tonight? I want to follow up on Tesla, the massage lady from the
club whom neither of us have met. I'd like to see what she has to say
about her fellow staff members. Then there's another task I've been
meaning to do."

"I'll join you. Ken is glued to the TV set watching a Heat game
tonight, so he won't mind if I go out."

"Great, I'll pick you up at seven-thirty. Oh, and one more thing:
wear something dark," she ended mysteriously.

"Why are we sitting in front of Slate's house?" Tally asked later,
when they were parked a few doors down from 501 Fairlawn Court
in Davie. Taking Marla's advice, she'd worn a black Spandex jump-
suit that made her look like a cat burglar. Wavy blond hair spilled
down her back, negating the anonymous image Marla wanted them
to project.

"Betsy implied Tesla lived here, and that's her dark-green Buick in the driveway." Her own outfit consisted of black pants and a matching zippered tunic top in stretch nylon. Hopefully, they wouldn't be too conspicuous if Tally covered her hair. It wasn't necessary now, but it would be in a short while if Marla carried out her other plan.

Tally's azure eyes glowed in the dim light of a streetlamp. "So Tesla and Slate are having an affair?"

"I'm not sure. When I called the club earlier, Sharon told me that neither one of them is on duty tonight. So let's see what happens."

"Why don't we just knock on the door?"

Marla shook her head, causing a length of bobbed hair to fall across her eyes. Shoving the strands away, she replied, "I don't want to tip them off. There's got to be a reason why Tess is so elusive."

"Speak of the devil; is that her coming from the house?" Tally pointed excitedly at the large-boned woman striding toward the Buick.

Marla's pulse accelerated. "Yes, I recognize her. She likes to wear those flowing garments. Funny, you wouldn't think Slate would be attracted to a big lady like her. He wanted Jolene, and she was slim compared to Tess."

"Maybe he doesn't like Amy because she's too petite. Should we wait until she leaves, then see if Slate's home alone?"

"Let's follow Tess. She might have more answers if we can talk to her." Turning on the ignition, Marla shifted gears, leaving the headlights off until they approached an intersection.

"Holy smokes, where is she going?" Tally wondered aloud as they cruised east on I-595 and then veered north on I-95.

Traffic on Monday evening was still fairly heavy, but since this was tourist season, Marla wasn't surprised. "I hope Tess isn't headed for Orlando!" she joked.

"You don't know anything about her except that she works part-time as a masseuse at the club. She could be going to night classes at BCC North Campus."

Education appeared to be the farthest thing from Tess's mind when they finally pulled into a parking lot at Pelican's on South Ocean Boulevard in Delray Beach. Inside, reggae music vibrated from a stage where the Stingrays performed live. A lounge held a dance floor filled with jiving guests, a karaoke platform, and an old-fashioned mahogany bar with glistening glassware. An adjoining barroom housed billiards, video games, and another seating area. At least a no-smoking policy provided clean air, Marla thought gratefully as the loud thrumming and noisy chatter assailed her ears.

Their arrival produced energetic male whistles and several offers to dance. Fending off their admirers, Marla gestured to a dark corner table. "Let's sit there," she suggested to Tally, hoping the dim illumination hadn't exposed them to Tess's view. Their target had taken a position at the bar, and Marla couldn't shake the feeling that her firm-jawed profile was somehow familiar.

"You know, I've seen that woman before," Tally hissed as they shouldered their way through the crowd.

"Yeah, I got the impression I'd seen her somewhere else besides Betsy's," Marla agreed. "Look who else is at the bar!"

"Why, it's Amy from the sports club! What's she doing here?"

"Taking a break from her job at the refreshment stand, I imagine." Marla led the way toward a corner table. When the waiter slouched his way over, she ordered a bushwacker, her favorite coffee-laced liquor drink. Tally requested a glass of chardonnay.

While waiting for their orders, Marla helped herself to a handful of salted peanuts from a dish on the table. "Amy told me Tess came here sometimes, but they're not really friends," she said, crunching on the nuts. "See how Tess is sitting at the other end of the bar?"

"Amy has quite a collection of guys hanging on. I thought you said she had the hots for Slate."

"Yeah, but he doesn't return her ardor. Maybe this is how Amy consoles herself, by picking up dates here."

"Tess appears to be watching Amy." Tally's shrewd gaze assessed the two women. "Look, that hunk just came up to Tess, and she's not interested in him. Why don't you go talk to her?"

Marla gave her friend an astonished glance. "Amy is too close. She'll see me and think I followed her."

"Tell her you came here to meet Tess." Tally's eyes twinkled playfully. "I should make an appointment for a massage with Slate. It would tickle my ego if he propositioned me!"

An hour passed while they nursed their drinks, tapped their feet to the music, and observed Tess keeping tabs on Amy. Finally, the Smoothie King attendant left on the arm of a blond, muscled surfer. Tess rose as though to follow, but Marla intercepted her.

"Hi, I'm Marla Shore, a member of the Perfect Fit Sports Club. You're one of the massage therapists, aren't you?" From the corner of her eye, she noted Tally paying their bill. She'd settle the tab with her later.

"Oh, hello, dear," Tess trilled, her heavily made-up eyes looking less than pleased.

Marla took a moment to size up the woman. Tall and broad-shouldered, Tesla Parr carried herself with an awkward stiffness. She seemed uncomfortable in high heels, wobbling slightly as she walked but holding her head high. Her dress displayed an ample bosom but slim hips, an almost incongruous match. After scanning her hairdo, Marla's gaze narrowed. Tess's luxurious ebony layers had a suspiciously vague hairline. *Bless my bones, it's a wig,* she realized with sudden insight. Tess's crimson lips parted as Marla's eyes inadvertently widened, and the woman's chalky white skin blushed. Her skin tone was due to a heavy application of light foundation and powder, Marla determined, openly curious about the woman's odd appearance.

"I wonder why I've never run into you at the club," Marla commented. "I was hoping to make an appointment for a massage."

"We have several other therapists, darlin'," Tess said with a strong Southern accent. "Ah'm sure you could see one of my colleagues."

"I've already had an hour with Slate." *Interesting how Tess's nostrils flared at the mention of his name.* "I gather Amy Gerard likes him. Quite a coincidence that you and Amy chill at the same club."

"Isn't it," Tess crooned in a voice that reminded Marla of the wolf in "Little Red Riding Hood." "Just as much of a coincidence as you bein' here tonight."

"I'm with a friend," Marla explained, nodding to Tally, who was walking in their direction.

Tess paled. "Ah have to go."

"Wait, I want to talk to you about Jolene Myers."

"What about her?" Tess backstepped toward the door.

"I heard Slate was angry with her because he'd asked her out and she refused. Do you think Slate's anger extended to violence?"

The woman's face clouded with fury. "You have no business askin' questions," she said, stopping to confront Marla.

"Why? Because Slate is your boyfriend? Where were you the night Jolene died? Or maybe Amy's jealousy led *her* to commit the dire deed. Is that why you're watching her, because you and Slate suspect she murdered Jolene?"

Tess's face purpled with rage. "Ah wouldn't go around town makin' accusations like that, darlin'. Y'all could land yourself in a heap of trouble."

"Oh, yeah?" Marla said evenly. "So could you, if I tell Detective Vail you're following one of his suspects."

The amber eyes cooled to a topaz hardness. "You do, Miz Shore, and you'll find your fuckin' ass sucked down a whirlpool worse than that Myers broad."

Her ominous words hanging in the air, Tesla Parr spun around and teetered toward the exit.

"Whew," Tally said, pretending to fan herself. "The temperature's risen in this place."

"Let's get out of here. I'm definitely going to tell Dalton about her. She's very strange. Did you notice her hair? It's fake, and she wears a ton of makeup, so you can't tell what she really looks like. Her eyes, though . . ."

"What about them?"

Outside, Marla glanced uneasily around the parking lot. It wasn't well lit at night, and she remembered the other incident at the athletic club. Could Slate have been the one who'd attacked her?

"Her eye color is uncommon. I know I've seen that woman somewhere else."

"Me, too. She must have left already. I don't see her car."

"She made a fast getaway." Retrieving her keys, Marla led the way to the Camry. Inside the car, she locked the doors before starting the engine. Belatedly, she thought of checking for telltale signs of tampering. Oh, well. If a bomb were going to explode, most likely it would have happened when she turned on the ignition.

According to the clock, it was nearly eleven by the time they reached Palm Haven. Perfect Fit Sports Club would be closing its doors in the next few minutes. Marla had doubts her plan would succeed, but she intended to give it a try.

"Do you have to go home yet?" she asked Tally, who'd been relatively quiet during the drive. She supposed her friend was reviewing events in her mind just as she was. "I know it's late. We both have to get up for work in the morning, but there's one more thing I need to do."

"Which is?" Tally grinned encouragingly, and Marla felt a surge of gratitude for her support.

"I have to get into Gloria's office. She has client records and may have personnel files as well. But if the club is locked, we'll try another time."

"Excuse me, did you say *we?*"

"You heard me. Are you game, or not?"

Tally shrugged. "I must be crazy to tag along with you, but it sure as hell beats staying home and watching TV. Let's go."

Thirty minutes later, Marla dropped Tally off at home. Their effort had been in vain. The sports club had been locked tight as a newly permed curl.

"We'll do it on Wednesday," Tally suggested before taking her leave. "I'll distract Gloria while you rummage through her office. It'll be easy if I pretend to be interested in a full membership."

Marla frowned. "How will that work? She'll want to do the paperwork in her office."

Her friend smiled wickedly. "Don't worry. I have a plan. We'll meet in the locker room same time as last week, okay?"

"You got it. Thanks for coming tonight, pal."

Weariness weighted her bones as she pulled into the garage of her town house. Erasing all concerns from her mind, Marla performed the routine of letting Spooks outside and back in again, checking her answering machine, and locking up for the night. After a refreshing shower, she pulled on a cotton nightshirt and collapsed into bed to review the day.

First stop, the real estate office. Eloise Zelman hadn't shown up for work, but her colleague Judy firmly believed the woman would reappear when ready. Vail had no luck tracing her, either. Was her disappearance related to Sam's mysterious dealings, as Judy had implied, and if so, how did that relate to Jolene's death?

Both Cookie and Eloise knew that Sam had been meeting secretly with Jolene. Had they shared an illicit love relationship, or were they conspiring together? If they were lovers, Eloise had a motive for doing away with both of them. But if not, was Eloise afraid that she would be the next victim?

If only Eloise would return, Marla thought as she twisted restlessly. That would solve a couple of problems.

Next came Hortense's revelation that the woman she'd met through Arnie was really Jillian Barlow, an actress and public relations specialist. She hoped Jill had learned something about Jolene from her coworkers. In the meantime, Marla had to keep quiet about the girl's identity so as not to tip off the killer. As for Arnie, Marla would protect him from being hurt, by having a private conversation with Jill to assess her intent. Arnie was a dear friend who needed a mate, but he didn't deserve a relationship built on lies.

Throwing off her covers, Marla got up and padded into the kitchen. Her mind was too active. She'd never fall asleep at this rate. Fixing herself a cup of cocoa, she sat at the kitchen table and sipped the hot drink slowly.

Dr. Crone's documents proved that Jolene had been falsifying lab test results—obtaining favorable data elsewhere and passing it off as her own. Jill might be able to trace the source—another reason to let the actress play her part.

And speaking of playing a part, her false engagement to Arnie still had to be resolved. They were deceiving Jill, so the deception went both ways. If Jill was truly fond of Arnie, how would she react when the truth came to light?

Don't tell her, Marla reasoned, scratching Spooks behind the ear when he nudged her ankle. *Stage the breakup with Arnie, and the matter will be settled.*

Personal issues aside, what about tonight's episode? Tess was clearly following Amy, but for what purpose? Tess and Slate appeared to have an ongoing relationship. Could Slate have been using Tess to trail Amy, and if so, why? Amy's behavior generated further questions. If the snack bar attendant was mooning over Slate, why did she pick up guys in a lounge?

Add Keith into the equation. He'd been talking to Slate about Amy. It was a tight-knit group, she concluded. If only she could get one of them to talk, secrets might unravel.

She rinsed out her empty cup, put it in the dish drainer, and headed back to bed. Feeling chilled, she pulled the covers up to her chin and turned on her side. A new moon provided no illumination through the drapes, leaving her bedroom in inky darkness. She felt the comforting weight of the dog's warm body when he jumped on the bed.

Letting her mind drift, she succumbed to a heavy drowsiness that enveloped her like a cocoon. Her eyelids drooped, and she floated into a sleep cycle, where strange dreams hovered in the wings.

Barking roused her as Spooks leapt off the bed and charged into the hallway. A crash of splintering glass was followed by utter silence, and then she smelled smoke. Bolting upright, she felt her heart race in panic.

"Spooks! Where are you? What's happened?" Tossing off the covers, she reached for a terrycloth robe and threw it on. Dare she go after the poodle? Breaking glass could mean someone had broken into her house. Or maybe it was a gunshot, and Jolene's killer was outside waiting for her to appear by a window. She reached for the phone, prudence taking precedence over her need to investigate.

"Police, fire, or medical?" asked the emergency dispatcher.

"All of them! Something smashed my window, and—"

Her smoke alarm blared, making her heart pound with fright. "Hurry," she cried. "If someone broke in, he might still be in the house! And please, notify Detective Lieutenant Vail."

Chapter Sixteen

Marla fled from her bedroom through a glass door leading to the backyard. Spooks appeared at her heels, yapping furiously until she scooped him into her arms. She proceeded cautiously toward the street, hoping the dog's bark had scared off any potential assailants.

Vail's arrival brought order to chaos, and she breathed a sigh of relief when he took charge. She spoke to Goat and Moss on the sidewalk while officers inspected the scene. About thirty minutes later, she spied Vail striding toward her, carrying a pile of clothing and a pair of black loafers. Heat suffused her cheeks when she noticed the bra strap poking out from between her jeans and a pullover top. *Get over it*, she told herself. *The man is a widower with a twelve-year-old daughter. He knows what it's like to live with women.*

Grateful that he'd been so thoughtful, she gave a watery smile as he handed her the bundle.

"Get in the car," he ordered, holding open the passenger door. "You can stay at my place for the rest of the night."

After he'd settled behind the wheel and turned on the ignition, he offered his findings. "Someone threw a Molotov cocktail through your kitchen window," he explained in a calm, detached voice.

"W-what's that?" Marla croaked, glancing at his stern profile. The only trace of emotion she could see was a muscle twitching in his jaw.

"It's an explosive device: in this case, a chemical fire bottle. You're lucky the thing didn't work right, or the damage would've been severe. Fortunately, the fire barely got started before it went out. You had more smoke than flames."

"That's enough," she said, her voice trembling. She cradled Spooks's small body in her arms, wondering how he'd get along with Vail's golden retriever. Goat had offered to keep her pet until she returned home, but Marla needed the comfort of Spooks's presence.

"Any idea who had it in for you?" Vail said. He turned onto West Broward Boulevard, heading east toward an older residential section where banyan trees shaded the roads like arms, protecting walkers from the blazing Florida sun.

Marla glanced at him warily. "I imagine I've ruffled a few feathers lately."

His hands tightened on the steering wheel. "Go on."

"Well, this morning I visited the Zelmans' realty office. Their assistant, Judy, said she expected Eloise to return unharmed."

He nodded, as though this wasn't news. "And then? You had the whole day off. I don't imagine you spent it doing errands like a normal person."

She ignored his sarcastic tone. "I went to Vero Beach to visit, uh, an acquaintance of Hortense."

A smile quirked his lips. "You mean you met the real Hortense Crone."

She gave up the pretense. "How did you find out?"

"Simple. I ran a check on *our* Hortense's license tag. Her car is registered to Jillian Barlow at an address in Vero Beach."

"If you'd have told me, it would have saved me a trip!" *Lack of trust is still an issue here, pal.* "What the devil do you know about Eloise? You don't seem so concerned about her. I thought you wanted her for questioning about Sam's death."

"Umm," he murmured, deftly avoiding a direct answer.

"She might be in danger. I hope you'll share the news if you learn she's safe."

"Are you planning to tell Arnie?" he countered.

"About what?" She gazed at him with perplexed eyes.

"Jill, a.k.a. Hortense." They'd entered his neighborhood, and he slowed as they approached his driveway. The brick exterior of his ranch-style home was lit by security spotlights.

"I don't plan to tell anyone her true identity for now," Marla answered. "Jill works at Stockhart Industries. She may be able to ferret out information not available to either of us. It's important that we don't jeopardize her position. As for Arnie, I think it's better for Jill to tell him herself. If she really cares about him, she'll reveal the truth in her own time. But I'm going to have a talk with her to see how she feels. I won't stand for Arnie getting hurt."

Pulling into the driveway, he cut the ignition. Spooks scampered from her arms to the backseat and peered out the window. "How about your little game? You and Arnie being engaged, I mean. Do you think he'll tell her the truth?"

"Oh God, this is such a mess. Arnie was meshuga to spread that news."

"Damn right." His eyes glittered as he faced her. "Worrying about you is giving me gray hairs. Things could have been a lot worse tonight at your place."

Why were graying heads such a popular subject lately? Her eyes fastened on his thick head of peppery hair, and all unpleasantries fled from her mind. The soft strands invited touching, and she remembered how silky they'd felt when she gave him a cut. A hitch caught in her throat. Her gaze, traveled downward, noted his polo shirt tucked into a pair of snug jeans. Warmth stole into her veins as his nearness penetrated her fogged brain. It was hard to swallow when she lifted her eyes and saw the way he looked at her.

When he leaned over to kiss her, she draped her arms around his solid shoulders, eager to release the fears of the night. She thought of nothing else but the press of his lips on hers until Spooks's jealous nudging broke them apart.

"Let's go inside," Vail said huskily, "or I'll start something I won't be able to finish."

Marla nodded gratefully, too caught up in the rapture of the moment to respond verbally. Cuddling Spooks, she opened her door while the detective retrieved her pile of clothing from the rear seat. At least she'd have an outfit to wear to work in the morning if Vail couldn't drop her off at home first. She'd need to call a window repairman and assess the smoke damage, which hopefully would be minimal. Plus, she'd have to get her car.

Trailing the detective to his front door, Marla wondered how they would explain her presence to his daughter. Wild barking sounded from inside. If the girl were sleeping, surely the noise would awaken her. She hoped the dogs got along, so they could all get some rest.

She'd needn't have worried about Brianna. The girl took their explanation in stride, giving Marla a curious look when Vail said she had been in danger.

"Where's she going to sleep?" was Brianna's only concern, glancing back and forth between the two of them with narrowed eyes. She appeared younger than her age, with disheveled long hair, and dancing bears on her flannel pajamas.

Vail's face colored as though he hadn't considered the matter. "We have a guest room, so she'll stay there. It has a sleep sofa," he told her in an apologetic tone.

"That's fine," she reassured him, putting Spooks down. The poodle yipped loudly in a barking contest with the golden retriever, and they raced around the living room chasing each other. While Brianna was distracted, Marla grabbed her bundle of clothes from Vail's arms.

"Brianna, do you have any makeup I can use in the morning? I'll need to get ready for work if your father is too rushed to take me home first." Shifting the garments, she hoped her underwear wasn't visible.

"Yeah, it's in my bathroom." The girl gave Marla a considering glance, as if just now realizing she was dressed in a robe. It didn't help that Vail was staring at her legs. "You know, Lucky barks if anyone moves around in the night," Brianna warned.

Marla felt her face flush. "I see. Will Spooks be all right? I'd like to go to bed, but he can sleep with me if you want him out of Lucky's way."

Vail cleared his throat. "Let the dogs get used to each other. They'll calm down eventually. You need to rest. It's been a harrowing night, and you'll be safe here." To emphasize his point, he reset the alarm, which he'd deactivated on their entrance. "I'll get you some linens for the bed."

"No, Daddy, let me," Brianna insisted—more to keep them apart than to be helpful, Marla decided.

Lying awake in bed, worries raced through her beleaguered faculties. How would she find time in the morning to take Spooks home, call a window repair service, and shower and dress for work? Tonight's incident highlighted her own jeopardy. Hereafter, she'd be extra cautious. Someone held a violent grudge against her, and more than one person came to mind straightaway.

Marla arrived at work nine o'clock on Tuesday to find Cookie Calcone pacing in front of Cut 'N Dye Salon with a stack of flyers in hand. "Oh, joy," Marla muttered, feeling her troubles compound like a cumulus cloud in the summer. Just what she needed after her *tsuris* last night: more aggravation. Already her plans for the day had gone awry. She'd planned to get here earlier, but after Vail dropped her off at home, time zipped by while she called a repairman, took Spooks for a short walk, and dressed for work. Now Cookie's presence heralded continued unpleasantness.

"Marla, when are you going to comply with SETA standards?" Cookie demanded, blocking her path. "You're still displaying the same products in your windows."

"I don't have time for this, pal. Move out of my way."

"I won't share any information about Jolene until you stop selling those brands," Cookie announced.

"Does that mean you've discovered something significant?"

"Maybe." Smirking, the shorter woman tossed back a length of strawberry blond hair. "I'll give you one tip. Jolene paid Wallace Ritiker under the table when he pushed through the zoning change for Stockhart Industries. She wasn't too happy with him lately because he'd voted against a measure that was important to her, and she had been counting on his support. I suspect Jolene was angry enough to threaten him."

"In what manner?"

"She might expose his other indiscretions. Jolene wasn't the only person from whom he'd accepted favors."

"Do you think he murdered her?" Marla couldn't conceive how Wally could slip sedatives into Jolene's bottle of capsules in the ladies' locker room, unless he had an associate in crime.

Cookie's moss green eyes cooled. "That depends."

"Go on."

"Sorry, you haven't met your end of the deal." Cookie jerked a thumb at the hair salon.

Marla gritted her teeth. "This involves a murder investigation. If you're withholding information, it could be construed as obstruction of justice."

"Says who, your boyfriend the detective? You seem to be seeing a lot of him lately. Aren't you engaged to the guy from Bagel Busters?"

"That depends," Marla mimicked, adding under her breath, *"Se zol dir grihmen in boych."* It wasn't nice to tell someone she should get a stomach cramp, but Cookie was a nudnick who had gotten on her nerves one time too many.

Grimacing with annoyance, she stalked into the salon. It wouldn't be long before the receptionist arrived, and then she wouldn't have the place to herself. Striding toward the storeroom, she considered Cookie's demands. Undoubtedly, laboratory tests performed on animals were cruel and unnecessary in cases where substitute trials were possible. But if she really liked a hair care product because of the results on her clients, would she stop using it because of manufacturing practices? Was she willing to waste time to scrutinize the ingredients lists and disclaimers on all chemical supplies?

Certainly, SETA supported a worthy cause, as long as its members didn't get fanatical. Marla might have considered complying just for the ethics and because she didn't care to see helpless animals hurt, but not because of Cookie. Blackmail didn't sit well on her shoulders. She'd been through it before. Mrs. Kravitz's knowledge of her shameful past had burdened her life in the past, and she wouldn't succumb to another type of coercion now that she was freed from the old lady's threats. Never again! She'd use whatever products she damn well pleased, and if she happened to order supplies hereafter from companies who didn't perform animal tests, that was her choice.

"Hi, Marla," called the receptionist as she entered the salon a few minutes later. "Your schedule is at your station. I put it there yesterday before I left."

"Thanks. I started the coffee brewing. Would you mind going for bagels?" *I'm not ready to see Arnie yet,* she thought as she put aside the stack of folded towels in her arms. Her nerves were on edge, thanks to Cookie's pacing outside the picture window. Would the police arrest the woman if she called them? Marla wasn't aware of the statutes regarding civil disobedience, if Cookie's actions could be construed that way. Better not to make a fuss, she decided. Loyal customers would walk right past the woman without glancing at her twice.

When her first client arrived, she didn't have time to think about Cookie or what she might have learned. Her day was booked solid, and Nicole had to take on the overflow.

"What formula should I use on Gail's highlights?" Nicole asked Marla.

She paused, shears in hand. "I used the gel lightener before, but it came out too light. Why don't you try Nexus eleven-N, and alternate every three or four packets with a darker color at the six-N level. It'll still be blond, but not as light as the gel."

Concentrating on her own client, she created a part at the occipital and separated a one-inch horizontal section of auburn hair at the nape. Holding it straight up, she flipped the strands over her fingers and cut an inch off the ends directly across. It took fifteen minutes to finish the shag.

Her next client was a young woman who wore her hair in long layers and wanted a new look. Marla studied her round features and assessed her chestnut color as a natural Level three.

"I'd like to do a cut that offers more movement and swing," she said, lifting a strand of hair. "I'd also lighten it two levels using color placement based on your cut, instead of highlights."

"That's lovely," her customer said after Marla shortened the length to just above the shoulders and used a shattering technique to break up the hair against her face.

"It's much more flattering," Marla agreed, pleased at how the new style brought out the girl's cheekbones.

The next customer wasn't so happy. It was an elderly woman with thick pearl gray hair. Her complaint was a yellowing on the longer portion of the crown and around the hairline.

"Do you take any medications?" Marla asked the woman.

"No, dear."

"Are you a smoker? Nicotine can stain gray hair."

"I should say not!"

"Then your problem may be due to sun damage." Marla lifted a section of dry hair. "White hair lacks melanin, which normally protects you from damage. Without that protection, exposure to sunlight destroys the keratin protein and causes other changes in your hair that result in yellowing. I'd advise you to use hair care products with sunscreen, and wear a hat when outdoors. I'll try a violet-based shampoo. It might get rid of the yellow for now, but you need to avoid direct sunlight."

Time blurred as Marla finished with one client after another. She didn't even realize it was time for lunch until Nicole asked if she wanted to order anything from Bagel Busters.

Arnie brought their order in person, marching straight toward Marla's chair, where she was completing a blow dry. Ignoring the knowing smirks of her staff, he dropped the container of food on her counter.

"Marla, we need to talk. Hortense called and said she could get away for lunch. I feel funny meeting her when you and I are supposed to—"

"What now?" Marla blurted, spying Vail strolling in through the front entrance. Hastily she sprayed her client's hair, then removed the cape. "Here's your bill, Babs. Have a good trip."

Babs Winrow, a steady customer, winked as she rose from the

chair. "I may not leave so fast. The sparks between you and the good detective are always so entertaining." She flicked her gaze between Arnie and Marla. "Of course, *he* may not agree."

Bless my bones; even Babs knows about our fake engagement.

"Hi, Dalton," Marla said. "What brings you into the shop? Have you learned anything new about last night?"

The tall lieutenant bore down on them, holding a brown paper sack. His peppery hair appeared ruffled as though he'd run his fingers through it instead of a comb. He appeared more imposing in his navy sport coat than a football player in full regalia.

"Hartman, what are you doing here?" queried the detective.

Arnie's mustache quivered as he grinned. "I'm visiting my fiancée. It's difficult to keep away from her when she's just a few doors down."

Vail gazed at him with an implacable expression, then handed Marla the bag. "Here's your robe. You forgot to take it when I drove you home from my house this morning." He delivered his remarks in a deadpan voice, but Marla noticed his gray eyes held a twinkle. "Your nightshirt is there, too."

Too stunned by Vail's audacity to respond, Marla vaguely heard the jingle of chimes from the front door as a customer entered. Arnie's glance darted toward the entrance, and his face reddened.

"Excuse me?" he said loudly, stepping closer to Vail. "Did I hear you say my fiancée's *nightclothes* are in that bag you just delivered?"

The detective towered over him by several inches. His gaze focused on the mirror for several intent seconds while Arnie's eyebrows furrowed worriedly. "You did," Vail announced in a stentorian tone. "An incident went down at Marla's place last evening. She spent the night at my house."

"What kind of incident?" Arnie snarled.

Work came to a halt in the salon as everyone's attention focused on the two men. Marla groaned inwardly. Why did Arnie have to choose now to pick their argument?

"Someone tossed a Molotov cocktail through her window," Vail explained patiently. "Fortunately, the damage was minimal, but I wouldn't let her stay home alone."

"You should have called me!" Arnie exclaimed to her.

Marla spread her hands helplessly. "I dialed nine-one-one."

"And *he* showed up? What's he do, monitor your phone lines?" Hunching forward, Arnie clenched his fists.

"Please, let's not get confrontational," Marla urged, feeling she was acting out a prescribed drama. From a corner of her vision, a familiar figure drifted into view. Hortense! Or rather, Jillian. As an actress, she was bound to unmask their pretense. She must have shown up at the deli and been redirected to the salon.

Jill sauntered forward, dressed in a short-skirted canary yellow business suit. Her hair was tastefully swept into a twist atop her head. "I'm on lunch break, and there's something I have to tell Arnie," she said, taking in the situation at a glance. "But I fear I'm interrupting."

Arnie, taking advantage, gave her a wounded-puppy look. "Marla spent the night at Vail's house."

"Oh, my!" Jill's eyes rounded in pretended horror.

"If you'd kept closer tabs on her, this wouldn't have happened," Vail said quietly to Arnie. "If she were my woman, I'd keep her safe."

How? Marla bristled. *By tracking every move I make? No way you're getting the chance, pal.* She eyed Vail resentfully. He'd started this!

"Maybe you two would rather spend time together," Arnie conceded, hanging his head. Gads, thought Marla, he's playing this for all it's worth. "I can't protect her like you can, lieutenant. I see how things are between you. I'm a schmuck for not realizing it before. Marla, consider yourself freed from any obligation to me."

"What?" she screeched, getting into her role. "Are you jilting me?" She emphasized the first syllable of *jilting*, pleased by the blonde woman's startled glance.

"I'm letting you go so you can be with him." Arnie spoke in a strained tone.

Marla whirled to face the actress. "Do you believe this? I only went to Vail's place last night because my house wasn't safe. We didn't do anything . . . unethical. His daughter was home, for God's sake!"

"It doesn't matter," Arnie whined, covering his face with his hands.

"You poor thing," Jill crooned, putting an arm around his slumped shoulders. "Marla may not appreciate you, but I do." Her voice lowered. "Let's go outside. I need to tell you what I found in Jolene's office today."

Chapter
Seventeen

"**I**'m coming, too," Marla said. "You and I need to talk, uh, Hortense." Aware of Vail trailing behind them, she accompanied Arnie and the actress outside. Cookie, who'd taken a break, had resumed parading in front of the salon.

"Don't I know you?" Cookie demanded, stopping to stare at the tall blonde. "Oh, yeah, you're a member at Perfect Fit. What are you doing here?"

"I came to see Arnie," Jill explained.

"Are you Marla's customer?" Cookie's green eyes narrowed. "This salon goes against SETA standards in using products from companies that do cruel animal tests. Do you know about the Lethal Dose Fifty? Rabbits, mice, and guinea pigs are force-fed or injected with household substances until half of them die. Cosmetic companies drip shampoos and hair sprays onto rabbits' eyes using the infamous Draize test that leaves many of them blind. More humane alternatives are available."

Jill gave a patronizing smile. "I'm aware of the options: computer assays, live cell cultures, and mass spectrometry, to name a few."

Cookie paused to give her a penetrating glare, then continued her tirade. "If you support those poor, helpless creatures, you'll shun this salon. SETA has been effective in causing cosmetics industry leaders to observe a moratorium on animal testing, but we still need your help. Only by speaking up and boycotting involved businesses can we heighten public awareness. Here, you can read more about it." Reaching inside her backpack, she pulled out a stack of pamphlets.

Jill squinted. "Hey, you're not involved with that animal rights group whose members sent booby-trapped letters to scientists, are you?"

Cookie planted a hand on her hip. "I don't hurt people, darling. I read about that in the newspaper, and it wasn't my group who claimed responsibility on the Internet. I would never condone hiding razor blades inside the top flaps of letters as a means of persuasion. It was a dumb move if someone thought that would force the release of monkeys held captive in laboratories. I demonstrate *against* suffering; I don't cause it."

"Good, then I'm already on your side. Listen, Arnie, I have information. Can we go somewhere private?"

"Hell, no," Marla snapped. "If this is about Jolene, I want to hear what you have to say."

Vail shouldered her aside. "This case is *my* jurisdiction."

"What's this about Jolene?" Cookie inserted.

Jill threw up her hands in capitulation. "I give up; you can all listen. I managed to get inside Jolene's office. In one of her drawers, I found an old newspaper article about Sam Zelman. Apparently, he'd been engaged in mortgage fraud on the West Coast a number of years ago. He'd put over fifty families into foreclosure. Sam offered people with bad credit a chance to buy homes through something he called an agreement for deed. Unknown to the homeowners, he never filed the deeds with the county clerk. Meanwhile, he falsified mortgage applications. When he defaulted on payments, lenders began foreclosing on the homes. Sam was charged with grand theft."

"He must have made lots of people angry," Marla said dryly.

"That's old news," Vail commented, "and it doesn't explain why Eloise vanished."

"Unless someone who was seeking revenge caught up to Sam, and Eloise is afraid she'll be next," Marla suggested.

"Did I hear you mention my name?" trilled a woman's voice from the parking lot.

Marla twirled around, and her eyes widened. "Eloise, where have you been?"

Eloise appeared none the worse for wear in dark Capri pants, a rust cotton blouse, and low-heeled sandals. Her disheveled hair appeared the only thing out of place. "I have a hair appointment today. Did you think I would miss it?"

"Your husband," began Detective Vail, his face somber.

Eloise's mouth tightened. "Sam's accident was unfortunate. I drove separately and left just before it happened." Her jaw trembled, the only sign of distress. "I got scared."

"Why?" Jill's voice was strong as she moved close to Eloise. "Because you knew Sam was meeting Jolene, and you were afraid you'd be accused of murdering them both? Why did you do it, Eloise? Were you jealous?"

Arnie interceded, clutching Jill's arm. "Let it go, honey. This is Vail's case."

For once, Vail gave him a grateful glance. "I need to ask you some questions," he told Eloise.

"She didn't do it," Cookie said in an undertone to Marla. "You get rid of those bad products like I advised you, and I'll fill you in on what I know. I'm going to check back here every day until you comply. But you'd better hurry, before someone else ends up dead."

Marla stared after her as Cookie marched off, but she couldn't consider the implications, because Jill swatted her shoulder.

"Is it over between you and Arnie?" the blonde asked, a hopeful gleam in her sapphire eyes.

Vail had taken Eloise aside and was speaking to her urgently. Marla focused on her rival for Arnie's regard. "Arnie and I are friends," she confessed. "We'll always be fond of each other, but that's where it ends. Just keep this in mind: honesty should be the basis for your relationship. I know who you are, pal. Your patron and I had a nice chat in Vero Beach. I hope you're no longer using Arnie as part of your act."

With those parting words, she turned to reenter the salon. Checking her schedule, she noticed Eloise was her next customer. With so many distractions, she hadn't given the name a second glance earlier. No matter. When Eloise departed with the detective, Marla had other chores to do until the next client arrived.

The shop kept her busy until the evening, when it was time to pick up Brianna and take her to dance class.

She began their conversation in the car. "I saw your father this morning. He came by the salon."

"Really?" Brianna faced forward, clutching a bulging dance bag in her arms. She'd swept her stick-straight dark hair into a high ponytail. Beneath a pair of jean shorts were tan tights that covered her long limbs like a second skin. An oversized T-shirt hung below her waist.

"When do you think he'll be finished with his night duty?"

The girl shrugged. "Who knows? If it's too much trouble for you to take me, I'll find someone else to give me a ride on Tuesday nights."

"I'm happy to help you." Marla glanced at Brianna's sullen expression. "I wish you'd trust me."

Brianna's lower lip quivered. "You've got your life; why bother with mine?"

Smoothing a length of bobbed hair, she gave a short laugh. "Good question. Guess I'm a masochist, if you know what that means." Traffic heading south on University Drive was especially heavy. Usually it calmed down after seven, but the light at Peters Road was holding things up. She should have taken another route. Annoyed as a driver cut in front of her, she gripped the wheel tighter.

"I'm not stupid," Brianna retorted, anger flashing in her eyes. "I get decent grades, and I'm in honors English."

"That's wonderful," Marla said quickly. "I'll bet your father is proud of you."

"That's why he discusses his cases with me." The girl jutted her chin forward. "We're a good team, and we don't need anyone to interfere."

Marla bit her lip, concentrating on driving. Talk about tough nuts to crack! Like father, like daughter. Vail didn't trust her yet, either.

"Hopefully, he'll discover who killed Jolene so he can close the case and return home in the evenings. Is he hanging his suspicions on anyone in particular?"

Brianna smirked. "You'd like to know, wouldn't you?"

Marla kept her tone casual. "I've learned that Jolene was tampering with lab test results."

"Someone named Cookie told my dad about that. She said she'd find the real source of Jolene's data."

"Has she?"

"Nope. Daddy thinks it's important. Actually, he's fairly suspicious of Cookie herself. She knows an awful lot, plus she hated Jolene for personal reasons."

Nodding, Marla felt compelled to explain. "Jolene fired her husband from his job, and their marriage broke up. Cookie blamed Jolene." She paused. "Cookie may be a big talker, but I don't think she has it in her to murder someone. The woman is too compassionate about animals."

"Daddy says people who are devoted to causes sometimes kill in the belief it's their calling."

"That's right, but I don't believe it applies in this case." They arrived at the shopping center where the dance studio was located, and Marla put aside further musings.

"You don't need to come inside," Brianna announced.

Instead of dropping her off, Marla pulled into a parking space. "I'd like to say hello to Lindsay. My friend Tally and I enjoy her Dancercize sessions at the sports club. I don't see how she has any free time between teaching classes here and working there as an instructor. Her evenings and weekends must be fully occupied."

Brianna cracked open her door. "She's a great dance teacher, but I don't think it's all she does. Lindsay may work somewhere else during the day before the studio opens."

"That's possible." A frown creased her brow. If she recalled, Dancercize was not listed on the club's daytime schedule.

Brianna slammed the car door shut and strode toward the brightly lit studio entrance. Swinging her purse strap over one shoulder, Marla hastened after her. The air felt chilly, and she shivered in her long-sleeved knit top. Darkness had fallen, bringing a cadence of insect sounds and a cool breeze.

"Hi, Brianna. Marla, it's great to see you again," Lindsay's cheerful greeting rang out when they entered. She straightened her leotard, which clung to her form like cellophane wrapped around a sculpture of the human body.

"Lindsay, how are you?" Marla said, speaking loudly to be heard over the pounding music and staccato sound of tap shoes coming from one of the classrooms. "You sure keep busy with all these dance classes. Do you teach here during the day, too?"

Lindsay's expression clouded. "The studio only opens when the kids get out of school. Brianna, you haven't turned in your ticket order for the recital yet. If you don't hand it in by next week, you won't get the seats you want."

Brianna plopped on a bench to change her shoes. "I don't know who can come. My dad might be working."

"When is the recital?" Marla asked, stepping toward her.

"May twenty-fifth. We have it earlier than most other schools. It's held at Parker Playhouse."

"Our performances are always fully booked." Lindsay gave Marla an appraising glance. "Will you be attending?"

She glanced at Brianna, who was taking an inordinately long time to tie her jazz shoes. "Am I invited?"

"Anyone can buy a ticket," the girl snapped, but Marla detected a faint plaintive note in her voice.

"I'd really like to come. Let me know how much it costs, and I'll reimburse you for the seat."

"Sure, if you don't mind being bored all evening."

"I won't be bored. I took ballet lessons in my earlier years, so I'm familiar with the routines. Besides, I like dance performances. My mother has a subscription to Miami City Ballet, but she goes with a friend. If I get tickets to a single show, will you keep me company?"

Brianna examined a spot on the floor. "Wouldn't you rather go to a cool dance club with your fiancé?"

Touché, Marla thought. "We broke up this morning. Arnie and I are just good friends. He's already got his eye on someone else. Didn't your father tell you our arrangement was, uh, temporary?" She glanced at Lindsay, but the instructor was already gliding down the hall.

"Dad said you were playing dangerous games."

"Oh, yeah?" *Dangerous from whose viewpoint?*

"Class is starting," Lindsay announced.

Brianna leapt up. "You don't need to wait around."

Before Marla could reply, Lindsay yelped. The dance instructor staggered to the side, her torso bent.

"What's the matter?" Marla called, rushing forward.

"Old back injury," Lindsay rasped. Her pale complexion indicated she'd never fully recovered.

Marla offered a steady arm. "Lean on me," she said while Brianna stood by, uncertainty written on her face.

Lindsay shook her head. "I'll be all right. Pills in my bag. I keep them with me, just in case. I can ask Tamar to start the warmups."

"Are you sure?"

Nodding, Lindsay compressed her lips.

"Nice nails," Marla commented, observing the teacher's fancy acrylics. "Who do you go to?"

"Denise at the New Wave."

"If you ever want to switch, we have a great manicurist at Cut 'N Dye."

"I'll keep it in mind."

Hunched over, Lindsay shuffled into the studio, gestured for Brianna to enter, then shut the door.

Lindsay's mention of pills reminded Marla that she'd never followed up on Hank, the pharmacist. Maybe his place would still be open. It was possible Jolene was one of his customers, and if so, she might have confided in him.

Unfortunately, when she passed by, the storefront was dark.

She'd look for him at the club tomorrow night when she met Tally there.

Her plans got waylaid Wednesday afternoon when she got home and found a message from Cookie on her answering machine.

"I have information that can't wait," Cookie's voice squealed. "I've got to work tonight. If you want to meet me, take the Royal Barge dinner cruise. I look after the birds on the island. It's crucial that you come if you want to know who killed Jolene. I've already made a reservation in your name."

Marla listened to the message twice more before phoning Tally. "I thought you wanted to snoop in Gloria's office tonight," her friend said in dismay.

"This is more important. If Cookie's information is valid, I won't need to sneak around the club. Wanna come along?"

"Me? Why don't you ask Dalton Vail? He's more appropriate as an escort. If he can't come, then I'll join you."

"Okay, I'll get back to you." Disconnecting from Tally, Marla dialed Vail's direct number at the police station.

"Marla, what is it? You know I'm busy," his gruff voice answered.

Her pulse accelerated at the sound of his low, masculine tone. "Cookie wants to see me tonight, and I thought you might like to come along. I believe she knows who killed Jolene."

"I wish I could get away, but I'm stuck here for a while," he said, regret filling his voice. "Don't you dare see that woman alone. If you can wait—"

"Thanks, Dalton, but I have to strike while the iron is hot, so to speak. I'll let you know if I learn anything."

Disappointed, she hung up and redialed Tally's number. "Vail can't come. You still want in?"

"Right on, girl. Dinner cruise, huh? Believe me, I'd rather eat than exercise any day."

Traffic along Route A1A was heavy as Marla headed south toward Bahia Mar. On the left stretched an expanse of beach ending at lapping waves. A veil of gray in a darkening sky blurred the horizon, but Marla wasn't interested in the scenery. She was anxious to discover what Cookie had learned. Signs directed her to park behind the Radisson Hotel. Stopping at a gate, she obtained a ticket, then drove toward a parking lot in the rear.

"I called ahead to add your reservation," she said to Tally as they strolled past a glass-bottomed boat charter. Her skin chilled in the nippy air, and she buttoned the suede jacket she'd worn over a cashmere sweater and dark pants. Tally looked snazzy as usual in a designer ensemble, her wavy locks fastened off her face with a tortoiseshell comb.

As they approached the ticket window, Marla examined her reflection. Her chin-length glossy brown hair curved inward at the edges, its wispy bangs gracing her forehead. She'd applied apricot lip crayon and mud shadow to complement her toffee eyes. *Too bad Dalton isn't here,* she thought regretfully. Tally was a good friend, but cruising down the river with the handsome detective would have been an interesting diversion. And in case things got rough—not that she anticipated any trouble—he would have been handy to have around.

The inside of the boat consisted of two rows of vinyl-strip chairs, six on each side of a center aisle. White overhead racks stored a supply of orange life vests. As Marla took a seat, she scanned the worn linoleum floor and faded blue paint peeling off the side walls that ended midway at a black railing, providing an open-air view of their surroundings.

"I hope it won't be too windy," Tally remarked, glancing at the family of tourists occupying a row in front. Seats were rapidly being filled, which surprised Marla since it was a weekday night. Then again, this was tourist season, so all attractions were bound to be crowded.

"Do you think Jolene's killer is on board?" she whispered.

A frown centered on Tally's brow. "That seems unlikely."

"You never know." She gave a furtive glance to the boat's occupants: a mix of families, couples, and prearranged groups. People chattered in French and German while seagulls soared past. A lady in nautical attire sat next to Marla. The woman wore a red, white, and blue striped shirt with a gold embroidered anchor; navy pants;

gold button earrings; and assorted necklaces that clinked when she moved. Great, thought Marla, now she and Tally wouldn't be able to talk in private.

The ship's horn blew, making her nearly jump out of her skin. Slowly, the boat backed away from the dock. Over a loudspeaker, Captain Randy introduced himself and the crew, mentioning there were three hundred people aboard. Heading west, they cruised by a yacht basin and into the Intracoastal Waterway.

"When will we reach the island?" Tally asked, checking her watch. "I'm hungry."

"You can enjoy the barbecue while I look for Cookie. If I recall from a previous visit, there's a number of parrots in cages hanging from trees around the walkways. Then again, maybe Cookie tends the animals in the show. She didn't give a specific place to meet her." Her gut clenched. "If Cookie uncovered a new piece of evidence, it's possible she tipped off the killer. Two people have died already. Someone is going to extremes, and I'm not even sure why."

Tally's attention centered on the million-dollar mansions facing the water shaded by sea grapes, queen palms, and spindly *Schefflera*. Banana plants hung over the river's edge. Descriptive commentary on the loudspeaker contributed to the background clatter of the ship's engine and the passengers' babble.

"What did Eloise tell Vail?" Tally asked.

"I'm not privy to that information. He doesn't confide in me. I should've asked Brianna. His daughter knows more about the case than anyone."

"Smart kid."

Tally's comment was meant to draw a reaction, but Marla merely stared at historic Stranahan House as they cruised by downtown Fort Lauderdale, known as the Venice of the South for its system of canals. Fortunately, the drawbridge was open, or they'd have been delayed. In her mind, an imaginary clock ticked away the minutes leading toward another disaster. The sooner they reached Cookie, the better.

Passengers exploded off the boat when they reached the island on the New River, where a barbecue dinner and a variety show awaited them. Marla veered away from the mob, spotting a beautiful white cockatoo in a cage. Raucous bird cries blended with songlike chirps as she found a pair of lovebirds and a toucan further along the path. No sign of Cookie.

Once everyone had herded into the main corral for the all-you-can-eat feast, Marla scoured the island. She and Tally split up to search the twisting gravel paths littered with dead leaves. Stars glinted in the night sky overhead, providing dim illumination for the heavily shaded trails. Skeletonlike branches stretched toward her, competing with thickly rooted ficus trees for domination.

Maybe she'd have better luck looking backstage where Cookie might be preparing for the show. *Wait, there's a sign partly hidden by that bougainvillea plant.* It led to an alligator pit. Wouldn't it be in Cookie's nature to feed the creatures?

With a purposeful stride, Marla ended up at the fenced-off crater. Peering over the edge, she wasn't prepared for the sight that greeted her: a woman's body, lying on the ground face-down, clad in jeans and a sweater. Even in the dim light, she could identify Cookie's strawberry blond hair.

Chapter
Eighteen

"I don't know how Cookie was killed," Marla commented to Nicole the next morning at the salon. "The police interviewed me and Tally. Cookie's body was still pliable when they arrived, meaning she'd met her end shortly before I discovered her, but there weren't any overt signs of violence."

Shuddering, Marla visualized the chaos that had followed after she'd notified the boat's crew. Then had come the fear that the murderer was still among them. Whoever had ambushed Cookie might stalk her next. Terror pursued her until she and Tally reached shore and the safety of her car.

"I imagine Detective Vail wasn't too happy to hear the news," Nicole said with a sympathetic grin. Cutting a client's hair at the next station, she snipped automatically.

Marla paused, hairbrush in hand. Her next appointment hadn't arrived yet, and she'd been cleaning her counter.

"All I heard from Dalton was how he'd warned me not to meet Cookie. Unlike the media, he's being very closemouthed about this case."

"Yeah, I saw the news report earlier this morning. A woman was found dead in the alligator pit at the Royal Barge dinner cruise. That's going to hurt their business! Tourists will shy away until the commotion dies down."

"Not necessarily," Marla commented. "It may have the opposite effect."

"Wasn't she the woman who picketed in front of your salon?" asked Nicole's customer, a scion of the community who'd been listening with interest.

"Yep, that's her." Marla clenched her teeth. No doubt the news story accounted for so many unexpected walk-ins today. Other folks wanted to assess her reaction. Normally, Thursdays tended to be quiet, but this morning had been incredibly hectic. While this wasn't the preferred method for increasing business at the cash register, Marla didn't begrudge the extra income.

Cookie's demise wasn't the only news making the rounds.

"Marla, I heard you and Arnie Hartman broke off your engagement," said Abby Whitehall, one of Marla's clients, later that morning. Possessing boundless energy, the taller woman used up calories faster than a marathon runner. She'd been thin as long as Marla had known her.

Giorgio piped in from across the room. "You should have heard Arnie moon over that blonde. *Mama mía!* I don't blame him." His hands imitated an hourglass figure.

"Is that so!" Abby exclaimed, her hazel eyes twinkling. "Arnie left you for another woman?"

"No, that's not what happened at all," Marla said. "I know Arnie likes Jill, I mean Hortense, and it doesn't bother me. He was upset because I'd spent the night at Dalton Vail's house."

"Oh! You're sleeping with the detective?"

"Marla, pick up the phone," yelled the receptionist from the front desk. "It's Tally Riggs."

"I'm in the middle of highlights. I'll call her back."

"So give me the juicy details," Abby urged, her gaze alight with curiosity. "Since when have you and Lieutenant Vail been a number? Are things really hot between you?"

"Pretty warm right now, *bubula*. He's mad at me for sleuthing on my own last night."

"Is he jealous over Arnie?"

"Our personal life is irrelevant until he solves this case. I spent the night at his house because someone threw a bomb in my window. He did me a mitzvah, that's all. Nothing happened between us—especially with his daughter, Brianna, playing chaperon."

"A bomb! Thank goodness you weren't hurt."

It was lunchtime when she finally returned Tally's call, dialing the number for Dressed to Kill Boutique. "Have you heard anything new about Cookie?" Marla said when Tally answered.

"No, sorry, I was hoping you'd spoken to Vail. That was so awful. I can't forget what the poor woman looked like, lying there like a broken doll." A heavy silence fell. "Anyway, that's not why I called. That man was here today, the one who buys clothes for his girlfriend and tries them on."

"What about him?"

"I realized why he looks so familiar. I think I've seen this guy at the club!"

"Perfect Fit?"

"You got it."

"Who is he? One of the members?"

"I'm not sure. Want to go tonight? I'll skip my aura class."

"Okay. That reminds me, I intend to stop by Eloise's office later. I'd like to know where she was last night."

As it turned out, Eloise wasn't to be found at her office, but she had signed in at the sports club when Marla and Tally showed up at seven o'clock that evening. Searching for her, they invaded the pool area, where a Splashfit class was underway—mostly senior citizens, it appeared from their uniformly gray hair. Steamy humidity mingled with a strong scent of chlorine as they passed the whirlpool, frothing and bubbling away.

"Marla!" hissed a nearby voice.

She whipped her head around and located the speaker, who was nearly submerged in the hot tub. Jill's blond hair was protected by a turban, and as she emerged from the water like a goddess, Marla noted that the head wrap provided more cover than her meager swimsuit. Jill grabbed a thick towel and draped it around her shapely torso.

"What are you doing here?" Marla demanded. "Have you seen Eloise?"

Jill waved a greeting to Tally. "I think Eloise went upstairs to use the machines. It's horrible about Cookie. You know, for a while I suspected her, but now . . ." Her voice trailed off.

Tally met her eye to eye. "You haven't talked to Detective Vail today, have you? Marla's not had any luck getting in touch with him."

"No, sugar. I had a nice shmooze with Arnie on the phone, though. That man is such a sweetheart. Do you know he asked me to attend his daughter's chorus concert?"

"Did you accept?" Marla had always thought school functions were the most boring events.

"Of course, and I'm so excited to meet his kids! I've always dreamed of having a family, but it didn't seem as though it would happen for me. Arnie may be a bit older, but that doesn't matter. He needs me."

"Oh, joy." Inwardly, Marla wished her luck. She had no desire to play mother to someone else's children or her own. Never mind that Brianna came with Dalton Vail. That didn't bear thinking about right now.

They walked together toward the women's locker room. Being next to two statuesque blondes made Marla feel like a shrimp. She entered the locker room under the arch of Jill's arm holding open the door. A cool rush of air-conditioning dried her skin.

"I wonder if Dalton is avoiding me. He blasted me on the phone last night for meeting Cookie. I told him you were with me, Tally, but it didn't make any difference. That man has to learn he can't control my actions. I'm not a shlemiehl he can push around."

"He cares for you," inserted Jill, a lopsided smile on her face.

Marla warmed toward her. The girl really could be nice when she exhibited her true feelings. "I know, but he shows it the wrong way." Luck was with her; Eloise sat on a bench in the locker room, sprinkling yellow powder on her toes.

"What is that stuff?" Marla blurted, seeking an answer to a question niggling in her mind.

Eloise glanced up. Her hair, normally coiffed after a visit to the salon, hung in wet strands as though she'd just showered. "It's an antifungal powder. Don't spread it around," she added facetiously.

"Oh, gross! You have athlete's foot?" Jill wrinkled her nose.

"Were you in here dusting that on your feet the night Jolene died?" Marla asked. "I saw some powder beneath her locker."

Eloise frowned, emphasizing the age lines on her round face. "I may have used it then, but I can't remember."

Plopping her bag on the bench, Marla signaled to Tally. "Go ahead and get changed if you want. I'll just be a minute." She turned to Eloise after her friend had walked off with Jill. "What happened when you left with Detective Vail yesterday? You didn't return for your appointment."

Hunching forward, Eloise hesitated before responding. "I was upset talking about Sam. The lieutenant seemed to think I might have been involved with his . . . accident. I know how it must have looked, my disappearing like I did. First Jolene, then Sam, and I'd suspected they were having an affair. Well, I got scared after what I saw in the parking lot."

Hoping to disguise her eagerness, Marla raised an eyebrow. "What was that?"

"I'll explain in a minute. After meeting you in the restroom, I had an argument with Sam over his involvement with Jolene. He wouldn't talk about it, and I was furious. I left the restaurant. We'd driven in separate cars, because I came directly from showing a client one of our properties. When I walked toward my car, I noticed a movement near his Chevy."

"You saw someone?"

She nodded. "Hank Goodfellow. I thought I saw your friend, too."

"Who?"

"Hortense, isn't it?"

"What was she doing?" Marla remembered Jill had excused herself from their table to retrieve a set of head shots from her car. She'd taken an inordinately long time in returning.

Eloise, a conspiratorial twinkle in her eyes, lowered her voice. "I think she was spying on Hank. He was tinkering with Sam's engine. I just assumed Sam had a problem with his car, and he'd spoken to Hank in the restaurant. I thought Hank was fixing it, but instead he might have been fixing the bomb. Later, I started putting two and two together. Jolene was one of Hank's customers. Maybe she'd threatened to expose his little side business. As a result, he may have killed her and then Sam because they were close."

Marla's gaze widened. "Did you tell Vail this?"

Reaching for a pair of socks, Eloise tilted her head. "The lieutenant is aware of Hank's extracurricular activities. His bureau's been investigating the illegal sale of drugs from Hank's pharmacy. Vail believes Hank may have some connection but is not the murderer."

"So why doesn't he bring Hank in for questioning?"

"He's waiting for evidence against him, so he can use it as leverage to get the man to talk."

"Is Hank here tonight?"

"No, I haven't seen him." Her eyes darted furtively about the room. "I wouldn't speak to him if I were you. He must be in cahoots with the killer."

"Doesn't Vail believe Hank set the bomb that killed your husband?"

"He mentioned something about trace evidence. I guess he's working on it but doesn't have solid proof."

"Hey, Marla, you getting changed or not?" Tally called, rounding a corner and peering at them.

"Where's Jill?" she asked. "Er, I mean Hortense. She prefers to be called by her middle name, you know."

"Hortense went upstairs," Tally explained patiently.

"Eloise, be careful." She felt the woman had been right to be afraid. Whoever killed Sam might believe his wife knew too much. "And if you have time, stop in at the salon tomorrow. I'll fit you into my schedule."

"What was that all about?" Tally asked while Marla threw on her gym clothes.

Quickly Marla reiterated what Eloise had told her. No one else was about, and they'd retreated to a distant corner of the locker room. "I'd like to get Gloria out of her office as we'd planned. Her files might tell us more about these people."

"Right. I'll tell her I'm considering a full membership, and I need her to go upstairs with me to answer some questions about the equipment. It won't give you much time."

Marla stuffed her bag into a locker and locked the door. After hoisting up her sweatpants, she pocketed the key. "Let's do it."

Waiting until she was sure no one else was about, Marla slipped into Gloria's office after Gloria left with Tally. Examining the clutter on her desk, Marla hesitated. She didn't want to displace items, but where to start? Stars rippled on a computer monitor as though a screen saver had activated. Personnel files might be listed there instead of in that locked file cabinet in the corner. It was a place to begin.

Seated at the desk, Marla swirled the mouse until the Windows desktop came into view. Looking under "My Documents" yielded unsatisfactory results. Perhaps she'd have better luck with a word processing program. Her heart rate increased when she hit the jackpot with a folder labeled "Staff" and another one, "Members." Scrolling down the staff list, Marla noted Tesla's address given as the street number she knew to be Betsy's house. Well, that wasn't much help. The rest of the details were rather mundane, with names, addresses, contact numbers, positions, and vacation schedules.

Turning to the member file, Marla found a reference to a spreadsheet program. Hoping it wasn't anything complicated, she brought up another window and noticed a discrepancy between members' initial fee dates and renewals.

She'd left the door partially closed, and when it was suddenly yanked open, she jerked upright in surprise. Slate's large form darkened the doorway. He glared at her with knitted brows. As he approached, amber eyes blazing like those of a tiger ready to pounce, Marla noticed those brows were unusually dark. They didn't match the medium-brown hair slicked back off his forehead.

Flushing guiltily, Marla clicked off the programs on screen, leaving the desktop icons displayed. Then she pushed herself up from the chair. "I, uh, was just admiring Gloria's computer system. I need to get a new one, and Gateway is one of my considerations."

"Liar." He stopped inches in front of her, fists clenched by his side. "What did you find out?"

She thrust her chin forward. "What are you hiding? Tesla lives with you, but her address given is your friend Betsy's."

"That's none of your business." A sheen of sweat broke out on his upper lip.

I'm getting to you, pal. "Tesla followed Amy one night. Did she tell you why?"

"I don't have to answer your questions." Grabbing her shoulders, he shook her until her teeth rattled.

"You'd rather talk to Detective Vail? Get your hands off me, or I'll charge you with assault." His height and shape merged with an image in her consciousness, and she gasped. "You're the one who attacked me with a broken bottle!"

Instantly, he stepped away. "I should've finished the job in the parking lot. A few cuts to your pretty face, and you'd have had a lot more to worry about. You're too nosy for your own good. I figured I could scare you off."

"Did you throw that Molotov cocktail through my window?"

"Huh?"

"Someone tossed a bomb into my house. The police have evidence. Would you care to confess now, or later in an interrogation room?"

"I don't know nothin' about that."

"Did you kill Jolene? Is that why you want me to quit investigating? You're responsible for the deaths of three people?"

His smug superiority was replaced by a look of fear. "What the hell are you talking about?"

Hearing voices outside in the corridor, Marla spoke quietly. "Sam Zelman and Cookie Calcone. Whoever killed Jolene might have murdered them, too. You have a history of violence, pal. The cops will want to bring you in, especially when I tell them how you've threatened me."

He stumbled backward, his bravado dissipated. "I only tried to scare you in the parking lot, nothin' else."

"Then what are you hiding?"

"Jolene knew. She knew a lot of things, like how Gloria rakes in extra money by manipulating commissions on the computer. Jolene figured it out when Gloria sent her repeated renewal notices."

"Is that what Jolene meant when she asked you if Keith was involved?"

"I never cut myself in for a share. Gloria would have broadcast what she'd learned about me."

Frustrated because he was revealing significant information, but not what she wanted to know about him, Marla shook her head. "What is that?"

"I can tell you," Tally's voice rang out loud and clear from where she leaned against the door jamb. "*He's* the man who comes into my boutique and changes into women's clothing!"

Striding into the office with Gloria at her heels, Tally pointed a finger at Slate. "I'll bet I know why such a mystery surrounds Tesla, the elusive massage therapist. You're looking at her. They even have the same letters in their names!"

Marla's mouth gaped. Gloria snickered, and Slate blanched.

"Is it true?" Marla croaked, even as the puzzle pieces mentally tumbled into place. Pantyhose in the massage suite, lipstick smeared on Slate's mouth, Betsy's obvious distress. No wonder, if her boyfriend preferred to dress in drag! "Why were you following Amy?" she demanded.

Slate's face crumbled. "Keith would have told our boss if I didn't do what he wanted. He's hot on Amy, so he ordered me to follow her to see who she hooks up with. The jerk doesn't understand she's not interested."

"That's because Amy likes you, stupid," said Gloria. "You're all a bunch of assholes. I'm the only one with brains around here." Her crimson lips pouted. "Now Marla, explain what you're doing in my office."

It was Marla's turn to feel cornered. "I understand Jolene learned you were cheating on customers and boosting your commissions. Did she threaten to expose you? Is that why you killed her?" She'd learned to go for the gut reaction, but she didn't really suspect Gloria. The girl wouldn't stoop to making bombs.

Gloria laughed raucously. "She couldn't have hurt me. But there were others whose reputations she could damage." Her glance flashed to Slate.

He raised his hands. "Hey, I didn't do it. I'd like to clear this up just to get the heat off. You were here the night Jolene drowned. Did you notice anyone other than Sharon and Amy in the lobby?"

"It was pretty quiet," Gloria admitted. "You might ask Lindsay who was in the locker room. She didn't leave until after Jolene went in for her massage. Maybe she saw someone else."

"Why was Lindsay still here?" Marla queried. "Hadn't Dancercize been over for at least a half hour?"

Gloria gave an evil grin. She was the type of person who enjoyed relating sordid gossip, Marla realized. "Hank Goodfellow had checked in earlier. I've seen the way those two act together. You should talk to him about it."

"Yes, I should." She signaled to Tally. "Let's get out of here. We've dug up enough dirt for tonight. These people need a shovel to cover up their sludge."

Chapter
Nineteen

Marla didn't get a chance to follow through on her visit to Hank Goodfellow's pharmacy right away. Hectic days at work and evenings out with friends consumed her time until the weekend was nearly over. A frantic call from Hortense in Vero Beach gave her the impetus she needed to carry on her investigation.

"Have you seen Jill lately?" Dr. Crone inquired. "She left a message on my machine Friday indicating she'd found the link to Jolene. I called her back, but no one answered."

Working in the kitchen, Marla cradled the phone on her shoulder. She slid on a pair of mitts to remove a lemon bread pudding that had finished baking in the oven. "Jill was at the sports club Thursday. I haven't seen her since, but maybe Arnie's gotten together with her. I can ask him for you."

A pause. "Have you told him about me? I mean, does he know about Jill playing my part?"

Marla detected a note of apprehension in Dr. Crone's voice. Did she still care about Arnie? "My lips remain sealed. Why don't I trace Jill and get back to you? If you hear from her in the meantime, please ask her to call me."

Putting the pan on a rack to cool, Marla puzzled over Jill's silence. Maybe the girl had accepted an audition out of town. Or perhaps she'd wanted to confirm her findings before returning Dr. Crone's call. Either way, she might have told Arnie.

Bagel Busters was on the way to Hank's drugstore. It was four o'clock on Sunday; both places might still be open. Rushed for time, Marla let Spooks outside to do his business in the backyard while she refrigerated the pudding. Fishing for a treat, she grabbed a piece of chocolate-covered halvah for a quick energy boost. A sigh of pleasure escaped her lips as the sweet sesame-seed candy melted in her mouth.

Spooks yipped at the door to be let back in. Stooping, Marla spared a moment to scratch behind his ears. "I'll pay attention to you when I come home," she promised, feeling guilty about leaving him alone again. After allowing him to lick her face, she straightened. Her purse was on the counter. Without bothering to check her appearance, she dashed out the garage exit. The denim jacket that matched her jeans should still be in her car. A chill wind whipped the air, and she shivered as she dove into the Toyota. Her long-sleeved silk blouse didn't provide much insulation, she thought, turning on the heater.

As she reversed from the driveway, she prayed under her breath. *Please don't let anything bad have happened to Jill.* Three people were dead so far. Even if Jolene's actions had brought about her own demise, that didn't explain why Sam or Cookie were targets unless self-protection was the motive. They might have uncovered Jolene's killer, which in turn made them a threat. Was that why a bomb had been tossed through her window? Someone feared she was getting too close to the truth?

Slate had admitted he'd attacked her in the parking lot. He'd been afraid her snooping would reveal his secret, but he'd seemed confused when she mentioned the Molotov cocktail. That indicated to her he wasn't the car bomber, either. He didn't possess the aptitude required to make explosives, regardless of how much instruction was available on the Internet.

Dr. Crone was a scientist, an inner voice whispered. And Jill worked at Stockhart Industries, albeit in public relations. Other than those two, someone had provided Jolene with lab reports she substituted for her own. Learning that person's identity was the key.

Wait a minute, she thought. Hadn't Cookie said her ex-spouse used to work at Jolene's plant before he'd been fired? What could have happened to cause his dismissal? Jolene had been his superior. Could he have discovered her deception? Or was he the source of those fake reports?

Dear Lord, another avenue to follow, Marla thought wearily. She wondered if the man had stayed in town, and considered how to find him. Relatives must have notified him about Cookie's death. Marla had been so wrapped up in her own concerns that she'd forgotten to ask about the woman's funeral arrangements.

A line of customers was waiting outside Bagel Busters when Marla arrived at the shopping strip where her salon was located. Arnie must be serving early-bird dinners, she thought wryly. The senior citizen crowd was out in force. She allowed herself the luxury of glancing into the rearview mirror to check her hair. The reddish highlights glinted in the fading afternoon light. Opening her purse, she withdrew a tube and applied apricot lip gloss. Now she was ready to conquer the world.

"Hey, Marla," Arnie called when she'd elbowed her way inside his establishment. Waving, he grinned in unabashed delight from behind the cash register.

Wondering how he always managed to look so manly in a T-shirt, jeans, and full-length apron, Marla approached with an answering smile. Ruth, one of the waitresses, greeted her while she waited for Arnie to finish giving change to a customer. "Have you spoken to Jill lately?" she asked at the first opening.

"We went out Friday night. I hope you don't mind." His dark eyes gleamed expectantly as though he would have liked her to protest.

"Doesn't bother me!" she said breezily. "I'm glad the two of you have hit it off. Has she, uh, told you anything new about herself?"

The grin disappeared from his face. "Hortense, alias Jillian

Barlow, confessed her secret identity. I was upset that she'd lied to me, until I remembered we'd done the same thing to her. Then I thought how brave she was to investigate Jolene's drowning."

"The real Hortense Crone—who is married, by the way—has been trying to get in touch with her, but Jill hasn't answered her telephone. Any idea if she went away for the rest of the weekend?"

"She was excited about something but wouldn't tell me more until she checked her facts."

"Ah! She left a message for Dr. Crone, who works at the Marine Annex in Vero Beach. Apparently, Jill found a link to Jolene's killer."

"Jill explained her role to me and how she's grateful to Hortense for helping her. She wouldn't do anything stupid, do you think?" A worried frown transformed his features.

"Maybe Dalton can enlighten us. I believe he's working today. I'll stop off there on my way to Hank's pharmacy."

Promising to let him know what she learned, Marla left to head for the central police station. As she'd surmised, Dalton was mired in paperwork when she was admitted to his office. Nonetheless, her heart somersaulted when his gaze brightened at the sight of her. He looked pretty decent himself, his broad shoulders encased in a white dress shirt. He'd loosened his tie and appeared relaxed, with his thick hair ruffled and a mug of coffee on his desk.

His glance scanned her denim-clad figure before settling on her face. "Sorry I haven't called lately, but I've been busy."

"That's not why I'm here." She plopped herself down on one of his chairs. "Dr. Crone has been trying to get in touch with Jill, who left a message on her answering machine that she'd found the link to Jolene's killer. When Arnie saw Jill Friday night, she was excited but wouldn't talk. He says she wanted to gather more information before coming to you."

A bemused smile curved his mouth. "You mean Arnie knows the lady's real identity?"

"She told him the truth. They like each other, Dalton. I'm so glad for Arnie."

His gaze captured hers. "Me, too."

She blinked, realizing she could easily get lost looking into the depths of his smoky eyes. "Jolene passed off someone else's lab test results as her own. My guess is, Cookie found the source. Jill may have pinpointed the same person, in which case I'm worried for her."

"You think Jolene had a deal going with someone else who works in a lab?"

"That's what Cookie implied. The question is who? The same culprit who sold Jolene the lab reports may be the person who designed Sam's car bomb and heaved that explosive through my window."

"Sold to Jolene? You mean someone made money on their deal?"

Annoyance puckered her brow. Was he being obtuse on purpose? "Why else would the perp contribute his own reports to be used by someone else in an unethical manner?"

Vail regarded her with a patient smile. "He could be unhappy in his job, wanting to get back at a colleague who wronged him. There are lots of reasons. Find the perpetrator, and you'll have your motive."

Marla brightened. "Possibly Jolene got disenchanted and broke off her end of the bargain. I don't think she would've exposed her partner in crime, because it would have brought forth her own duplicity. But she must have angered or threatened this person somehow."

Picking up a pen, Vail studied her, as though weighing how much to say. "Have you spoken to Hank Goodfellow lately?"

Her jaw dropped open. "He's a pharmacist. Do you think he's—"

"Goodfellow doesn't work in a lab."

"So why . . . wait, Slate implied Hank and Lindsay were interested in each other. Isn't Hank married?"

"Hank's got problems, and his rocky marriage is only one of them. We're about to bust him wide open."

"What exactly is he messed up in?" she asked encouragingly, as though Eloise hadn't already told her.

"Illegally selling prescription drugs. One of his clerks has turned informant, and we've obtained a list of his private customers. Apparently, Hank thinks he's doing them a service, but the law doesn't see it that way."

"That must've been what made Wallace Ritiker so upset. He was afraid he'd be implicated. Is his name on the list?"

Vail shook his head. "Not on that one, but he may have been paid to turn his back on the scheme. Jolene was one of Hank's customers. She'd been pretty vocal about protesting his recent price hike. You'd mentioned Lindsay. Isn't she Brianna's dance teacher? She takes some sort of pain med Hank supplies."

"She hurt her back a while ago," Marla replied, "and it still bothers her. Was Sam one of his customers, too? I don't see how he enters the equation. What did Eloise tell you?"

"Not much I didn't already know." He clicked the ballpoint pen in and out.

Marla sat forward as another idea flooded her mind. "Could Hank have supplied Jolene's gelatin capsules?"

A muscle in his jaw twitched. "That's a distinct possibility."

Scraping her chair back, she stood. "I'm going to see him."

"You are not." His bulk rose. "This investigation is nearly a wrap. He's about to go down for his little side business. Steer clear, understand?"

"Are you giving me orders, lieutenant? I don't believe I'm a member of the police force."

"Marla, please."

His pleading tone wormed into her heart. "I won't screw things up for you, but I'm concerned about Jill. If she knows who the killer is, she's in danger."

Walking to her car, she realized they hadn't identified any new suspects, other than Hank, who possessed the skills to make a bomb. Dr. Crone? Heck, she lived in Vero Beach. Besides, she'd sent the actress to learn who had harmed Jolene.

Wasn't there another chemical plant in town? Maybe their personnel files held some answers. Certainly it was worth a try, but most likely, they wouldn't be open until tomorrow. Hank's pharmacy seemed the best bet.

Fortunately, he hadn't locked his doors when she arrived. Ignoring the "Closed" sign in the window, Marla pushed through the entrance. Obviously figuring he'd seen the last of his customers, Hank had removed his white coat and was securing the cash register when she coughed to announce her presence.

Hank glanced up, his blue eyes looking startled at first, then relieved. "Oh, it's you."

"Who were you expecting?" she replied. *The cops, maybe?*

Giving a sheepish grin, he ran a hand through his thinning hairline. "I'm just about to lock up, but since you bring your mom's prescriptions in a lot, what can I do for you?"

Marla leaned on the counter. "I've been having headaches lately, and over-the-counter medicines aren't working. What have you got that's stronger? Forget my insurance card. I'm willing to pay cash."

He leveled an appraising stare at her. "Don't you hang around with that police detective?"

"I've helped him with a couple of cases."

"I think you'll have to see a doctor."

She smiled in a beguiling fashion. "Hank, I understand you've helped people. It's not exactly a secret. You probably figure you're doing them a kindness, especially with the way managed-care plans deny benefits these days."

His guarded expression didn't soften, so she tried another tack. "Look, I know law enforcement doesn't take kindly to folks supplying certain medications without a prescription. It's a shame, because patients can't even get a doctor's appointment unless they're dying. You're treading the line between healer and druggist. In some cultures, that's acceptable, but not in ours. In fact, if I were to give you a word of warning, I'd say the shit is about to hit the fan. Get my drift, pal?"

"Why are you here? You don't usually have headaches, do you?"

"Wally was afraid you'd drag him in. Did you bribe him so he'd look the other way? He was mighty upset after that break-in."

"The thieves stole my money," Hank said. "Ritiker felt I should've been more security-conscious."

She raised an eyebrow. "Are you sure you didn't stage that robbery yourself to cover up your cash flow imbalances? I'd heard you raised prices recently, and Jolene didn't approve. Did she threaten to blow the whistle on your lucrative sideshow?"

Hank slammed a fist down on the counter. "Don't implicate me! I don't know anything about her death."

"She swallowed a couple of capsules, thinking they were gelatin, but they contained sedatives. Did you supply them, Hank?"

His oblong face sagged. The pinkish jowls reminded Marla absurdly of a turkey's wattle. All he needed were a few tufts of hair standing on end. "I knew I'd get into trouble. *She* said to make up a bottle of capsules that looked like Jolene's. If I didn't, she'd produce evidence against me. She was angry because I hadn't filed for divorce like I'd promised."

"Is that why you fixed a bomb in Sam's car, because your friend ordered it?"

"No, I knew what she'd planned. I opened his hood to see if I could dismantle the device, but I'm no good with wires."

"Eloise saw you. She figured you'd bumped off Jolene to keep her silent, then murdered Sam. Eloise suspected Jolene and Sam were having an affair, and she gathered you knew about it and were afraid Jolene had confided in Sam."

"That's absurd. Of course, Jolene was seeing Sam. *She* told me that Sam was their contact person."

"Huh? Who are you talking about?"

A sly look entered his eyes. "You don't know, do you?"

"Eloise also saw Jill in the parking lot. Hortense," she added at his perplexed frown. A sinking feeling knotted her stomach. "Was she . . . the one who ordered sedatives that looked like Jolene's gelatin capsules?" Jill hadn't come to town yet, unless she'd arrived earlier than she'd let on. But she hadn't been in the locker room at the sports club that day. Whoever switched the containers had to be present.

Hank picked up his keys and rounded the counter to face her directly. "Ask your police friend. I'm outta here." He headed for the door, gesturing for her to follow.

"Cookie Calcone is dead."

That stopped him cold. Pivoting, he glowered at her. "That bitch should have minded her own business. She always was a troublemaker."

"Cookie discovered Jolene's supplier of test data. You *are* aware Jolene was falsifying lab reports?"

He shrugged. "I don't know the details."

"You said Sam was Jolene's contact, but she had to have been buying test results from someone at another chemical plant."

"Maybe Sam acted as their go-between." His brows knitted pensively. "That does make sense, when I add in what you've been saying."

A snort of exasperation escaped her lips. "Will you tell me who you mean?"

He reached for the doorknob. "Since you were so kind to pass on a warning to me, I'll pass on this tip to you. Denise at the New Wave knows the details."

She'd heard that name before. "Who?"

"The manicurist. I remember my . . . friend was real angry the week before Jolene died. She'd mentioned hearing some gossip while she was getting her nails done, and that's what made her ask for the capsules."

"I don't get it."

"You're a hairstylist. Ladies confide in you, right? I'd guess they talk to their manicurist, too."

"Hank, this person whose name you won't reveal, she's dangerous. Three people have been killed. Whether or not you innocently supplied those sedatives, you're implicated, and I have a feeling the police already know. Why don't you get a lawyer?"

His mouth tightened, and he ripped open the door. "It'll be a relief at this stage. I could never have kept her in the high-mannered way she wanted."

Pausing, he regarded Marla with a hooded look. "Marla, please don't think ill of me. I've been doing people a service, giving them what they need and what our health care system isn't providing. It's tough enough to remain competitive with the big chains and with insurance companies limiting payments. I could have been doing worse."

How? By dealing in cocaine traffic? Disgusted with his attitude, she watched Hank drive away while contemplating her next move. The New Wave wasn't likely to be open on Sundays, so her visit to the manicurist would have to wait. Realizing she was close to the truth, she bit her lower lip. If only Jill were here, they could compare notes.

Walking along the deserted shopping strip, Marla found a pay phone and dialed Vail's house to see if he was home yet. No one answered, not even Brianna. The girl should be there doing her school work. Vail's daughter needed a guiding hand, she thought, but that wasn't her job.

Feeling forlorn, she decided to head for home. Dusk invaded the winter sky, and she didn't relish being caught in another empty parking lot. Storefronts receded like so many frozen sentinels as she marched forward, footsteps echoing on the pavement. A prickly sensation ran up her neck, making her hesitate in front of her Toyota. Should she look for stray wires beneath the hood? She'd been occupied with Hank for nearly a half hour, enough time for someone to tamper with the vehicle.

Unable to ignore a sense of foreboding, she crouched on the ground and glanced underneath the car. Nothing unusual dangled below. *Examine the engine*, she told herself, hoping she remembered how to open the hood. Being mechanically impaired, she'd always relied on Stan for car maintenance. Since their divorce, the local dealership did the job.

Spreading her fingers, she found a latch and exposed the engine. She leaned forward, but her purse strap slid off her shoulder and she fumbled to grab the handbag. Before she completely regained her balance, the hood crashed down on her shoulders, knocking the breath from her lungs. A small, hard object jabbed the small of her back.

"Turn around real slow," said a husky female voice.

The pressure eased from her shoulders as her assailant lifted the hood. Waves of pain assaulted her muscles as she straightened. Marla turned carefully. When she saw who stood in front of her, aiming a gun at her head, her heart skipped a beat.

Chapter
Twenty

"What's the matter, Lindsay? Doesn't teaching dance classes give you enough money? Just what is your day job anyway?"

With her crystal blue eyes, the waves of soft blond hair clipped back off her face, and her slender body encased in a jogging suit, Lindsay barely looked a day over eighteen. Certainly not like a killer, Marla thought.

Lindsay's face contorted in a twisted smile. "I work at Listwood Pharmaceuticals over by Sawgrass Mills Mall in the Industrial Park."

"So you're the one!" Dozens of questions sprang to her tongue, but she held her silence.

"You think you're so smart, don't you?" Lindsay sneered. "Let's see how well you follow directions. Get in your car. We'll drive to the sports club."

"It's closed by now!" On Sundays, the place shut its doors at five o'clock.

"How convenient," the dance teacher observed. "It makes things easier. It'll appear as though you were using one of the machines and didn't notice the club was closing. What a shame no one was there to help you when you had an accident."

Lindsay gestured with her gun, and Marla complied by slipping inside her car. But any intention of sliding out the opposite door was halted when Lindsay grabbed her wrist.

"You do anything foolish, and you're dead." Lindsay maneuvered beside her on the passenger seat and aimed the gun at her head.

Keeping calm, Marla started the engine. Neither of them wore seat belts. Perhaps she could swerve the car or sideswipe a utility pole to knock Lindsay off balance. Then she'd throw open the car door and tumble outside. Wrestling with Lindsay over the weapon seemed an unattractive option. Although she'd never had a gun pointed at her before, she realized it might go off accidentally. She didn't know enough about the things to determine whether this one had a safety or not. Vail could help her. Where was the man when she needed him?

"Why did you kill Jolene?" Marla asked, heading south on Pine Island Road.

Folds creased Lindsay's smooth brow. "No harm in telling you now, since you won't be able to repeat my story to anyone. I didn't have much money when I grew up, and I was determined to accumulate enough to be comfortable. My boss at Listwood Pharmaceuticals didn't advance me fast enough. I thought I'd impress him by obtaining formulas from a rival company. Sam Zelman, who helped me find an apartment when I moved to town, told me about this woman who worked at Stockhart Industries."

"Jolene," Marla rasped, hoping for a break in the traffic so she could make a move to freedom.

Lindsay's aim didn't falter. "Jolene was unhappy because she'd been passed over for promotion. She'd been griping to fellow members at Perfect Fit Sports Club where she belonged. Sam picked up on her dissatisfaction and asked if she wanted to earn the raise she would have had in a higher position."

Understanding dawned. "So Sam became the contact between you and Jolene."

"That's right. My boss, Rudy, was pleased when I presented him with our competitor's formulas. As a reward, he gave me twenty percent and Jolene got the other eighty percent of his payment. I felt I

deserved more, so I made an offer to Jolene to sell her our test results, which were more favorable than hers. She paid me better than
Rudy, but it wasn't enough for the risks I took.

"Jolene was too greedy. She wanted more money for the formulas
she provided to Rudy, maybe to compensate for the payments she
gave me. Up until that point, she didn't know my name. Sam got a
cut to act as our go-between. But one day, Denise opened her big
mouth."

"Denise at the New Wave?"

"Yeah." Lindsay's glacial expression told Marla what she thought
of gossip mongers. "The stupid manicurist blabbed about her other
client who worked in a laboratory and how she was screwing her boss.
Jolene looked me up and demanded more money, otherwise she'd
stop our exchange. I couldn't risk her telling Rudy what was going on."

"So you decided to eliminate the threat."

"My job was at stake. You don't know how hard it was back when
I had to scrape to survive. I'd come too far to give up everything I'd
achieved."

The traffic light ahead turned yellow, and a car in front zoomed
forward. Reaching the intersection, Marla slammed on the brakes at
the same time she reached for the door handle.

Something hard crashed into the side of her head as she prepared
to catapult herself from the vehicle. White-hot pain exploded behind her eyes, blurring her vision. While she slumped, immobilized,
Lindsay tugged her to the passenger side and traded places.

"Try that again and I'll pull the trigger. I'd rather not do it that
way, but I will if necessary." Lindsay pressed the accelerator when
the light changed and sped toward the turn for the sports club.

Marla's head reeled. "If you think I'm just going to let you murder me, you're mistaken," she croaked, her mouth dry. "You won't
get away with it. Jill is onto you."

Lindsay gave a raucous laugh. "That bimbo won't be bothering
me. I paid a friend to call her, pretending to be a former associate of
Jolene. He implicated Dr. Crone. Jill took off for Vero Beach first
thing Saturday morning."

"But Hortense called me. She hadn't heard from Jill all week-end."

"The girl is probably sneaking around, trying to collect evidence. I'm not worried about her showing up."

Marla grew more desperate as Lindsay turned in to the entrance to Perfect Fit. The parking lot was deserted, offering no protection when she emerged from the car with Lindsay jamming the weapon in her back.

"I suppose you have a key to the place," Marla commented wryly. She clung to her purse, mentally assessing its contents for some-thing she could use in self-defense. Too bad she hadn't kept her ex-pensive shears. They'd come in handy once before in an unpleasant situation. Metal nail file? Maybe.

Marching forward, she stood stock-still as directed while Lindsay keyed the lock. Running wouldn't get her far if she tried to bolt. Her knees wobbled, and her head felt filled with cotton. She'd probably topple over at twenty paces. *Keep her talking.* Surely there must be some way she could escape.

The interior of the club was brightly lit, and Lindsay prodded her toward the left, past the massage suite and administrative offices to a staircase.

"How did you manage to switch Jolene's gelatin capsules for the sedatives?" Marla asked, wincing from a shooting back pain as she slowly climbed the stairs. Her leg muscles quivered, and she grip-ped the railing to steady herself. Her temple throbbed from the blow she'd received.

Lindsay grasped her shoulder from behind. "Hank made a bottle with capsules that looked exactly like her gelatin supply. I wanted something lethal, you know, but he tricked me. No matter; it did the job."

"Hank said you were angry that he hadn't filed for a divorce." She stumbled and almost fell, but Lindsay steadied her. The top of the stairs was just ahead. This area of the gym was dark, with machines rising out of the gloom like misshapen cypress stumps in a swamp.

"We were lovers," Lindsay confessed. "He was afraid I'd go to the police with what I knew about his money schemes. That's why he gave me the sedatives. Did Cookie tell you I left in the middle of Dancercize ostensibly to make a phone call? I exchanged the capsules then."

"Is that why you killed her?"

"She didn't remember right away. Later, when it came back to her, Cookie realized I'd had the opportunity to enter the locker room while Jolene was occupied in the studio. It didn't take much more for her to figure out my connection to Jolene."

"How did you do it? There wasn't any blood."

"We keep syringes in our labs. Easy to fill one with potassium cyanide. She wasn't expecting me to jump her on that island."

Reaching the top landing, Marla hesitated. "What about Sam? And how did you switch the gelatin back for the bottle of sedatives?" Pivoting, she faced Lindsay and put on a brave front she didn't feel.

Lindsay climbed the last step and aimed the gun point-blank at Marla's chest. "I didn't leave the club that night after Dancercize. Jolene had mentioned she was going for a massage. I waited in an unoccupied office and then sneaked into the locker room from the back entrance."

"You left some resin beneath her locker. I should've picked up on that, but I thought it might have been Eloise's foot powder."

"Go on over there," Lindsay pointed. "You're going to have an accident with the weights." When she was satisfied Marla was obeying, she continued. "Eloise was a real fool. Sam didn't die because he was having an affair with Jolene. I fixed that bomb because he was the only one who could connect me and Jolene."

"Why didn't he say something to the cops?"

Lindsay snickered, a malevolent expression on her face. "Sam had already spent time in the clinker, and he didn't want to drag his name through that muck again. The shlemiehl thought he was saving his wife further disgrace by keeping quiet, but he asked me for more money. Me! Why should I have to sacrifice?"

"If the manicurist hadn't alerted Jolene to who you were, would you have killed her?"

"Probably not. Proves it can be dangerous getting your nails done, huh?"

Intent on listening, Marla stumbled over a flat bench. Before she could regain her balance, Lindsay hurtled forward, slamming her in the chest. She tumbled backward, hitting her head on a horizontal weight bar and ending up sprawled on the green vinyl pad. She lay on her back, staring at her assailant.

"This weight bar will crush your ribs," Lindsay gloated, dropping the gun. "Whoever finds your body will believe you overstretched your abilities and lost control."

Marla heard a strange gurgling cry that seemed to come from across the room. "What's that?" she said, rolling to her side and out from Lindsay's grasp.

"Oh, that's just Brianna."

"What?"

Lindsay seized the moment to grab a clump of her hair. Twisting Marla's head, she thrust her neck against the protruding metal bar. "The little brat asked me a question Tuesday night. My back hurt so I wasn't paying attention, and I told her where I worked. That was a mistake, because I realized she might tell her father. When no one was home today, I knocked on her door and told her you needed help to solve this case. It was a lame excuse, but the stupid child fell for it. You'd think she'd know better with her father being a cop."

Dear Lord. Tears choked Marla's throat, which Lindsay forced against the bar until it dug into her skin. "No!" she screamed even as her breath was cut short.

Her windpipe was slowly being crushed. Pain no longer became an issue when her lungs wouldn't fill. Rage energized her, and she used the boost of adrenalin to kick backward. Her foot connected with something solid. Lindsay howled, loosening her grip. Marla staggered upright, clasping her throat. A raspy breath provided oxygen. Another breath brought clarity of purpose. She had to get to the girl and save them both.

"Brie, I'm coming," she shouted, taking a swing at Lindsay. The blow glanced off Lindsay's chin. Marla spun around and ran. Metal poles sticking out from machines turned the room into an obstacle course. She crashed into a Gravitron 2000, shaking its pulley but not its stack of weights.

Snarling, Lindsay retrieved a heavy chrome dumbbell and charged. Marla sidestepped past a Reebok Body Trec and leaped aside when Lindsay whipped the dumbbell through the air by her ear. If only she could find something to use as a weapon. She'd dropped her handbag when Lindsay had first assaulted her at the top of the stairs, and Marla doubted she could lift a free weight as easily as Lindsay could. Her only hope was to reach the exit. But where would that leave Brianna?

Her heart hammered as she dodged Lindsay's repeated attempts to bash her brains in. She reached the treadmills, where Brianna was bound by the wrists and gagged. One flick of a switch, and Lindsay could put the machine on lethal overdrive. Dropping to her knees, Marla followed the wire and yanked the plug. That was quicker than fumbling with knots. The girl's dark eyes glistened with fear as she tried desperately to free herself from the nylon cords binding her arms.

"Hold on," Marla urged. "I'll get us out of here." She thrust her body between Lindsay and Brianna.

Lindsay raised the dumbbell. Marla knew she had to disable her, but how?

She'd be top-heavy holding up that weight. Crouching, Marla darted sideways, then reversed course. With a wild yell, she butted Lindsay in the side like a rampaging bull. Lindsay gave her a startled glance before tumbling to the floor. Shrieking when an end of the dumbbell bounced on her ribs, she lay flat on her back. Marla followed through by kicking Lindsay's chin and was gratified by the sound of her teeth cracking.

"Don't mess with Brianna," she growled, "or you'll answer to me." She turned her attention to the child. "Hang loose, honey. I'll call for help and then find something to cut you free. Let me take that gag off." Wincing, Marla peeled the duct tape as carefully as she could.

Her mouth quivering, Brianna tugged at her bonds. Her braided hair swung with her efforts. "Don't leave me," she pleaded. Gone were the bratty, defiant mannerisms. Her face, gazing up at Marla's, displayed a vulnerability that she'd kept hidden before.

Marla never thought she could care this much for a child after Tammy's tragic death. That chapter in her life had been closed, but now she realized it had only lain dormant. Dammit, Brianna had awakened feelings that she hadn't wanted aroused. It only brought pain when someone you loved was hurt.

Unable to repress her surge of emotion, Marla patted the girl's arm. "Don't worry. I'm taking Lindsay with me, and I know just where I'll put her."

Lindsay seemed to have forgotten about the weapon she'd left on the other side of the room. Since she was subdued for the moment, Marla trotted to the bench press and retrieved the gun. She used it to prod Lindsay from the floor. Like two drunken sailors, they stumbled downstairs and into the women's locker room. Marla remembered the metal tanning booths from before. Three of them carried red-and-white signs warning of danger from ultraviolet radiation.

When Lindsay realized what Marla intended, she regained her senses. "Bitch!" she screamed, ignoring the weapon Marla brandished. Lowering her head, she rushed forward.

Marla swung the gun, banging it against Lindsay's ear. Stunned, Lindsay staggered back. Realizing she still needed to stop the woman, Marla raised her knee and thrust a foot into her assailant's stomach. With a grunt, Lindsay careened backward into the booth. Its interior, surrounded by ultraviolet lights arranged in vertical rows, and with a metal mesh floor, permitted standing room only. Marla slammed the door shut. Spying a tall Detecto scale nearby, she shoved it along the floor until it blocked the booth's exit.

There, she thought, *that should keep Lindsay temporarily.*

Noticing her fingers trembling as they held the gun, Marla dropped it into a receptacle. First she'd call for help from the reception desk, then she'd find a tool to cut Brianna's bonds. Maybe Vail would consider bringing his paperwork home on weekends hereafter. It wasn't wise to leave the girl alone—not that he'd listen to her advice.

When the police finally arrived, Vail was driving his own car. The first words out of his mouth reminded her of Stan.

"I can't trust you to stay out of trouble, can I?" His remonstrative tone set her nerves on edge. "No sooner do you walk out of my office door than you step in sheep dip."

Marla wasn't quelled by his furious glance. Standing in the lobby, she squared her shoulders. "You mean *drek*, don't you? Shouldn't you be more concerned for your daughter?"

"Huh? What's Brianna got to do with this?"

Brianna chose that moment to pop into view. Marla had opened one of the massage suites and suggested the child rest until the authorities arrived. At the sight of her slim figure in jeans and sweater with her braid askew, Vail's face paled. Hadn't he ever considered that his family might be vulnerable because of his job? *A good reason not to get more involved with him*, Marla's inner voice replied. But her resolve dissipated as Brianna came to her defense.

"Give her a break, Daddy. Marla just saved my life."

Vail's eyebrows lifted heavenward, while Marla felt tears threaten for the second time that night. Would wonders never cease?

Chapter
Twenty-one

"So why did Lindsay do it?" Arnie asked, his arm draped around Jill's shoulder.

Marla, who sat next to Dalton Vail at the Macaroni Grill, regarded Arnie and Jill across from them. Also part of their group celebration were Tally and Ken, and Dr. Crone and her husband, who'd driven down from Vero Beach so Hortense could finally confront Arnie in person.

"She had a deal going with Jolene," Marla explained. "Both of them felt as though they should have received more recognition at work. Jolene sold trade formulas guarded by her company. In return, Lindsay sold lab test data that Jolene substituted for her own reports. Their deal went sour when Jolene learned Lindsay's identity through their mutual manicurist and demanded more money."

"Ironic, isn't it?" Tally put in, her long hair secured in a French twist. "People you confide in, like your manicurist or hairdresser"—she glanced at Marla—"can blab to the next person and seal your fate."

Marla sipped her Coke. "Professionals don't spread gossip. That won't happen in my salon."

"Yeah, right!" Tally laughed. "Where else do you get some of the best information to help you solve these cases?"

"Marla's not a schnook," Arnie said, coming to her defense. "She's talking about her staff, not the customers."

Marla addressed Jill, who seemed perfectly happy nestled in the curve of Arnie's arm. "Please stop in for a complimentary session. Your highlights look as though they could use a lift, and those ends need trimming. I'd like to show you what I can do." She smiled graciously.

"Sure, Marla, when I have a chance. Work is keeping me busy, and I've talked my boss into giving me flexible hours so I can go to auditions. This past week has been hectic."

In the week since Lindsay was arrested, Jill had blossomed into a truly delightful person. No longer putting on false airs to gain information, she'd become a frequent visitor to Bagel Busters during her off-hours. Her trip to Vero Beach last weekend had been fruitful in that she'd finally convinced Hortense, once she realized Lindsay had set her on a false trail, to visit Palm Haven to meet Arnie.

Their meals arrived, and everyone dug in voraciously. His mouth stuffed, Arnie fielded a question to Hortense. "Do you feel satisfied now that your cousin's murderer is in jail?"

The scientist wiped a dribble of tomato sauce off her chin. "Yes, I do, and Jill helped explain to Stockhart Industries executives how Jolene had been falsifying reports. They agreed to make amends in their animal testing methods. From what you told me about her, I think Cookie would have been happy."

Marla's appetite lagged. Three people were unjustly dead, and Eloise had lost her husband. She'd stopped in to get her hair done and told Marla how she'd already felt estranged from Sam. His loss didn't disturb her as much as his involvement in another nasty scheme. He could have exposed Lindsay, but he didn't do so because it would have meant revealing his role. Yet if he'd talked, he might still be alive. Eloise had wondered whether they might have been able to reconcile his past and move on.

That opportunity was gone now, but there were others. Arnie glowed in Jill's presence, and their relationship seemed headed in a good direction. He'd finally met the real Hortense, who'd laughingly admitted her high school crush on him.

The only downside was Brianna, who'd wanted to drop out of dance school. Marla figured a different teacher would take over Lindsay's classes. She'd encouraged the girl to finish the year, buying a ticket to her recital to clinch the argument.

"Is Brianna okay?" she asked Vail, who'd been unusually quiet. He'd brought his daughter to the restaurant, unwilling to leave her home alone. She was sitting at a separate table with Josh and Lisa, Arnie's children.

"She'll be fine." His molten gray eyes avoided hers.

She noticed he'd barely touched his meal. This was the first time any of his cases had hit home, and it had struck him hard. Doubtless there were counselors in his department who could help if necessary, but he'd probably rebound on his own. He'd need to rewire his thinking about his daughter's safety without getting obsessive; that's all.

"I'm sure you've warned her about strangers," Marla said, covering his hand with hers. "But someone you're familiar with is trickier. My mom and I used to have a special code. If anyone said my mother had sent for me, I could believe them only if they gave the proper phrase."

"That sounds like Anita." He smiled and squeezed her hand. "Brianna said you bought a ticket to her recital. That was kind of you."

"Actually, I bought two tickets. I thought I'd bring my mother along. She likes dance concerts." *And it won't hurt for Ma to meet your daughter—not that I'm getting so involved with you.* Her brow creased as a memory tugged at her.

"What is it?"

"My mother left a message on my machine. She has something important to tell me. In my haste to get ready for tonight, I forgot to return her call."

"Want to use my cell phone?"

"No, thanks. I'll get back to her in the morning. She'll want to hear about this evening anyway." She gave him a coy glance. "I'm glad you're not working late hours these days."

He grinned, his eyes lighting up with pleasure. "I was putting in too much overtime. It feels good to lighten the load for a change. Now I'll have more time to spend with the people I care about."

His affectionate gaze made her squirm. "Brianna got you a seat for the dance recital. I hope you won't have to work late then."

"I'll make it a point to be there. By the way, didn't you mention you'd help me plan Brianna's thirteenth birthday party?"

She groaned inwardly. "I guess I did. When is it?"

"After yours, which is in a few weeks, I believe?"

Arnie interrupted. "Remember, Jill and I have a date with you guys for Marla's birthday dinner."

"I'll just gain more weight," she griped, but a smile lit her face.

Vail's gaze leisurely traveled her body, which she'd shown off to advantage in a black sheath. "It looks to me as though those workouts have been beneficial. Are you and Tally intending to become permanent members at Perfect Fit?"

"I don't know about you," Marla said to her friend, who was grinning at them, "but I've had enough exercise classes to last a lifetime."

"Me, too," Tally agreed, "but what else can we do to stay in shape?"

"I have a great idea. Le't speed-walk in the Fashion Mall. It'll be more fun to climb the escalators at Macy's than struggling with a Stair Master. Besides, I'm in the mood for a shopping binge."

AUTHOR'S NOTE

Following Marla's example, I joined a health club for a trial membership. My conclusion is the same as hers: I'd rather speed-walk in the mall or take my dog for a stroll! Regarding Marla's excursion to Vero Beach, this seaside town is one of my favorite Florida weekend getaways. Back in Fort Lauderdale, if you want to experience the same dinner cruise Marla took with Tally, check out the Jungle Queen.

If you're interested in learning more about animal testing, visit the web site for PETA (People for the Ethical Treatment of Animals), at *www.peta.com*. For a discussion of animal testing in the cosmetics industry, see this useful book *Don't Go to the Cosmetics Counter Without Me* by Paula Begoun. Her Web site is *www.cosmeticscop.com*.

As for Marla and Dalton, stay tuned for the fourth installment in the Bad Hair Day Mysteries to see what happens next in their developing relationship. Her pretend engagement to Arnie is nothing compared to the masquerade she plays in BODY WAVE. Someone close to Marla is in trouble, and when she investigates, it seems her friends harbor more secrets than the suspects.

I love to hear from readers. Write to me at: P.O. Box 17756, Plantation, FL 33318. Please enclose a self-addressed, stamped #10 business-size envelope for a personal reply.

E-mail: *ncane@att.net*

Web site: *http://nancyjcohen.com*